ASH
FORGED

ASH FORGED

DEATH SMITH BOOK TWO

Joost Lassche
aka Osirium Writes

Podium

To my two little ones, the echoes of my heart.

Copyright © 2024 by Joost Lassche

Cover design by Daniel Kamarudin

ISBN: 978-1-0394-4586-4

Published in 2024 by Podium Publishing, ULC
www.podiumaudio.com

ASH
FORGED

Prologue

February, 13 AR
East Bulgaria

A crackling fire waged its war against the frigid night sky, its dancing flames casting flickering shadows that painted the surroundings with an eerie glow. Sparks leapt into the air, their brief existence fading into nothingness. That evening, the Rift-site carried a lingering scent, a mixture of burning plastic, wood, and the unmistakable tang of spilt blood. In mere minutes, the once-secure and well-maintained site was now gone, overrun, and ravaged. The sudden emergence of cloaked figures from the Rift had caught both the site personnel and the Rifters off guard.

Confusion and shock had played a role, but it was the staggering gap in ability that had sealed their fate the moment the intruders had emerged. The Rifters, armed with modern weaponry and high-quality armor, had proven to be no match, their resistance lasting mere seconds. Both high-caliber bullets and explosives barely seemed to slow down the cloaked figures, if the Rifters even hit them. The projectiles that had found their mark encountered an invisible barrier, abruptly halting their momentum and rendering them ineffective.

After the sudden onslaught, a lone Rifter clung to life, her trembling hand applying desperate pressure to her wounded stomach as she bled out onto the cold ground. Kneeling beside her, a cloaked stranger observed her gradual descent into the clutches of death. There was no trace of hatred in his golden eyes as he witnessed the woman's futile struggle. Throughout this ordeal, his countenance remained resolute, undisturbed by all the death around him, as if numb to it all.

"It will be over soon, youngling," the stranger said, his tone masculine and almost regal. His hand rested gently on hers, his four fingers carefully guiding her hand away from her fatal wound, hastening her fate. "Surrender to it," he whispered, witnessing the gradual disappearance of color from her visage until she lay motionless, her eyes losing focus. *We all end the same*, the stranger thought, his gaze fixed upon her fading form, etching the image of the female Rifter into his memory. Moments later, his cloaked companions converged, wordlessly signaling that it was time.

With measured steps, the stranger guided them toward the vicinity of the Rift itself, where a smaller figure remained seated on the ground. Vibrant energy surged from the figure, distorting the air and stirring a whirlwind of dust. The sheer intensity of the wind thrust the hood backward, unveiling her unmistakable features. In that moment, he recognized his own reflection in her, a shared lineage that extended beyond mere blood. The two of them bore the weight of duty and an unbreakable oath to what remained of their family and people.

"I . . . found it," she said between gasps. Exhaustion and pain had ravaged her body as she had woven more of herself throughout the process, strengthening her connection with her surroundings until it finally stopped. It was the price a seer had to pay to read the flow of fate itself. Pebbles and dirt fell downwards as she felt her energy leave her. Gravity forced the seer onto her hands and knees.

"It is here . . . The harbinger of their ruin," she told him. Her golden eyes were wide with fear and disgust. "I felt its destruction, the sheer brutality of it . . . Heard the echo of countless souls lost in a single moment. The people of this realm . . . they have no inkling of what kind of weapon they've brought into existence," she explained, forcing herself upright, as he physically supporting her.

Embracing her, the stranger sensed his companions' approach. His gaze lingered on each of them, fortifying their connection and resolve. They shared an unspoken understanding of the gravity of the situation, the very reason they had stood by his side all these years throughout countless realms.

United in the aftermath of the havoc they had unleashed, nine souls stood resolute, driven by a shared purpose. And with a mere seven words, he would set in motion a sequence of events that would defy the course of fate itself: "The Seer has spoken. Locate this weapon."

CHAPTER ONE

Closure

Two weeks after Rift 7
March, 14 AR
St Lucas's Hospital
London, England

DANIEL

There was an uncomfortable silence in Room 5-A, broken only by the sound of the clock above the doorframe. Seconds passed, threatening to turn into minutes before the young man nodded understanding.

"I'm sorry, I know that this news must be unpleasant for you," the GRRO representative said, trying her best to make eye contact with the young man.

Daniel observed the exchange in silence, while internally grappling with his emotions. Constance Grand, the representative, had just disclosed to Lance and him that the GRRO had concluded their investigation into the "incident." Two weeks of deliberation had resulted in all charges against the three individuals involved being dropped. While Daniel had anticipated such an outcome, the harsh truth still pierced his heart.

Daniel's eyebrows shot up in disbelief. "Are you serious? Is that all?" His voice started to rise but quickly settled as he recalled Lance's fragile state of mind. "Will the GRRO really leave it at that?" Daniel asked, forcing himself to maintain a composed, respectful tone, despite his growing frustration.

He wanted to know what the GRRO would do about this matter. Kira, Connor and Louis had given their initial statements to an official when they had first exited the Rift, yet afterwards everything had gone wrong. There was video footage of the woman, Kira, entering the GRRO vehicle on-site, but she had never arrived at her destination. There had been no trace of her afterwards. Not long after that, the GRRO concluded that the identification documents she had provided RAM were forged, thus making her identity a mystery.

As if one unknown element wasn't bad enough, Connor had lawyered up within hours. At first, he had been cooperative, but after entering the GRRO HQ, several lawyers who worked for his guild had swept him up in an ocean of red tape and legal loopholes. Officially, the American Rifter had fully cooperated with the investigation, yet Daniel couldn't help but imagine the limited options the GRRO faced against such an adversary. With Connor's brother ranking as the fifth most-powerful Rifter in the United States and a powerful guild bolstering him, Connor became virtually untouchable.

Louis, the Frenchman, had fully cooperated, attending numerous hearings and offering assistance whenever possible. Yet, ultimately, his account mirrored the initial statements given by the other two: their party had been ambushed by monsters, and they believed the rest of their group had perished. The severity of the situation had forced them to retreat to their camp for reinforcements. Although cooperating, Louis had returned to France after seven days, having remained in contact with the GRRO through the branch in his home country.

"I'm afraid so," Constance said, answering Daniel's question. Her tone was neutral. However, her eyes occasionally glanced at the young man sitting in the hospital bed, devoid of any emotions. "Mister Turner, the GRRO deeply regrets what has happened to you, and offers their condolences to you and the friends and families of the fallen," she said as she slowly got up, realizing that Lance didn't have any further questions. She handed Daniel her card and excused herself, letting him know they could contact that number anytime if they had further questions.

In the end, Daniel had accepted the card and thanked her for her time, realizing that now wasn't the time to ask the hard questions. He'd choose his battlefield somewhere away from Lance. He inhaled deeply before he turned his attention to the young man. "How are you feeling, lad?" Daniel asked carefully as he observed Lance staring out of the window, his bloodshot eyes betraying his inner struggle, even though his face divulged little of it.

"I don't know," Lance admitted before the door to his room swung open abruptly, unleashing a colossal Rift-hound that bounded inside. The creature wasted no time, its gaze fixed on Lance, leaping onto his bed and pressing against him affectionately. A moment later, Dieter followed suit, acknowledging Daniel with a nod before heading toward Lance. With his broad arms, he ensnared the young man, enveloping him in a powerful embrace.

The Rift-hound, Little Hans, burrowed his head underneath Lance's arm to rest on his lap. Both Dieter and the hound looked exhausted, no doubt having just returned from another Rift. Daniel then stepped outside of the room, hearing Lance's voice break as his hands ran through the creature's fur. The animal slowly coaxed Lance down the path of grief and toward healing.

As Daniel closed the door behind him, he grabbed his phone and texted Samuel Jones, asking him to meet up later. He figured the head of the GRRO London branch might give him more answers.

Several minutes later, Dieter joined his friend outside of Lance's hospital room. He grabbed some coffee and the two of them made their way to a nearby bench. The loyal Rift-hound had refused to move, intent instead on keeping Lance company. Dieter was still wearing his Rifter outfit, minus the armor he usually wore over it. He was unshaven, dirty, and had some minor bruises on his arms and face. The man looked as if he had simply dropped everything and rushed over as soon as he'd exited the Rift and learned what had happened. Knowing his friend as well as he did, Daniel figured this was probably the case.

"You could've at least washed," Daniel said with a grin as he leaned back against the wall, closing his eyes briefly.

"And you could've gotten me a coffee, instead of using the whole one-hand excuse," the large German said, gently nudging his friend in the ribs while sipping coffee.

"I'll try to remember," Daniel said with a smile while glancing down at the hot coffee in his cup. "Any trouble in the Rift?" he asked, changing the subject.

"Nope," Dieter replied before taking another big sip. "Just a run-of-the-mill Level Four Rift nestled in the countryside. Found ourselves in a cursed jungle realm, hacking through the dense foliage for weeks to reach the bloody event. Had I had known . . ." The German suddenly stopped, as if unsure what he wanted to say. The two of them sat in silence for a while after, Dieter ignoring any nurse or doctor that stared at him and the state of his clothes as they passed by. Finally, he broke the silence and asked the one question Daniel did not know how to answer: "How is he doing?"

Daniel let out a heavy sigh, his mind grappling with how to explain Lance's state. There were so many aspects to cover, and nearly all of them were bad. "Poorly," he finally said as he opened his eyes. "Physically, there's been some improvement. He had several broken bones, multiple lacerations, and his left hand needed extensive surgery to fix. Still, he is young, healthy, and has been using his Skill to speed up the healing process. His doctors expect a full recovery, though there might be some lingering numbness in his left hand, if at all."

"And mentally?" his friend asked.

"An absolute train wreck filled with survivor's guilt. No other way to describe it. It took both the GRRO and me hours to grasp the truth—that Lance, not Thomas, had survived and made it out of the Rift before driving away from the Rift-site. It was bad. The GRRO had even contacted Thomas's family with incorrect information about who had survived. By the time I had found him, nearly ten hours had passed," Daniel said as he sipped his coffee. He could hear his friend mutter things under his breath, no doubt feeling terrible for the Walker family.

"The lad was a mess. I found him on his sofa, next to Thomas's broken shield. He wasn't in a good state of mind at that point. Blood loss, injuries, and shell shock had eroded much of him. And you know how internal the lad usually is. The things he said at that moment were mostly incoherent," Daniel said. He knew the story would get even more complex when he had to explain to Dieter what had "officially" happened inside the Rift and what Lance's testimony had been. The young man's account of things had been about poor leadership from the fighters and them abandoning the porters to fend for themselves. Thomas had sacrificed himself to save Lance.

While they drank their coffee, Daniel explained what had happened in terms of the investigation and the events afterwards. The hardest part was retelling how Thomas's family had reacted upon arriving at the hospital. Both a GRRO spokesperson and Daniel had been there to break the news, to let them know it had been Lance that had survived, not Thomas. He could still remember how every word they uttered fragmented the family even more. The mother had simply collapsed in tears while Thomas's father remained upright, devoid of any emotion as he supported his family.

"And how are you doing?" Dieter asked. His hands were gripping one another and exerting a tremendous amount of force. He was no doubt dealing with his own grief. Daniel knew that Dieter would have more questions about the investigation and what had happened to the three fighters who had left Lance and Thomas to their fates. For now, the large German focused on what he could do for his friend.

"About the same as you, I think. I . . ." Daniel stopped as he leaned backwards again, exhaling deeply. "Those boys didn't deserve this. They were supposed to do some boring jobs to get some experience under their belt. I figured if they did a dozen of these Rifts, I could persuade you to let them join your guild."

"*Our* guild. I still haven't accepted your official resignation. And you know full well that we would've accepted those boys in a heartbeat and treated them like family," Dieter said as he ran a hand through his dirty blonde beard to distract himself somewhat. "When is the funeral?" he asked eventually.

"The day after tomorrow. Thomas's father expressed his wishes for us to be there as well if you're up for it?" Daniel said. His friend simply nodded.

Thomas's father had frequently spoken with Daniel to hear how Lance was doing. He had wanted to visit, but Lance had either been in surgery, therapy, or the GRRO had taken up too much of his time with their investigation. The death of so many Rifters needed to be investigated from all angles. Beyond that, Lance had refused most visitors during his stay until now.

"I'm meeting Samuel later today," Daniel said, ignoring the disapproving grunt from his friend as he continued. "I'm going to see if the old man has some more information for us about the investigation. Can you look after Lance for now? The doctors said they could discharge him tomorrow morning or later in the afternoon."

Dieter nodded once more. There wasn't anything else left to say after that. They both felt the loss of Thomas, having spent a long time together during his first Rift. While Daniel had continued to be a large presence in the young man's life, taking on the role of mentor, Dieter had bonded with Thomas differently. Both he and Thomas were quite similar in their behavior and had regularly kept in contact, with Dieter frequently receiving messages from Thomas for advice or inquiring about any potential openings in Dieter's guild.

Both Rifters sat a while longer together, each staring at a different random spot on the floor as they drank their coffee in silence mourning the loss of a good man.

A few hours later, Daniel sat at the bar with another man, each holding a glass of scotch. The amber liquid reflected their faces as they each gazed into its golden depths. They lost themselves in it as if it might reveal the answers they sought. Daniel had placed a folder on the bar between them, containing the GRRO logo and a case number.

"What the hell am I going to tell the lad?" Daniel said finally. He took a large sip and felt the liquid burn his throat as it went down. It felt fitting, as if he was chasing the demons out of his mind. They would no doubt make their return in a short while, but it didn't stop him from trying. They would come nipping at his heels, festering his mind with self-loathing and guilt.

The guilt at not having been in the Rift with Lance and Thomas or not having pushed them to Dieter's guild sooner. *Even with one arm, I might've made a difference*, Daniel chastised himself before taking another sip.

"That's up to you. I think the truth will hurt as much as any sugarcoated variant of it," Samuel Jones answered as he eyed the one-handed Rifter at his side. The document between them contained all the information about the Rift "incident" that had resulted in the loss of six people. There was the official report of the Rift-leader, supporting R.A.M. personnel on-site, and eyewitness accounts of several Rifters who had been inside the Rift. "No version will make it any better, or bring back lost friends," Samuel said as he swirled his drink.

The impulse to smash the wooden bar with his fists surged through Daniel like a lightning bolt, but he clenched his hands tightly, determined to keep his emotions in check. The day had sapped him of his mental strength, leaving him drained and disheartened. The GRRO's announcement, closing the investigation and reducing it to a vague "incident," stoked the flames of his frustration. It was a convenient label, a shield to hide the unsettling reality.

"Did Mr. Turner say anything else about what happened inside?" Samuel asked carefully, aware of how protective Daniel could be of loved ones.

"No, nothing more than the basics. Monsters cornered their group because of poor leadership and greed. Three of the Rifters fled. Thomas got Lance to safety at the cost of his own life," Daniel said, closing his eyes. It still puzzled him how Lance had survived exiting the Rift, other than chance and a lot of luck.

Daniel had tried to talk to Lance about what had happened, but Lance had frozen up each time. Questions about the state of his current Level or Class remained unanswered. Lance had told him he didn't want to open his status screen or deal with anything Rift-related at the moment. It was one of the few triggers capable of jolting Lance out of his mental haze, igniting a feverish anger whenever the topic was pressed.

Daniel felt Samuel's gaze on him, his mind no doubt busy in taking it all in. The old man was a keen observer and had been around Rifters long enough to know how to read them. Proceeding with measured words, Samuel ventured forth. "I heard he is to be discharged tomorrow?"

"I think so," Daniel said, rapping his knuckles on the bar a few times. "I tried to convince him to stay longer, talk about his experiences with a professional there, but he refused each time. The doctors said it is probably PTSD and that it would be beneficial for him to see someone at a later stage," Daniel explained as he shook his head, knowing how hard it could be to help a Rifter.

Most of the Rifters that Daniel had encountered had endured some sort of trauma. It was an intrinsic part of their existence, a consequence that accompanied the transformation into becoming a Rifter. Just like soldiers on the front lines, Rifters were thrust into brutal combat scenarios, enduring hardships that could break most people. Yet, Rifters' challenges extended beyond normal, rational boundaries. They faced unforgiving environments that violated all logical explanation, encountered savage flora and fauna that defied description, and confronted merciless and monstrous adversaries hell-bent on eradicating them.

Plenty of people had suggested that Daniel himself undergo therapy after the many bad Rifts he had been in, yet he had refused each time. It wasn't a matter of dismissing the value of professional help or lacking trust in their intentions. Rather, it stemmed from the challenge of conveying the realities of a Rifter's experiences to an outsider. That was precisely why Daniel had found solace in his guild, surrounded by fellow Rifters who understood the horrors he had faced firsthand. Their shared understanding and support served as a lifeline for coping with the horrors of a Rift.

Samuel got up and finished his last drink as he signaled to the bartender that Daniel would be paying. "Daniel, sometimes there are no words left beyond those that hurt us. But you can be there for him as he's facing the pain," he told him as he grabbed his coat from the chair and made his way to the door. Upon opening it, Daniel could see a black car parked outside. The driver was already getting out to open the passenger door for Samuel.

"Take care of yourself. And take some time to reconsider my offer of employment," Samuel said, as he waved at the Rifter, as per usual ignoring Daniel's outright refusal to work for the GRRO. That Samuel didn't take the folder with him was a sign of trust between the two men, and an unspoken assumption on his end that Daniel would end up working for him. The old man hadn't ended up as the head of the GRRO's London branch by not having a sharp instinct when it came to people.

With Samuel gone, Daniel was left to his thoughts and the sound of the bartender cleaning glasses. He felt the stump of his right arm twitch and irritate him again. *How the hell do I tell Lance that even the GRRO is powerless here, despite understanding what happened inside the Rift? To explain that truth and justice, at times, gets buried beneath layers of corruption?*

He remembered Lance's reaction when the GRRO official had broken the news to them. The folder on the bar only made that news even darker. The document contained numerous detailed examples of Connor's lawyers actively working against the GRRO investigators. It showed evidence of the R.A.M. officials purposely having chosen to take on a higher-level Rift instead of a safer one. The worst part was about Kira, the Rifter who had disappeared. They had found ties between her and several contract killings over the past five years. *All of this would chip away at what little Lance has left if he ever were to find out. Losing a friend is bad enough, but losing one because of other people's negligence, greed, and evil intentions?*

He stared at both the drink and the folder for minutes as he went over his options and weighed their potential outcomes. Finally, he recalled something his wife used to say to him: *A kind heart endures.*

The memory of her pulled at his heart. The image of her holding their child right until the end . . .

Refusing to let more of those memories bubble up to the surface, he finished his drink in one quick motion. Afterwards, he grabbed his phone and dialed Dieter's number. Moments passed before he heard the man's voice. Feeling his right arm throb in pain, he brought the phone to his ear, making his choice.

"It's me. We need to talk."

CHAPTER TWO

Closure

The following morning
March, 14 AR
St Lucas's Hospital
London, England

LANCE

Flashes of pain ran through Lance's body as he felt the constant icy sting at his side. Fear gripped his heart, but not for his own safety. *Don't think about it! . . . I have to!* Lance thought, his heart racing. His grip tightened around the knife's hilt as he pulled it from its scarlet sheath. Pain, fatigue, and uncertainty threatened to consume him, though a singular need dwarfed them all. He gritted his teeth and threw the knife, watching it glide toward a man who was fighting for his life. "Lance! Use it!" he screamed, only to realize that it was Thomas's voice uttering those words.

A second later, Lance woke up screaming, reliving the last moments of his nightmare. His arms thrashed around him, fighting off the things that haunted him. He felt a figure lay a hand on his chest while pushing him back into his bed. Compared to Lance's strength, this hand felt like an unmovable mountain.

"Easy there," a voice said soothingly, triggering Lance's memory by doing so. He recognized Dieter's voice, sensing the man next to him in the dark room. Dieter's hand kept gently restraining his movement until Lance finally relaxed and his breathing gradually calmed down. After opening his eyes fully, he took in Dieter along with a large creature who jumped over from a nearby bed and was now leaning against Lance.

"I . . . I felt . . . I saw . . ." Lance said, unsure how to even explain what he just experienced. He thought it was a dream, but it had felt so real, as if he had lived

Thomas's last moments. He had seen and felt how his friend had made the decision to pull the knife out of his body in order to save him.

"Just shadows and scars," Dieter said as he patted Lance's chest. He could feel the young man's heartbeat slow down, no longer threatening to burst out of his chest. "Easy now. Just shadows and scars, nothing more. Most of us have them," Dieter continued, as Lance felt the man's hand slowly slide to the side, gripping Lance's shoulder before he got up. The tall German then opened the curtains to let the morning sun inside, vanquishing the remnants of nightmares.

"Get up, lazy bones," Dieter said playfully, arms tightly folded as he observed the young man's sluggish movements. "You've had your beauty sleep. Time for us to get something to eat and hunt down a fancy quack in a white coat to give you the all-clear." Then Dieter began folding Lance's clothes, but his interest swiftly waned, prompting him to shove them carelessly into the bags instead.

A part of Lance hated that Dieter was seeing him like this. Another part was glad. Ever since leaving the Rift, Lance occasionally experienced nightmares like this, always chaotic, always real as if he was reliving Thomas's memories. This night had been a particularly bad one. The fact that Dieter didn't pry into what had happened and instead simply ordered him to get out of bed was reassuring. Lance usually felt shame whenever a nurse or doctor found him like that, so distraught and vulnerable.

"Sure," Lance replied as he pulled off his shirt and grabbed a fresh one. As he did so, he could feel Dieter's gaze on his back. No doubt, it was tracing the network of scars etched into Lance's flesh—some still fresh, while others had begun their gradual fade.

Although Lance had only been a Rifter for a short while, he didn't know many who didn't have scars or other permanent wounds. Still, he had collected quite a few in his brief career as a Rifter. "I thought the doctor would see me in the afternoon?" Lance asked as he slid into his pants and sweater before fumbling with his left shoe.

"And in the meantime, I'm going to let you will waste away in bed?" Dieter asked, shaking his head and pointing at Little Hans. He snapped his fingers, signaling to the large Rift-hound that he was to stop chewing on Lance's right shoe and return it to him. "You had a full two weeks to indulge in that luxury, princess," he remarked with a grin, tossing Lance's bags into his waiting arms and making his way toward the door.

Lance was glad that Dieter had refused to leave him alone last night, instead opting to sleep in a chair while Little Hans slept in a separate bed. Still, the man's excuse of being "too tired to go home" was anything but convincing. Lance usually felt at ease with Dieter. The man could make you step away from your problems for a while and focus on something minor, to get your bearings again. He reminded him of Thomas. Those two were both quick to act and feel but also knew instinctively that some things needed time to heal. In the end, Lance did as Dieter asked and put on his drool-covered right shoe and made his way over to German and Little Hans.

Opening the door, Dieter led the young man and his four-legged friend out of the room toward a nearby office to find a doctor.

Two hours later, Lance found himself staring at a wall that was covered with dozens of framed news articles alongside photographs. Every one of them was a person who Dieter had saved over the years, including a picture of Lance and Thomas. It pained Lance to look at it, but he understood why Dieter displayed them all on his wall.

"Did most of them become Rifters?" Lance asked, tracing his fingers over several of the pictures, almost feeling what these people had felt when they survived their first Rift. The news article on the middle of the wall was of Dieter himself, from several years ago. Although it was in German, Lance understood some of the words.

"No, only a few of them became Rifters," Dieter said, his voice echoing from his kitchen. Every few seconds, Lance heard a loud whining noise as Little Hans kept begging the German for food, even throwing his empty bowl at Dieter's shin to get the message across. The two of them were perfectly in sync on the battlefield, but they obviously had conflicting ideas about proper food portions back on Earth.

Lance stepped away from the pictures and toward a small cabinet that contained things from inside a Rift, ranging from Rift-shards and Mana stones, to more unique ores or dried-up exotic plants. Lance noticed a few broken or dented weapons in the cabinet next to it that Dieter had either used or collected as trophies. Among them was a large mace with a black and red hue. His gaze fell upon the many nicks, dents, and signs of wear that adorned most of these items. Lance quickly moved away from them after remembering a broken shield that held a permanent position on his couch back in his flat.

"It smells good," Lance said as his heightened Perception skill picked up on the ingredients Dieter was using.

"It will taste even better."

"I never pegged you for a proper cook," Lance said, stepping into the kitchen and seeing Dieter hard at work, preparing sizable portions of sausages, eggs, bread rolls, cheese, lettuce, sliced tomatoes, and two glasses filled with orange juice.

"What nonsense has Daniel been filling your head with?" Dieter scoffed, shaking his head as he silenced the stove's sizzle. Afterwards, he placed Little Hans' filled bowl on the floor before sitting down on a barstool and handing Lance a plate. "Despite what Daniel might've been telling you guys, I used to be quite normal, and I enjoyed cooking. I was a senior salesperson in a local carpet shop and was living a quiet life until a Rift happened to me," he explained before biting into his bread roll.

"It is hard to picture you and Daniel as anything else but warriors. How could I not after how you two saved me and Thomas back then?" Lance said, remembering the way Dieter and Daniel had cut through ranks of Lizardlings to save him and the other people inside the hospital.

"Hmph, you're way off the mark. Believe it or not, my life used to be pleasant and blissfully dull. Honestly, my biggest concern revolved around choosing between a winter holiday or a summer getaway. Daniel had a similar tale to tell—once a bakery owner, living a simple existence with his wife, until fate intervened," Dieter recounted, skillfully swiping a small slice of bacon from his plate by accident as if it had slipped, and smiling at hearing the gratifying canine grunt that echoed from below.

Lance smiled, imagining Daniel baking bread or Dieter selling someone a new carpet. The thought of Dieter mercilessly bashing in a monster's skull with his formidable mace felt more natural than envisioning him trapped within the confines of a suit and tie. The two of them continued to eat in silence afterwards, a large snout occasionally bumping into Lance's knee, trying to persuade the young man to spare some more bits of bacon. When Lance extended a bit of lettuce as an alternative, he couldn't help but detect a dissatisfied snort escaping from Little Hans, as if signaling betrayal.

Lance focused on the Rift-hound, remembering all he had read about animals that had survived a Rift and the Rifters that bonded with them. Whereas humans could actively distribute points to certain areas and grow stronger, Rift-animals simply grew organically in the direction that made the most sense. Little Hans had started off as a large English mastiff, but he had grown a lot since then. Ropes of muscle adorned his legs and Lance remembered how the animal had used its teeth to rip apart thick Lizardmen scales.

"I did the cooking. The two of you are on clean-up duty," Dieter declared, a satisfied grin spreading across his face as he proudly tapped his full stomach. He then sauntered toward the living room to watch some television.

With no choice but to do so, Lance cleaned up, letting the Rift-hound lick up the scraps from each plate before placing them in the dishwasher. Once he had finally cleared the table, Lance closed the machine with a sigh.

Ever since his escape from the Rift, a repeating status screen notification had kept irritating him. Lance could ignore it for a while, but it always popped back up after a few hours. He had refused to interact with it because of his survivor's guilt, along with the torrent of other emotions that ravaged him. However, with Thomas's funeral looming on the horizon, Lance knew he could no longer evade the source of his guilt—the item now housed within his inventory. Determined to preempt any emotional breakdown during the funeral, he resolved to face the

notification head-on, opening his status screen and bracing himself for what lay
ahead.

[You have unspent Attribute points]

He had gained three Attribute points after he had survived the last Rift. These
points taunted him for a while with what they represented. He ignored how they
made him feel as he focused on how to spend them. His Endurance was currently
his highest Attribute, with Strength and Agility tied in second place. Perception
was in third place, and Wisdom and Luck were last.

It tempted Lance to put those three points into Endurance. After all, it had
been a vital part of how he had survived the hazardous, rock-filled underground
river, as well as his fast exit from the Rift. Strength and Agility had been useless
then; same for Wisdom and Perception. *The fact that I survived at all was pure
chance,* Lance thought as he shook his head. Some Rifters considered the Luck
attribute a waste, while others swore by it. The Attribute helped nearly every action,
increased the chances of a good Item drop, and could mean the difference between
a normal hit or a potentially critical one.

[Luck:] [20] (+3)

In the end, Lance placed all three points into his Luck. Not because of any
strategy, but more as a statement to himself. Afterwards, he made his way over to
Dieter to watch some television, eager to distract himself from what he had just
done.

"Really, I'm fine," Lance lied. Dieter and Daniel were lingering at his door later
that evening, holding it open. Lance loved them for it but wanted nothing more
than to have some time for himself. Lance had spent most of his day with Dieter.
They had watched a movie together, done some grocery shopping, had Lance's
GRRO identification updated at the London branch, and afterwards made their
way over to Lance's flat. The updated ID now listed Lance as a veteran.

The GRRO listed new Rifters as Survivors until they reached Level Ten and
gained their Class. After that, they would get the rank of Veteran until they reached
Level 100. Some agencies relied on proof of Rank. Other nations relied on complex scanners that used exotic elements found in a Rift to measure the radiation
emitted from a Rift-shard. The greater the output, the higher the Level.

GRRO simply kept testing as optional for the lower-ranked Rifters such as
veterans, allowing a Rifter to update it when they felt it necessary. The higher a
Rifter's level, the more job opportunities they usually had. When Lance had
seen his new credentials, having read the word "Veteran," he nearly chucked it

in the nearest bin. He felt far from a veteran during his last Rift or every day since then.

Lance and Dieter had cleaned up his apartment earlier, explaining that Daniel would join them later. When Daniel arrived, the mood had instantly soured. It seemed like good news at first. Daniel had explained he had visited R.A.M. to negotiate the outstanding loans Thomas and Lance still had with the company. They had been standard loans for equipment, a backpack, and tools. Because of the rarity of Rift-materials, it was worth several thousand pounds. Daniel had explained that he had gotten R.A.M. to drop the loans for Thomas and only charge Lance a third for the damages and loss of the equipment he had borrowed. In return, Lance had to sign a document not to go to the press about the "incident."

It had hurt Lance to sign it, but he knew that in the end, it meant thousands of pounds didn't suddenly burden Thomas's family or put them in debt. He knew how often Thomas had chipped in, even back when he had still been a nurse. It had been Thomas's way of supporting his father after the man's medical discharge from the military because of a back injury. Signing the document had felt both nauseating and right at the same time for Lance. In doing so, he hoped it would bring the Walkers some rest.

Afterwards, Lance had expected the tension to go away, but Daniel had surprised him when the man had placed a large folder on the table in front of him. Daniel had hesitated a moment before he let go of the folder, explaining that he had spoken to Samuel Jones. Upon hearing the full details of the investigation, the near immunity of Connor, the shaky testimony from Louis, and the bloody enigma that was Kira, Lance had wanted to rip the document in half.

He wasn't sure what he felt at that moment. There was rage, fear, guilt, and despair. Everything hit him at once, numbing him again, like how he had been for the last two weeks. Lance felt like nothing had changed.

"Lance, you know, we could always stay the night. It might be easier to drive to the funeral together, right?" Daniel asked, as Dieter gave an encouraging nod. They had no illusions of what this news meant to Lance and the Walkers.

"I'm fine," Lance lied again, flashing them a broken smile. "I think I expected this. I . . . want some time by myself . . . for now, at least. I'll see you two in the morning." Then he slowly closed the door. His heightened senses could hear them on the other side of the room, the shifting of weight on the floorboards as they finally moved away from his door and left the complex.

The young man then waited a few minutes in silence before he steeled himself and opened his Inventory, bringing forth the reason for most of his guilt and self-hatred.

[You have combined and retrieved two items]

Lance watched the pale figure appear in the seat in front of him, dressed in a torn R.A.M uniform. The figure stared through Lance with empty eyes, a dullish gray Rift-shard embedded in the center of a gray chest. Lance braced himself as he looked at the figure, at the pale man that looked so much like Thomas.

Lance forced himself to remember every detail, permanently engraving then in his memory before opening the folder again and grabbing three pictures, which he placed in between the two of them. Photographs of the people who had wronged them. Lance slid each picture toward the pale man, seeing the gray gaze shift downwards at them. Remembering his oath to Thomas, Lance broke the silence.

"I'll keep my promise, Thomas, even if it means I have to get it for you on my own."

CHAPTER THREE

Scented Memories

The day of the Funeral
March, 14 AR
Lance's Flat
London, England

LANCE

The lingering traces of cedarwood, citrus, and lavender filled the surrounding air. The mix of scents clung to Lance's body until it became a part of him. Months ago, he would've thought of the cologne as just "nice," but now that he was a Rifter, he could pick out nearly half of the ingredients just from a single whiff. Lance wasn't the type to wear cologne, but today was different.

He had put on a dark blue suit with a black tie and a black shirt underneath, rather than his usual jeans, T-shirt, and hoodie combination. The last time he had worn it had been a few years ago when a distant relative had died. He still remembered how the suit had been too big for him and that it hadn't done his figure justice. Now, the black shirt clung to his body, hinting at his strength while remaining tasteful.

Lance ran his fingers along his jaw, feeling the smooth skin underneath his fingers. Slowly, he moved them upwards, charting a soft line over his lips. Then he brought his hand out in front of him, making a fist while staring at the firm muscles and. He could hear his joints groaning as he increased the pressure, feeling the strength flow through his fist.

A few hours ago, Lance had turned his hands into a bloody mess against a wall in his room. He had punched it until the brickwork got damaged and blood and stone dust had mixed with one another. The pain had served as both punishment and catharsis, an outlet for his brewing emotions. Afterwards, he used his "Mend Wound" Skill to recover, fixing the numerous cuts and lessening the pain.

"Today is the day we bury you, Thomas," he murmured, his voice a solemn whisper hanging heavy in the air. A gentle breeze slipped through the open window, ruffling his tousled brown hair. His gaze fixated upon his own reflection in the mirror as he went over his appearance once more, hoping it looked respectful enough. As teenagers, the two friends had joked about who would die first and how the funeral would go. Both men would make wild claims and demands of the other in terms of speeches, clothing, and how to act.

The very notion of speaking, of paying homage to his departed friend, threatened to induce a gut-wrenching upheaval within Lance. The reasons behind his unease were all too clear, his conscience weighed down by what he had done to his best friend. He had turned Thomas's body into something else, twisted into an abomination that denied his mourning family the chance to lay him to rest with the dignity and closure they deserved.

In the mirror's reflection, Lance's gaze darted to the ghostly figure standing near the corner, its gray eyes staring back at him. The visage had been with Lance throughout the night. He had gotten no sleep since Dieter and Daniel had left, and the ghostly figure was similarly restless. Lance could feel the effects of fatigue but suppressed it using his Healing Skill to temporarily recover some of his energy.

The pale man was different. Lance had realized that figure didn't need to sleep, drink, or eat. He had stayed awake all this time, staring at the three pictures on the table and later at Lance hurting himself against the wall. Lance had clothed the man in his old bathrobe, covering him up better than the ruined R.A.M uniform could. Not that he seemed to mind. The pale man was content to just sit and watch Lance, seemingly expectant of something. It was as if he needed something from Lance.

Now, minutes before Lance was to be picked up by Dieter and Daniel, he addressed the pale elephant in the room. He sat down on the table in front of the man, staring into his gray eyes, desperate to see some hint of Thomas. Sadly, he found none. "You aren't Thomas," he said finally as he leaned closer to the pale man, inspecting his features once again. It was hard not to want to treat him as Thomas, but that felt like betraying his friend's memory. "No, you're not him. But you can be something to honor his memory," Lance said as he watched the pale man react to his words.

Lance remembered fragments of how he got his Class, how he had felt like he was burning up from the inside. He remembered the moments after surviving the Rift, when the two of them sat on the sofa and shared Thomas's last cigarette until only ash remained. This man reminded Lance of that, of something that was burned up and turned into something else, something devoid of color. A mere echo of what had once been.

"Ash," Lance said finally as he stared at the man in front of him, nodding as he did so. "Your name is Ash," he said, more determined this time, again nodding as he reaffirmed his words. Mentally, Lance accepted the name he was giving the silent man. He noticed "Ash" nod once, either out of a confirmation or due to simply mimicking Lance. It drew Lance's attention immediately, as he wanted to see if it was just coincidence, but he stopped when he heard Dieter and Daniel's car pull up outside.

[You have stored an item in the Inventory]
[You have named this item "Ash"]

"We'll pick this up later, Ash," Lance said as he placed his hands on the man's shoulder and accepted storing the "Item" in his Inventory. The bathrobe fell to the ground afterwards, no longer supported by a frame.

There was a stony silence within the Walker residence that day. In the past, it had been a beacon of warmth and love, but now it felt devoid of that. It was muffled by the silence of loss, looming over all of them on the day of Thomas's funeral. Though the sun hung high in the sky, loss had wrapped the house in darkness, the drawn curtains blocking out the light. The only constant sound was that of the wind blowing through the trees, rattling the windows, and the sound of a mother sobbing upstairs in her room, along with the gentle tones of her daughter comforting her.

Most of the family had gathered in the living room. Cousins, aunts, and uncles accompanied them, offering their support, or sharing the grief. They were all mourning the loss of a young man who hadn't deserved to die at such a young age. Occasionally, relatives or friends of the family would throw glances toward Dieter and Daniel, who were standing near the kitchen. Some of them looked at the Rifters with curiosity or neutrality, but a large portion of them simply stared at them with anger. A confused rage at having no one else to blame for Thomas's death. The glances Lance occasionally got from those people were worse, since he knew they felt pity at seeing him.

I hate this, Lance thought as he glanced at the empty casket surrounded by flowers. People had written things on the wooden panels, as per the family's request. Some wrote mere words, others short stories. Shared memories were mingled amongst other various tributes of love for Thomas. Lance had simply written two words: "Oath keeper." There was nothing else to write beyond it, no words to offer to ease the suffering of the family and loved ones.

So, Lance sat in a corner of the room, minding his nerves while fighting the urge to run. He could feel the worried glances thrown in his direction by Dieter and Daniel, knowing full well he'd do the same if he had been in their shoes. A part of him felt ashamed, having them worry about him like that, since both were mourning as well. They had all fought together during their first Rift. There was no way that those two men weren't feeling the loss after all the time they had spent with Thomas.

Lance's focus shifted as he heard the groan of worn knees and a bad back as Thomas's father, Jacob, slowly got up and fought back a pained groan. The man appeared to make his way over toward Lance but changed course along the way toward Daniel. Although there was some distance between them, Lance heard the occasional bit of dialogue as the man addressed the two Rifters.

". . . expressed his wish . . . pallbearer . . . empty caskets are . . . heaviest . . ."

Lance watched the Rifters nod respectfully as they promised they would help in any way they could. Afterwards, Lance could feel three sets of eyes land on him, weighing him at that moment. Forcing his head down, he suppressed the emotions that came bubbling up to the surface. Even now, Thomas's father had to be an enduring pillar for his family. Grief had shattered his wife while his daughter and his youngest son were now suddenly without their sibling. To top it all off, Jacob had to worry about Lance, to prevent Thomas's best friend from cracking under the weight of responsibility and loss.

It was only a few moments after Jacob returned to the sofa to take care of his youngest child when Daniel made his way over to Lance. "Lad, we were asked—"

"I know," Lance interrupted him before giving a soft smile. Afterwards, he moved past Daniel and up the stairs as he tried to suppress his emotions. Lance reached the landing that gave way to the many rooms on the first floor of the Walker residence. His eyes narrowed on the worn white door that had a bright red "T" painted on it, marking it as Thomas's room. He moved toward it and was about to open it when the door leading to the master bedroom opened, followed by Kate stepping outside. She closed the door behind her, leaving her grief-stricken mother alone in the dark room.

When Kate made eye contact with him, he immediately felt the weight of his guilt threaten to undo him. He remembered the first days in the hospital, unable to explain what had happened. He had wanted to give the Walkers closure, but the GRRO and the hospital had allowed no visitors at first because of his traumatized state and the ongoing investigation. When they finally allowed Lance to receive visitors, it had mostly been Daniel and Jacob, how had told him how badly the family had taken the loss of Thomas.

He figured Kate would no doubt hate him, or at the very least resent him for not being able to protect her brother. Lance had been the one who had persuaded her brother to become a nurse, to work in the same hospital. Afterwards he had persuaded Thomas to keep working for R.A.M. when they had become Rifters. Lance might not have wielded the blade that killed Thomas, but he played a significant role in the road leading to that blade.

"Sorry, Kate, I'll go downstairs," Lance said in a hushed voice, stepping away from Thomas's room as if burned by it. He barely made his first step when a pair of arms wrapped themselves around his neck, waves of autumn strands blocking his vision. He could feel Kate pull herself into him as her body shook, suppressing the need to weep. "I . . ." Lance continued, only to be silenced when Kate's hand cupped the back of his head and forced him closer to her.

Her breath rushed over his neck as tears streamed down her cheeks, demanding the same of Lance. Kate's chest heaved with quiet sobs as he wrapped his arms around her, breathing in the smell of her hair. Eventually, both broke down like that, supporting each other's weight and grief as they wept in silence for what seemed like hours.

Kate only pulled away from Lance when her father called her, letting her know it was time for the procession to start.

Several hours later, Lance was back in his own flat. He caught the rugby with his left hand, snatching it out of the air. He could feel the fabric groan underneath his powerful grip. He inspected the ball and remembered when he had bought it during a match between England and New Zealand. Jacob had bought tickets and had taken the two young men with him.

Lance noticed the worn-out letters on the ball before he threw it in an arc toward a pair of pale hands who caught it from a seated position before Lance closed his eyes again. Doing so, he could almost pull off lying to himself, pretending for one moment that Thomas was still alive, and that they were back in the hospital, throwing a ball back and forth.

Upon returning home, he had taken off his jacket and tie and folded up the sleeves of the black shirt. The memory of Kate still lingered on his clothes, reminding him of the funeral as well as confusing Lance in a different way. He remembered how devastated Thomas's mother was and how distraught her daughter had been when she stepped out of the bedroom.

"The funeral was nice. You would've hated the casket. It was far too humble for your tastes," Lance said with a wounded grin, seconds later catching the ball again. He pulled his arm backwards and forced a slight curve in his throw, forcing the pale man to react faster. Ash barely caught it, but he was improving. It was impressive what the man had learned in a few hours.

"Your father is keeping the family together," he continued, addressing the memory of his friend. He remembered the fortitude and determination Jacob had shown in his home and at the funeral itself. *It's going to undo him eventually*, he thought, knowing that Jacob Walker's behavior wasn't healthy. Lance hoped that the family had found some sort of solace during the funeral, once again feeling guilty about what he had done with Thomas's body.

I'm the reason that casket was empty. I'm the reason a mother couldn't hold her child one last time.

Holding out his hand, Lance caught the rugby ball without looking at it. Although he had taught Ash how to throw it, there wasn't much variation in his throw at this point. The pale man had no purpose or function at first but was clearly learning by example. Lance had witnessed him pick up things on his own and mimic what Lance was doing. Compared to before, Lance was now paying far more attention to what Ash could do.

"I hope your family will be alright," Lance's words whispered into the void, carrying a hope that his friend could hear them. Taking part as a pallbearer, shoulder-to-shoulder with Thomas's father, younger brother, and uncle, he had tried to pay homage to his dear friend. Flanking him had been Daniel and Dieter, unwavering in their support. A part of Lance wondered whether Jacob had asked the Rifters for help carry the casket as a last tribute to Thomas, or if the man thought Lance was too unstable without their support.

"Thomas died because I wasn't strong enough to protect him. It is all because of those three," he said as he pointed at the folder on the table in between them. He watched Ash's gaze follow where he was pointing. By now, both men had etched the three pictures within that folder into their minds, the flames of memory searing the images into their consciousness.

Daniel had agreed to let Lance borrow the document for now, to help him get some closure by providing all the information that was out there. Daniel would no doubt collect the document later that week, although it mattered little to Lance. He had already memorized what he needed and had made copies with his smartphone.

"I need to do this," Lance said as he made eye contact with Ash. The pale man stared at him before nodding once, copying him. "I know . . . I know that this isn't healthy . . . I'm fragmented and unhinged," Lance explained, knowing full well that the events from the last Rift still haunted him and held dominion over his traumatized mind. He wasn't grieving properly, and he was all over the place emotionally. Even worse, he barely understood his own Class and the unknown traits that had been granted to him.

Lance only really found solace when he suppressed all that guilt and grief that he was feeling, bottling it all up inside until it turned into an icy rage. He was only stable when he was focusing on a single task. "They need to confess what they've done. They need to face justice," Lance said as he moved his arm forwards and extended his hand.

"And we'll be the ones to make them do so."

Ash watched Lance's hand for a few seconds before he extended his own. He clasped Lance's hand as he nodded once more, this time not copying the man that had created him.

Status Compendium

Name:	Lance Turner
Level:	11
Class:	Death Smith

Attributes

Endurance:	35	**Agility:**	26	**Wisdom:**	20
Strength:	26	**Perception:**	23	**Luck:**	23
Health:	650	**Mana:**	135		
Stamina:	215	**Inventory:**	25		

Traits

Taint of death:	Able to use Rift corpses as items	Prolonged use results . . . -ERROR UNREADABLE!-
Shard instability:	Prolonged use results . . . -ERROR UNREADABLE!-	Prolonged use results . . . -ERROR UNREADABLE!-

Skills

Mend Wounds	Lvl 1	Restores minor wounds	+10 Health +4 Stamina	−10 Mana
Death Forge	Lvl 1	Allows (re)forging of death related items	+1 Item	−Raw materials −Black-shards −50% Stamina regeneration −50% Mana regeneration
Repair Item	Lvl 1	Restores durability on items	+1 durability per 1 item per 1 minute	−Raw materials −Black-shards −25% Stamina regeneration −25% Mana regeneration

Retainers

Ash	1x	Human

CHAPTER FOUR

Boot Camp

Two Days After the Funeral
March, 14 AR
Lance's Flat
London, England

LANCE

Warm, gooey cheese and the crunch of grilled bread filled Lance's mouth as he bit into the sandwich. He could taste the garlic in the butter, mingled with the velvety texture of bread and milk. Lance closed his eyes as he ate the meal, knowing full well that it would turn sour the moment he opened his eyes again. He could feel his right foot keeping pressure on Ash's knee, maintaining the connection. As long as Lance did so, he could continue to use his "Repair Item" Skill on Ash.

Lance had already used this Skill on two occasions but never with Ash outside of his Inventory. The physical connection during this third time felt more intimate as he watched the damage slowly mend. Lance's sense of guilt swelled within him, heightened by the sight of Ash's expressionless face, a flicker of confusion in his eyes. After savoring every last bite of his sandwich, Lance meticulously licked the crumbs from his fingers before finally opening his eyes again.

Lance's gaze landed on Ash, clad in his old gym attire. The faded gray jogging pants and black T-shirt did little to compliment Ash's unnaturally pale complexion. Despite the lingering signs of a partially dislocated shoulder, the "Repair" Skill had fixed most of the damage already. Lance now found looking at Ash's shoulder much more tolerable.

Lance placed his plate beside him and met Ash's gaze. "Look, I've already apologized three times. Please, don't give me that look," he implored, his voice filled with remorse. Ash's stare lingered on Lance before shifting back to his dislocated left shoulder, silently assessing the state of it.

"Come on, you know it was an accident during our training," Lance said, hoping his apology would soothe his own troubled conscience. Despite the incident being unintentional, guilt still consumed him. For the last two days, Lance had been working hard with Ash to see if he could teach and train his companion.

Over the span of a day and a half, Lance had patiently taught Ash how to stand properly, maintain balance, and even increase his pace while walking. It was a journey that encompassed both frustration and excitement, as Ash evolved from a motionless husk into something that could follow Lance around. The pale man could now even grab things in the room that Lance had pointed to.

The learning process had been far from seamless, with Ash colliding into a wall on one occasion and crashing face-first into a table on another. These mishaps had resulted in minor cuts and a broken neck, respectively. On both occasions, Lance resorted to repairing Ash within his Inventory, though the latter incident had freaked Lance out beyond what words.

[Repair Item: Lvl 1]
[Cost per usage: −25% Stamina/Mana regeneration (Temporary)]
[Effects: Allows the user to repair items
At Lvl 1 restores 1 Durability per minute on 1 item]

Lance had read the Skill description and its effects about a dozen times. It seemed straightforward at first, but reality was never that simple. His "Mend Wounds" Skill was similar, in that it was just a minor healing ability, but it also blinded the recipient. The "Repair Item" Skill was also more complex than what the description listed.

"Let's focus on the positives, alright?" Lance offered as he gestured toward the hastily scrawled notes on the paper, positioned next to his teacup. "This is what we've learned thus far," he began, sharing his thoughts while ignoring the fact that Ash seemed more interested in the cup than the notes.

"First off, 'Mend Wounds' doesn't apply to you, since the system categorizes you as an item." Lance vividly recalled the countless attempts he had made, exhausting his Mana in the process. He had also experimented with his Skill on Thomas's shattered shield and tattered R.A.M. uniform, yielding comparable results. "It's only able to heal living people or animals."

Eager to keep Ash's attention, Lance tapped on the next series of scribbles on the paper. "Number Two," he said, making sure to emphasize the number, "to repair an item, I either keep it in my Inventory or maintain physical contact with it." As if to demonstrate this, he lifted his foot from Ash's knee. Almost instantly, he spotted the notification on his status screen, indicating that the "Repair Item" Skill had ceased. Promptly, he placed his foot back on Ash's knee, activating the Skill once more.

"Thirdly," he said, pointing at the next scribbled line, "repairing takes time, and I can only mend one item at a time." To illustrate his statement, he rested his hand on the torn R.A.M. uniform beside him, attempting to activate the Skill. Yet, a notification swiftly confirmed his words, indicating that it was currently impossible.

"Four, the Skill only repairs one durability per minute for a small repair. If an item is heavily damaged and missing large bits, it either needs additional suitable materials or enough black-shards to serve as a substitute," Lance explained as he glanced at both the R.A.M. uniform and the shield. The severely damaged shield was missing a lot of steel. Lance had tried to repair it but was missing the raw resources and the additional shards needed to repair it.

The R.A.M. uniform, though torn and ragged, retained most of its fabric, granting Lance the chance to mend it without acquiring additional materials. While contemplating repairs, his attention briefly turned to the cracked screen of his smartphone, but he decided against it. Each crack in the screen served as a reminder of the first Rift he had survived alongside Thomas, each fracture mirroring the hardships they had both endured during that ordeal.

He then glanced at Ash and realized how different his companion was to the average Rifter. Ash had broken his neck several hours ago and lost most of his durability, which had marked him as "broken." Still, Lance had repaired him just fine, since Ash had lost no parts of himself. Daniel was a prime example to serve as a comparison. A torn arm was something Daniel could survive, yet a broken neck was beyond healing. For Ash, it was the opposite.

"And lastly, Number Five. The reforging of a deceased Rifter into . . . well, whatever you are, doesn't create an item of similar strength," Lance remarked, thinking of the "sparring match" he had engaged in with Ash mere moments ago. The force of one of his punches had dislocated Ash's shoulder. Lance had initially thought that Ash's current capabilities were like those Thomas had as a Rifter, so he hadn't held back. In reality, Ash was now comparable to how tough and agile Thomas had been *before*.

The decrease in power and speed will make things harder for me, Lance thought, but he refrained from complaining. *Still, I can't deny that having an extra pair of hands and eyes around will be an immense help within a Rift.*

Lance recalled how he and the other weak survivors had assisted Daniel and Dieter during their first Rift. *We may not have been able to take down the monsters one-on-one. But as a group or as a distraction, we contributed a lot.* Shifting his attention back toward Ash, Lance inspected the strange man again. "I still don't know how I even created you in the first place, or if I am missing something here. But black-shards alone don't work. Perhaps a corpse is required?" he mused, recalling his attempts at that route.

"Considering your strength matches that of an average non-Rifter, we'll have to maximize your technique and experience to level the playing field," Lance declared, as he waited for the "Repair Item" skill to finish mending the damage he had done to Ash.

As Lance waited, his fingers instinctively reached for his smartphone, eager to begin planning his companion's training. He quickly lost himself in the task as he contemplated the next steps. He realized that having proper training gear was vital. Without it, he'd run the risk of another "training accident" like what had happened earlier.

A few hours later, Lance was waiting patiently inside a large store, doing his best to not feel the judgmental eyes of the woman next to him. "There are a lot of items there," the woman said, glancing into Lance's cart, which was struggling to contain all the hefty weights, steel bars, ropes, elastic bands, and other sport-related equipment within it. Even then, Lance had finished getting everything on his list. Several items were still being fetched by other employees.

He looked back at the middle-aged woman, noting her blue and black company jacket with its obligatory nametag. *She* does *looks like a Margret*, he thought as he felt her icy gaze upon him. "I'm sorry about taking up so much of your time. I swear I'm nearly finished," Lance said, ignoring Margret's concern about whether he could get it all to his car in one trip. Although she tried to sound genuine, Lance could almost taste the judgmental tone in her voice.

He then spotted two other employees returning with tennis balls, archery equipment, and some boxing and hockey gear. "Thank you!" Lance said with a warm smile as he grabbed the items and placed them in his car, only to spot the third employee running over, holding onto several folded, empty boxing bags.

Unlike Margret, there was excitement in these employees' eyes and one of them was sweating, as if he had rushed through the store to get the things on Lance's list. *Dammit*, Lance thought, chastising himself for not buying the items in several different stores to draw less attention.

He had gone to a store that was an hour's drive from his house to prevent running into an acquaintance, or—God forbid—Dieter and Daniel. The last thing Lance needed were rumors circulating in his neighborhood about a weird Rifter buying sports goods in bulk. It would have made no sense since the GRRO could provide anything that he wanted in terms of training within one of their facilities.

Lance thanked the employees as he grabbed the rest of his items, afterwards pushing the cart toward the cashier. The cashier struggled a bit with moving the heavyweights but scanned every item in Lance's cart. He smiled but figured small talk wouldn't lessen their suspicions of him. He could feel the eyes of several onlookers as he placed the items back in his cart, handling the weights with relative ease. As a Rifter, these items were useless to him in terms of equipment, seeing as he couldn't bring any of it with him inside a Rift. But to help train Ash, they would be vital.

He could use those weights in a dozen ways, from slowing down Ash's movement, to teaching the man how to throw a heavy object effectively in combat. The boxing and hockey gear would hopefully lessen some of the damage when the two of them sparred and get Ash used to gear that might hinder mobility. The steel rods, archery equipment, and other items would mimic distinct threats. Lance would blunt some of the arrow tips and wrap layers of cloth at the ends of the steel rods—all this to make it less lethal, thus preventing unnecessary repair time. Ash might only be as strong and quick as an average human, but Lance would make sure that Ash got as much of a combat and survival education as the pale man needed to survive a Rift. Or at least as much as Lance could force in a short period. *I'm putting myself and Ash through all of this based solely on the hunch that I can bring Ash along into a Rift*, he confessed to himself.

Lance noticed the successful transfer icon appear on the register, showing that he had just spent over a thousand pounds on items. This didn't even include the amount he spent to rent a car for a few days. He suppressed the urge to groan as he slid his wallet back in his pocket and said goodbye to the cashier. In the grand scheme of things, a thousand pounds was pocket change for an average Rifter. Basic provisions for bringing inside a Rift were usually even more expensive than that.

Still, training with Ash and buying the equipment was helpful for his emotional wellbeing. He could focus his mind on the task ahead, rather than deal with whatever emotions and memories he was trying to bury underneath the anger and the oath he had sworn.

So, Lance made his way over to his rental car with an overflowing cart.

"There we go," Lance said a while later, after he and Ash had unpacked everything and hauled it all inside an abandoned factory. He placed a box on the floor next to the others. Ash simultaneously put down a bag full of tennis balls. He couldn't help eyeing the strange circular objects as he did so. It had taken some time to get used to, but the quiet, observing nature of Ash had its charms.

Lance had tried to teach Ash how to speak, but the sounds he produced were akin to stone grinding against metal, like some sort of unnatural growl. Lance had stopped teaching Ash afterwards, deciding he'd spend more time on training instead.

Lance smiled as he stepped backwards, seeing the sorry state the old factory was in. Thomas and Lance had been there a dozen times when they were younger, daring one another to smash in a window with a brick or to risk their lives by traversing the rusty old walkway on the second floor. *God, we were proper idiots back then.*

From what Lance remembered, the abandoned building used to be a biscuit factory before competition had driven it out of business many years ago. The city had scheduled the place for demolition several times, but eventually just left it alone to rot, out of sight. Lance had decided to make it their training ground because of its abandoned state. That, and it was nearby, allowing easy access for him either by bike or simply after a short walk.

"This will work for now," Lance said both to himself and to Ash. Hardly anyone ever visited this place beyond the occasional daring teenager. Because he knew the place well, he figured the two of them could barricade the entrances and windows with a few heavy steel beams or some old crates. If anyone wanted to enter it, they could hear them coming and allow Ash to hide. That, or Lance would scare them off.

Just in case, he made sure that Ash was always wearing regular clothes and a hoodie to hide most of his unnatural features when they went out. At a distance, Ash looked like a pale person, something that wasn't all that strange in the United Kingdom.

Lance took another look around, seeing dozens of sharp edges, moldy wood, and rust-stained metal. If he wanted to train in a safe environment with all the equipment and opportunities he would ever need, his best course of action would be to go to one of the many GRRO training facilities. For only a minor fee, he would have access to swimming pools, climbing walls, obstacle courses, VR-chambers, gun ranges, and all the professional personal trainers he could ever need. But Lance didn't want a safe environment. He had seen just how different the GRRO facilities were from an actual Rift. There wasn't any risk of a cave collapsing or a Rifter stepping into jagged thorns or crashing through brittle terrain.

To prove his own point, Lance pulled on a nearby handrail, only to rip half of the steel support pins out of the wall, clearly rusted and broken from decay. This place could fall on their heads at any moment. That constant fear would make it the perfect place for them to train. The best part was that no one beyond Lance would know where to look for them. No one would link this place to him. Not the GRRO, nor Dieter and Daniel. He could train Ash here every day with no one noticing.

The two of them could hide the equipment they used in some of the nearby boxes, stash them on the second floor, or simply keep it where it was. Worst-case scenario was that some teenagers would steal his bow or gloves. He figured no one in their right mind would take the heavy fitness weights. And if they did, he felt that they would've earned it at that point.

Beyond training Ash, Lance realized that he would need to develop as well. Connor, Kira, and Louis were all dozens of Levels higher than he was, if not hundreds. He would need to grow both in Experience and Levels if he wanted to get justice for Thomas. Just tagging along with a company such as R.A.M. and following strict rules wouldn't work anymore. He needed more freedom and flexibility to do what he wanted and to get as much Experience as he could within a short amount of time. Ash would help him with that. Beyond that, Lance's own abilities had to be honed to perfection as well.

Then, with a wolfish grin, Lance grabbed the protective boxing helmet and a chest piece as he turned toward Ash.

"Ready for round two?"

CHAPTER FIVE

Gum, Cash, and Toes

The Next Day
March, 14 AR
The Workshop
London, England

LANCE

Lance stepped past the metal detector and body scanner, following the security officer's instructions. On the adjacent table lay a small plastic container, bearing a printed number and containing an assortment of items retrieved from his pockets upon entering the Workshop: a piece of chewing gum, car keys, hastily scribbled notes on paper, a car rental receipt, and a bottle of water.

The guard documented and took a photo of each item. Afterwards, he sealed the container and placed it into a slot in the wall that was guarded by another security officer.

Probably the most secure piece of chewing gum in the world, Lance thought, suppressing a smile while following the officer's instructions and getting into a T-pose. He had bought the piece of gum for a few pennies but could've sold it for a lot more if he had found it in a Rift. He allowed the man to pat him down and make sure that he had nothing else on him. Although it might've looked like what one might expect at an airport or any other security point, there were some differences. The guards in the back were heavily armed, with weapons far exceeding normal lethality.

In the queue next to him, Lance could see another Rifter storing her things. A large stack of blades and maces were sticking out of her pack. She had proper documentation and labels for all of it so the guards would allow it inside. The Workshop didn't mind you bringing in anything dangerous, explosive, or corrosive, as long as it was made from Rift material and had accurate documentation.

Beyond simply storing and retrieving things from an Inventory, it was hard to prove what was a legitimate Rift item and what was just being sold as one. Someone could use specialized instruments that could measure the faint radiation given off by such items, but that was expensive. This meant that most non-Rifters would have to take a gamble when buying an item or go through more secure channels such as the Workshop, where people checked and verified everything constantly. Rifters could find employment as appraisers of sorts, being able to verify the legitimacy of an Item for a client who wished to stay away from the GRRO or other agencies.

Lance thanked the security officer and collected the tag for his container. As he walked past the checkpoint, the large, open space that was the Workshop greeted him with its sheer complexity. He could still recall when Daniel had given Thomas and him their first tour. It had overwhelmed him then, but even now, he couldn't help but be in awe. There were over a thousand people on this floor, with a substantial portion of them being Rifters.

He could see people with similar guild uniforms and company logos, or simply individuals that were selling or buying at the behest of a Rifter. The Workshop had several floors and side sections, each with its own shops and specialities. GRRO engineers had designed and built this place like a fortress, with thick, armed concrete pillars carrying the weight of the sections above it, the dullish gray concrete a stark contrast to the many brightly painted shops, banners, and flags, all desperately trying to get a buyer's attention.

Lance had saved up quite a bit of cash after several successful Rifts while working for R.A.M. He had used up a portion of it to pay off any outstanding debts he had back when he was still just a nurse. At the moment, he had around £29,000 to spend. *First off, basic equipment,* he thought as he made his way toward the stairs and up to the second floor.

It took him a few minutes to find what he was looking for, but eventually he located a small store that offered the more "mundane" items. Stepping inside, Lance noticed another customer who was simply browsing, allowing him to introduce himself to the shop owner. Typically, Rifters displayed their credentials as a courtesy, assuring sellers they weren't some clueless civilians who didn't know what was going on. However, the simple act of Lance summoning a smartphone into his hand out of thin air served as sufficient proof during their initial encounter.

After going over a shortlist of what he needed, as well as a price range, he realized just how expensive all of this was when a basic blanket would set him back around £600. In the end, Lance settled for three twenty-liter steel canisters and a smaller one of ten liters. An average person would need around three to four liters of water per day, give or take. Rifters needed more depending on the climate, activity, or if they needed the water for other things such as cooking, cleaning, or rinsing out wounds.

With these items, Lance could store around seventy liters worth of freshwater or other liquids with him. The best part was that the Inventory registered each container as just a single item, so it didn't matter if the container held one liter or the full amount. This meant that Lance wouldn't have to carry around his entire weight in water. Beyond that, he bought a small steel canteen and a sturdy, flexible camp blanket he could tie together to make a sleeping bag.

Having reached an accord on the price, Lance submitted his identification tag for scanning, all the while suppressing the urge to widen his eyes in astonishment as he glimpsed the total of around £9000. The staggering figure hit him like a weight, signifying a merciless drain on his savings, nearly a third of which had evaporated in an instant. *The sad part is that it is only going to get more expensive from now on.*

His time working for R.A.M. had been arduous work, but the company had taken care of the rest. He'd worked long hours, mining rocks until he was exhausted, but he never had to think about food, water, and shelter. R.A.M. provided it all for its Rifters. Moreover, they extended their support by offering equipment for acquisition or rental, ensuring that each Rifter had access to the tools required for their tasks.

The downside of working for R.A.M. was that everything Lance had collected or killed had automatically become their property, save for the occasional item he had dared to keep for himself in the past. Now that he wanted to focus on Leveling Up, it meant that he had to look for different jobs and Rifts, ones that allowed him more freedom. This also meant that he had to take care of everything by himself now.

Saying goodbye to his savings, Lance went toward the next shop to get the things he would need.

I'm so broke, Lance thought. He still had enough to pay for rent and food for two months, but it didn't compare to the costs of buying Rift items. For now, he was done with spending money on anything worth more than a candy bar. With an internal groan, he opened his Inventory and took stock of what he now had in terms of items.

[Inventory slots: 25/25]
[Damaged smartphone 1x]

Lance figured it was wise to keep the phone in his Inventory, since it was the most expensive item he possessed. By doing so, he could safeguard its battery life, shield it from harm, and keep it dry. While the thought of selling it for additional funds had briefly enticed him, he ultimately chose against it, recognizing the significance the phone held beyond its monetary value.

[20-Liter steel canister filled with water 3x]
[10-Liter steel canister filled with water 1x]
[1-Liter steel canister filled with water 1x]

Considering the considerable space the five water canisters would occupy in his Inventory, Lance weighed their worth. Opting for efficiency, he secured the smaller canteen to his hip, ensuring both accessibility and conservation of space. This arrangement granted him the capacity to carry approximately seventy-one liters of water, a provision he hoped would endure for at least two weeks, possibly extending further with careful rationing.

[Camp blanket 1x]

Lance figured a single blanket would be enough for his first expedition. It meant that he wouldn't have to sleep on the rough floor or in the cold, provided there wasn't any rain. It came with a sling so that he could carry it. But it was bulky and would hinder his movements.

[Ash 1x]
[R.A.M. Work uniform 1x]

It would take him two slots to bring Ash with him inside a Rift and get him at least dressed. Shoes, weapons, and armor would take up too much space. Not that Lance had the cash for it. The uniform itself had been Thomas's R.A.M. uniform that Lance had wrapped around his torso when he escaped the Rift. It was worth at least £3000 and was technically still R.A.M's property. But Lance figured he could borrow it a while longer before he returned it. Beyond that, the company had already dropped Thomas's loan, so Lance felt like it wasn't technically stealing on his part.

[5kg of dried Red bark fruit 4x]
[5kg of Trejo roots 4x]
[5kg of dried Rirkling meat 4x]

Food rations would either play a significant role or hardly at all. He still remembered his other Rift experiences and the occasional wildlife or edible plants he had seen there. If he were lucky in his next Rift, he could live off the land for a while. The fruit he had bought was both hydrating and rich in vitamins, the roots rich in fibers and carbs, and the meat fatty, oily, and rich in proteins.

And the best part is, everything tastes horrible! Lance thought as he remembered the "sample" he had tried in the shop. It was the cheapest option that Lance could find that was still healthy and edible. He would've preferred already cooked and prepared meals, but that would take up more space in his Inventory. Better to cook on-site. As a last resort, he could even consume the food raw, although at that point, it seemed more appealing to fling oneself off a cliff rather than endure such culinary torture.

[Leather raincoat 1x]

It was a crude and poorly-stitched-together leather raincoat. It reeked and was uncomfortable to wear, but it was cheap and waterproof. In case of a downpour, it would come in handy. If not, Lance figured he could use it as a waterproof roof to sleep under. The worst-case scenario was that he could rip it apart and boil it, to serve as a last-ditch meal when everything went wrong.

[Steel entrenching tool 1x]

Bulky, tough, and easy to use. It was a simple tool, with an option to turn the head into a small shovel or pickaxe. He could strap it to his belt if he wanted to. The tool weighed a fair bit and could hinder his mobility if he didn't wield it. Lance figured he could also use the pickaxe as an improvised weapon of sorts. If not, it would help mine ores or make digging up roots easier. He could also turn the shovel part into a makeshift grill to hold over a fire.

[Broken steel shield 1x]

Lance had decided it was wise to bring Thomas's shield with him. Though cracked and no longer offering its former level of protection, the thick steel composition still provided a measure of defense. He decided that training Ash to use a weapon and shield would work best for the earlier Rifts, so a steel shield would come in handy.

With all slots filled, Lance would have to carry the rest of it with him. For footwear, he held onto the sneakers he had worn during his first Rift experience. While not the most robust option for survival, they still provided basic protection for his soles. Lance had torn his former tattered nurse's uniform into thick strips and rolled it together into makeshift bandages, hand wraps, and bindings to help tie things down. He had also bought a cheaper variant of the uniform that R.A.M. used, with much less padding or protection.

In terms of offense, he had bought a steel hand axe and a small utility knife. The former was useful for chopping wood, while the latter was like a Swiss Army knife, only longer and sturdier. All of it made him look woefully unprepared, but it would do for now. He still had around £500 to spend. He could've gotten some extra socks or something, but Lance had spent it on an information broker and facilitator.

What made the GRRO so successful was in part the way they allowed Rifters to find one another and to help in clearing a Rift. There was the obvious monitoring and policing element to it, but most of the time the GRRO helped facilitate Rifters in whatever they needed, be it buying or selling items, securing travel options, or finding suitable parties.

Lance could've used the information the GRRO had on hand, but he instead preferred to spend the £500 on a specialist, searching through the hundreds of options for a suitable match. In the end, Lance had settled on a broker that Matt and another Rifter had told him about. He would hear back in a few days, hoping that the broker could find a good match for him that ticked all the specifics he required.

He had been tempted to buy a sidearm such as a pistol, but he knew he lacked the funds for it. Daniel and Dieter had explained why they didn't use guns, since most Skills wouldn't work with modern weaponry, making them far less effective when facing higher-Level monsters. Still, Lance had seen during his time with the R.A.M. how effective a machine gun could be on the lower Levels.

So, with an empty wallet and a filled-up Inventory, Lance went back home after retrieving his things from the security checkpoint, including his well-protected bubblegum. Hopefully, the minty flavor would wash out the sting of spending nearly £30,000 in a single day.

[You have stored an item in your Inventory]
[You have combined and retrieved four items]

A few hours later, Lance watched Ash suddenly spring into existence, fully dressed and wielding a shield and axe. Ash's eyes scanned his surroundings and his own hands as he got into a defensive stance, just like they had practiced.

"You need to be faster, buddy. Don't just look for the weapons in your hands. Feel the weight of the shield and how your hand grips the handle of the weapon," Lance said as he moved over toward his companion while pointing at the axe.

Ash was wearing the repaired R.A.M. uniform with the broken shield in one hand and the axe in the other. The pale man looked silly, but Lance knew just how effective an axe and shield combination could be.

[You have stored an item in your Inventory]
[You have combined and retrieved two items]

Again, he stored Ash and the equipment, only to bring him out again. This time, Ash was wearing just the uniform. To his credit, the man stayed still and composed, no longer pausing and hesitant. Beyond training Ash during the last few days in combat, survival skills, and basic tasks, Lance was also teaching him to adapt to being retrieved from the Inventory. He needed Ash to react quickly to his environment, either to protect and shield people or simply to remain neutral and blend in.

Lance continued to store and retrieve Ash, each time switching things up. One moment Ash had a knife in his hand, the other moment it was a steel canister, or he was suddenly wearing a raincoat. Each time it happened would be another experience for Ash. It was slow going, but the pale man was getting better at it. Beyond that, Lance was also teaching him how to hide and only to come out when he gave Ash a signal.

His idea was to bring Ash with him during his next Rift. Lance knew he still lacked the experience, training, and equipment to survive a weak Rift on his own, so he needed to party up with actual Rifters. "All right, try to hide again," Lance said as he closed his eyes and counted to ten, allowing Ash the time to scout his surroundings and pick a spot.

Ash's current capabilities and Lance's lack of Rift experience were the reason he had used a broker. He needed to partner up with a group that had plenty of Rift experience so that he could learn from them. But the group had to be more defensive, more hesitant to go out. Lance figured that a more defensive team would allow him more freedom to explore on his own and to bring Ash out in the field. Teaching the pale man how to hide from monsters and Rifters would be a valuable skill to have during that time.

I hope this works, Lance thought as he opened his eyes. He glanced sideways and instantly spotted Ash's toes sticking out underneath the curtains as the man tried to hide in a way a child might.

God help me . . .

CHAPTER SIX

Kickstarting Ash

The day Before Rift 8
March, 14 AR
The Abandoned Factory
London, England

LANCE

Lance's fingers released the tension of his bowstring, propelling an arrow forward. The projectile whizzed through the air, aimed at the sprinting figure of Ash. Yet, just as the arrow closed in on its target, Ash swiftly evaded the projectile, ducking beneath it. A grin spread across Lance's face as he retrieved a second arrow, quickly nocking it while stealing a glance at the charging man.

Ash's momentum was impressive, matched by his improved form. Though not yet reaching Thomas's intimidating skill, Ash had evolved into a skilled combatant, capable of posing a substantial threat to most non-Rifters. With the added weaponry of shield and axe, his potential magnified further. The next arrow left Lance's bow at a frightening speed, aimed directly at Ash center mass. Anticipating the attack, Ash raised the steel shield in front of him, deflecting the projectile just in time. Lance then moved to the next spot on the rusted steel catwalk overlooking the obstacle course he had made for Ash.

From this elevated position, he observed how Ash sprinted and maneuvered himself over wooden crates, leaping from one marked floor to the next. Lance, the architect of this challenging gauntlet, unleashed moments of chaos and urgency onto the obstacle course. Every so often, Lance would surprise Ash with a boxing bag hidden around a corner, or another one that would come crashing down from the ceiling when Lance cut a nearby rope that had kept it in place.

Lance had painted the bags with either human or monstrous faces on them. He had tasked Ash to ignore the human-looking ones, or even hide from them. When it came to the ones painted to resemble monsters, the pale man was to always go for the kill. Lance had filled some boxing bags with sand, while he filled others with rocks, just to throw Ash off balance when encountering them.

Adding another layer of challenge, Ash now had to contend with the occasional archer that Lance was portraying. Initially, Lance employed cloth-covered arrows fitted with blunted tips, their surfaces coated with paint. This allowed them to easily tell if Ash had successfully blocked an arrow or if it had just bounced off his body. Following exhausting days of practice, Lance transitioned to actual arrows, heightening the stakes of Ash's training. A part of him felt bad for doing so, but he knew he would need Ash's help in the coming days. Despite the heightened danger, Ash never exhibited signs of pain, only discomfort at being rendered immobile.

Lance calmly nocked another arrow, biding his time for the perfect opportunity. Just as Ash scaled a wooden obstacle, Lance let the arrow fly, aiming for the pale man's torso. Ash swiftly leaned to the left, evading a direct hit but not escaping entirely unscathed. The arrow pierced his right arm, embedding itself into the wooden surface below.

Undeterred, Ash promptly shattered the shaft by slamming the steel shield against it. Without missing a beat, he then climbed upwards again before leaping off the other side. Ash landed amidst a cluster of boxing bags adorned with monstrous faces that Lance had positioned there.

Lance's companion rushed first, slamming into the bag with the shield before throwing his axe at another bag. Ash then grabbed the bag he had slammed into, holding it upright to block Lance's next arrow currently speeding toward him. Moments later, Ash was on the move again, having retrieved the axe that he had thrown earlier. Now with both axe and shield in hand, he rushed forwards, rounding the corner and stumbling upon a steel barrel that had a printed-out picture of Connor taped on the side of it.

Lance wanted to see what the man would do. By suddenly introducing that picture in their training regime, Lance would quickly learn whether Ash would or wouldn't attack it due to it being a human. To Lance's surprise, he noticed Ash speeding up. With an explosive leap, the man propelled himself toward a solid brick wall, rebounding off it with tremendous force, hurtling toward the unsuspecting barrel from the side with all the kinetic force the man could produce.

Lance watched a shield-wielding Ash crash into the barrel, sending it on its side with enough force to create a loud impact noise. Without pause, Ash then followed up with a relentless barrage of punches and strikes upon the barrel again and again, his commitment evident in every blow.

"And stop!" Lance shouted. In response, his companion paused his assault and return to a standing position, waiting for another command. For a few seconds, Lance simply watched him, peering down from his elevated position. A sense of pride washed over Lance as he witnessed Ash's instinctive, decisive actions. The man's commitment to the task at hand left a good impression. However, a seed of doubt sprouted within Lance's mind, whispering that the magnitude of violence displayed was perhaps venturing into the realm of excessive force.

Ash mirrors what I share and teach. I'm doing this to get justice, not vengeance. Lance remembered the many nights he had spent with Ash going over the three pictures, memorizing their every little detail and how they made him feel. Rather than lose himself in a complicated ethical dilemma of justice versus vengeance, Lance focused on the here and now.

"You did great," Lance said as he placed the bow and arrows down on the ground before jumping off the catwalk. He landed on the floor in a crouched position a few paces away from Ash. He slowly rose to his feet as he flashed his pale companion a smile. "Now, let's see how you'll do against an opponent who fights back."

Lance's smartphone lay on its back, no longer propped upright because the crate it had been leaning against was now broken. A mixture of red and gray blood marred the surface of the cracked screen, although one could still vaguely make out the song title on display: "Mötley Crüe - Kickstart my Heart."

With a sluggish ascent, Ash rose from the ground, a trail of gray blood dripping from his broken nose. He wiped his nose across the sleeve of his R.A.M. uniform before reassuming his fighting stance. The protective boxing and hockey gear he wore showed a lot of damage from all the sparring. Both men had been going at it for the better part of five hours already, only stopping occasionally to put on a new song, or heal or repair when the situation required it.

"I told you I would get even," Lance declared, giving his companion a satisfied, albeit admittedly immature grin. A grin that was stained red by Lance's own bloody nose. Despite Lance being stronger and faster than Ash, it didn't mean that he was exempt from taking any damage. The first two hours Lance had dominated their sparring match, with him having to constantly hold back in order to not damage Ash or risk wasting time waiting for the man to get repaired. Still, the longer things went on, the more fatigued and wounded Lance got. Ash didn't tire, nor did he seem to get distracted by pain or discomfort.

"Unarmed once again," Lance said, circling Ash and teasing him with the occasional fast jab. It was still surprising to see just how skilled his companion had gotten in such a small timeframe. Ash was adequate at using a shield and one-handed weapon but was horrible with ranged weaponry or when grappling. But boxing was something that he picked up fast. The more Lance noticed these developments, the more he became convinced that some bits of Thomas endured within Ash, beyond just the physical similarities.

Dodging the oncoming punch, Lance contorted his body, narrowly escaping the impact against his face. Yet, before he could regain his footing, Ash's subsequent strikes connected, battering against his defensive guard as he retreated. Lance rubbed his bloody nose and tasted blood, remembering the nasty uppercut Ash had given him a few minutes ago. After having spent most of his day training Ash, his Stamina was no longer regenerating as quickly as it should be. Ash could simply keep going for a long while, only suffering damage if he constantly went beyond his limits.

I need this. This style of training is exactly what I need. Pain, hardship, and enduring it all, Lance thought, adjusting his stance before lunging toward Ash. His fists unleashed a barrage of rapid, powerful jabs, each punch resembling a haymaker due to his enhanced Strength. *I'll use that pain to reforge myself into something stronger.* A bloodstained grin stretched across Lance's face as he observed Ash's arms rising to block the onslaught, momentarily obstructing his line of sight. Seizing the opportunity, Lance closed the distance in a swift dash, ducking low before explosively springing upward.

By the time Ash registered Lance again, he had already maneuvered himself next to him. Grabbing onto Ash's pale neck and arm, Lance skillfully disrupted his balance. Then, in a fluid motion, Lance's leg descended like a thunderous axe, sweeping Ash's leg out from under him. The powerful momentum catapulted the pallid fighter's head into a collision course with the unyielding ground. Fortunately, Ash's layers of protective gear prevented Lance from shattering the man's skull and spine upon impact with the unforgiving concrete floor.

"The Osotogari needs work," Lance told himself as he backed off, remembering the correct name of the leg sweep he had just performed. The dazed Ash gradually registered what had just happened to him as he got up again. While Thomas had spent several years learning how to box from his old man, Lance had done some judo in his childhood. He wasn't all that skilled in it, but he remembered enough of the basics.

Both Daniel and Dieter had encouraged Lance to pick it up again during his training in the GRRO facilities. There, Lance had learned the basics of several fighting styles, all adapted to fight monsters that were beastlike or humanoid in appearance. While most Rifters preferred a spear, sword, or other tools for fighting up close, one couldn't underestimate the amount of kinetic force a person performing a large leg sweep could generate. This was without factoring in how much a strong Rifter could further increase that lethality.

"Shield and sword," Lance ordered as he watched the man head toward a crate to pick up a broken steel shield and a thick metal pipe that had cloth wrapping at the tip. Lance grabbed his smartphone and pressed the repeat button, ignoring the bloodstains on the screen. He still found it silly to be sparring with this type of music, but it had been a song from Thomas's collection. A part of him was enjoying his friend's choice of music more and more. *You sure know how to pick them, Thomas*, Lance thought, suppressing a chuckle before he faced Ash and nodded, letting him know they would continue their training. Lance then held his right hand to the side as he activated his Inventory.

[You have retrieved an item]

The hand axe appeared in his hand as he rushed toward Ash, taking a few swings at him with the back end of it, both to prevent any major damage to Ash and to stop the axe from chipping when steel hit steel. With both using weaponry, Lance had to hold back a lot more of his power, knowing full well that Ash had more trouble with this type of fighting. Still, Lance only held back so much, preferring to keep his companion in constant survival mode.

Lance swung a few times, seeing Ash block it with his shield before the pale man slammed his own weapon toward him. It barely missed Lance as he backed off. They exchanged steel several more times, each fighter going in for low and high strikes, feinting left, or suddenly rushing in from the right. Ash hit Lance on the arms and on the sides a few times. But it was nothing compared to what Lance did to him. Just as the song was nearing the four-minute mark, he went for the proverbial kill.

Lance came in with a wide swing, letting the axe zero in on Ash's right arm. The pale fighter instantly brought his own weapon up to block it, as he had done several times before.

[You have stored an item in your Inventory]

The axe suddenly disappeared, Ash's weapon meeting no resistance as his swing went wide. Lance simply kept his momentum going as his axe swing turned into a balled fist that hammered into the side of Ash's ribcage with enough force to crack bones and send the pale man down on the floor.

[You have retrieved an item]

The axe then returned a few seconds later, Lance pinning the dazed man onto his back. He kept a foot on his chest to keep him in place. Lance then brought the axe down, stopping just short of his neck before the timer went off and the song stopped playing.

Retrieving an item wasn't instantaneous. While skilled Rifters could improve their speed, the process of retrieval always took longer than simply storing an object. Lance's actions had carried inherent risks, leaving him momentarily defenseless, yet they held the potential to an enemy off guard.

Lance extended his left hand, assisting the injured man to his feet. "You did great, mate," he praised softly, gesturing toward the nearby crate, indicating that they should stow the weapons. As Ash complied, Lance stored his own weapon in his Inventory. With a sigh, he retrieved his bloodstained smartphone, storing it for a moment. When he retrieved it again, its surface was miraculously wiped clean.

It was one of the many benefits of using an Inventory system like this. A Rifter could only store what the Inventory system classified as an Item. You couldn't store anything clinging to an Item such as blood, dirt, or grease. This made it harder for a Rifter to apply oil or poison to a weapon, but it made it that much easier to clean something or dry wet clothes.

He checked the time as he sat down against a nearby crate and caught his breath. His body wanted to scream out from all the bruises and fatigue he had built up in the last few hours, but it felt right. Each cut reminded him of the dangers of a Rift, each bruise felt like a reassuring sign that he had prepared as well as he could, and his aching muscles reminded him of what would happen tomorrow: his next Rift.

Mend Wounds
[You have used Mend Wounds Lvl 1 at the cost of 10 Mana]
[Current Mana 31/135]
[Mend Wounds has reached Lvl 2]

As the blue light enveloped his body, he could feel his nose itch and get warmer, as the wave of healing energy desperately tried to fix his battered face and the other injuries he had sustained. It took him a few minutes to realize that he had received a status update, noting the upgraded version of "Mend Wounds." Lance opened the menu, checking to see the difference now that it had reached a higher Level.

[Mana cost] [+5]
[Additional Health restored] [+10]
[Additional Stamina restored] [+4]

An increase of ten Health and four Stamina at the cost of five extra Mana? Not bad, Lance decided. He double-checked it just to be sure. The increase in his Skill Level was a surprise, but one that he had been expecting for some while. As Rifters used Skills inside or outside a Rift, they would grow more comfortable with it, as well as tailor their bodies to it. When they reached a certain point, their Skill could increase in Level and potency. Because Lance had been using this Skill for a long time, not to mention the frequency of use the last few days due to the constant damage from sparring, it had only been a matter of time before he improved the Skill.

The increased Mana cost was a downside, but Lance was still making a net profit in Stamina and Health recovery because of efficiency. In theory, this would mean that he would have to cast the Skill less often to heal up, resulting in him not constantly blinding himself from the healing glow.

When Ash was done, he took a seat next to Lance, leaning against the crate and mimicking the way Lance was sitting. The pale man had removed his protective hockey and boxing gear, revealing the mess of nicks and cuts that covered his body. Feeling guilty, Lance moved his elbow against Ash as he activated two Skills at once.

Mend Wounds
[You have used Mend Wounds Lvl 2 at the cost of 15 Mana]
[Current Mana 16/135]

Repair Item
**[You have used Repair Item Lvl 1. Reducing Stamina and
Mana regeneration by 25% until completion]**

A flash of blue light blinded him as he felt the restorative energy flow through him, mending bruises and minor cuts. It felt stronger than before. Although he hadn't counted on the increase in Skill, it came at a perfect time, because they would head into another Rift tomorrow.

"Are you ready for your first Rift experience?" Lance asked his companion when the healing Skill had stopped, seeing the pale man contemplate before carefully nodding his head once. Lance wasn't sure whether Ash had simply nodded because he thought it was required of him, or if the man had formed an opinion on his own. For now, it didn't matter to Lance. He simply chose to believe it was the latter and take it as a sign that the omens for tomorrow were at least favorable.

"Let's try not to die tomorrow," Lance said finally to Ash and himself as the two men began to prepare mentally for the following day.

CHAPTER SEVEN

Bottom Feeders

The Following Day
March, 14 AR
Ipswich, England

LANCE

Lance checked the time on his phone as he calculated whether he'd make it to his destination, Ipswich, on time. It was a habit of his when using public transportation. It didn't matter if he took an earlier train, he'd still unconsciously wonder about what time he'd get there or if there would be a delay. He noticed his reflection on the cracked screen, the tired expression on his face, hinting at the horrible night he had suffered through. They were happening more frequently.

Similar to what he had experienced in the hospital, strange, lifelike dreams had tormented him. This time it was Thomas fighting a Lizardling, back during their first Rift. It wasn't so much a dream of his friend, as it was like a memory seen through his eyes. His dreams were forcing every feeling, thought, and ingrained instinct from Thomas onto Lance, demanding that he relive those moments. By the time he had woken up, he had been a mess of sweat and aching muscles, Ash standing over him with a curious expression.

As he pushed the memories of his horrible night away, he forced his mind to focus on the task at hand. The broker he had hired back at the Workshop had come through and set up the meeting for him and the party he would be joining, the White Clovers. Lance had studied all the information about them, as well as the information about this Rift.

From what Lance had learned about the Clovers, there were always three core members with others joining them now and again. They had only lost one member in the last four years and that had happened during the closing of a Rift-event, when a Rifter exited the Rift at an unfortunate angle and speed. Beyond that, the group only took official GRRO Rifts and focused on closing Rifts that were ranked as Level One or Two. The list stated other variables such as their average payment per Rift, typical expenses, interaction and standing with other Rifters, and their recorded modus operandi.

It was a lot of data. The GRRO kept track of a lot of things, maintaining a steady supply of information about the coming and goings of items, materials, and Rifters. At the moment, Lance wasn't as interested in what the White Clovers' financial score was but how they operated.

"Bottom Feeders," Lance whispered, tasting the insult that was associated with the term. The White Clovers were a party that specialized in clearing Rifts, meaning they would constantly enter and clear the Rift-event until the Rift itself destabilized back on Earth and collapsed. These types of Rifters were called "Closers" depending on what region of the world you were in. On paper, it was a very important job, because they removed a Rift from a location, allowing normality to return to the area. Sadly, some Rifters looked down on these types of Rifters, claiming that they were too weak, unskilled, or cowardly to clear anything higher than a Level Two Rift, giving them degrading names such as "Bottom Feeders" or "Tremble Shards."

Lance wasn't sure what he'd make of these types of individuals, having only encountered Rifters who worked as employees for companies such as R.A.M. and those belonging to larger guilds such as Dieter and Daniel. In the end, he figured that there were positives and negatives for many jobs and types of Rifters. He decided he should instead focus his attention on what he had to do right now: learn and get stronger, quickly.

Eventually, Lance felt the train slow down as they arrived at Ipswich station. He steeled himself for what was to come before collecting his things and throwing his rucksack over his shoulder, making his way to the nearby exit. He smiled as he passed by the train conductor, clocking the confused look on her face. An hour ago, she had asked him to show his ticket, only to be met by a GRRO-sanctioned Rifter ID. It meant that he could travel freely to and from Rifts without question, although in most cases this meant the airport or taxi. No doubt the conductor hadn't seen a lot of Rifters who used the train, not to mention preferred standard class.

"Have a nice day," Lance said as he exited, his senses picking up on the unique sounds and smells that made Ipswich the town that it was.

Because Lance had arrived early, he had about two hours to spend on his own. Having never visited Ipswich, he did a bit of sightseeing. He did this both to get a feel of the place and to calm his nerves. It was a Level Two Rift, and he had been inside higher-Level ones, but each Rift carried a unique set of threats and dangers, be it terrain, climate, or life forms. And this Rift would be the first one without Thomas.

Lance had bought and finished a sandwich, some chocolate bars, and ice cream, stuffing himself as full as he could. While Rifters could only bring Rift-related Items with them inside a Rift, they could eat and drink normal things on the day of them entering a Rift, provided there was about a solid six hours of time in between. There had been studies done on why this was so, a scientist by the name of Michelle Eldrin being the first one to document the process. Eldrin had figured out what things a Rifter could eat and drink beforehand and how long it would take before the radiation from their white-shards would have changed and affected those nutrients. With eight hours to go before he would enter the Rift, Lance ate as many calories as possible, while also treating himself a bit.

When it was time to meet up with the others, he made his way to where the Rift was located, just a short walk from the town center. It wasn't hard to spot it because of the many barriers in place, preventing average citizens from nearing it. From what Lance had read about the Rift, it had appeared in a large apartment complex, swallowing it up whole along with parts of the adjacent buildings. It had happened during the day, so the Rift had caught only a handful of people when it appeared. A few other Rifters had cleared the Rift already, but only to stop it from growing beyond a certain point. Afterwards, most Rifters stopped caring when the Level of the Rift had gotten too low.

From what Lance could see and what he had read, this had been going on for about a year now, with a section of the town now inaccessible because of the Rift. It wasn't in a favorable location where companies could buy the rights to mine or farm it. So it simply stood out like an eyesore here in the heart of Ipswich, constantly reminding people of a horrible day in their lives. All the while, the town bled resources because this section of town was blocked off.

It feels weird that in a short while this Rift will go away, Lance thought, remembering the deal the broker had bartered between Lance and the White Clovers. Apparently, the party had signed up for two consecutive clearings.

Lance passed a corner and noticed a small crowd waiting outside of a small restaurant. *Found them,* he thought. He could see several reporters and locals standing outside, peering in with both eagerness and curiosity. Sighing, Lance grabbed his rucksack more firmly before he walked toward the restaurant, slowly making his way past the onlookers. He ignored their irritated comments and questions. No doubt most of them were thinking he was just a random civilian who wanted to get a closer look. Lance continued to move forwards. It wasn't like any of them had the strength to prevent him from just slowly pushing his way inside.

Lance closed the door and saw the people inside. Most of them were staring right at him. It wasn't hard to figure out who was a Rifter and who worked for the GRRO or for the restaurant. The chainmail, leather, swords, and axes quickly gave it away. *Myles Howard, Noel Burke, Claudia Young,* Lance told himself repeatedly as he made his way over to them. He hated this, meeting new people, and introducing himself. It was the reason he preferred to only have a handful of friends and acquaintances rather than dozens. He felt a slight ache in his chest, catching him off guard as he neared them, feeling an unusual instinct take over. A second later, he flashed a warm smile as he grabbed Myles's hands. "I'm assuming you guys aren't here for the ravioli," he said, his smile strangely confident and infectious.

Myles and the others laughed and they all proceeded to shake his hand, introducing themselves one by one. All the while, Lance made mental notes, trying to produce a picture of each of them in his head, combined with the information the broker had provided. *Myles Howard. My height, white skin, gray eyes, blonde hair, late thirties. Warrior class. Around Level Eighty,* Lance thought as he examined Myles's chainmail and thick leather armor. It wasn't a fancy design but rather one of practicality. Someone had designed it to not hinder movement, and it displayed signs of being used in the field. Beyond that, Myles had a shield on his back and a one-handed sword on his hip. Lance could see a pistol and a knife secured at his side.

The woman next to Myles wore mostly leather armor with thick padding underneath it. Her arms and legs had steel plates woven into leather guards. *Claudia Young. Shorter than me, tanned skin, green eyes, brown hair, early thirties. Warrior class as well. Around Level Seventy,* Lance recalled as he took in the sight of her axe and mace on her hips, hinting that she might be a dual wielder. Slung around her back was a shotgun, big and sturdy and designed for a Rifter.

In the back sat Noel. The man was busy finishing his coffee while rubbing a hand through his thick gray beard. *Noel Burke. Average height, dark skin, brown eyes, graying hair, in his late fifties. Mage class. Around Level Eighty-Five,* Lance noted. Noel's outfit included layers of cotton, leather, and a scale-like material. What stood out most were several shaped Mana stones embedded in his gauntlets. Most Mages preferred having these stones on hand to serve as Mana batteries. Beyond that, Noel carried a large spear and several throwing axes.

"Good of you to join us," Myles said as he offered Lance a seat.

Noel nodded at that. "Always better with a fourth. The broker mentioned you had a healing Skill?" the older man asked, his gaze somewhat hopeful.

"Yeah, I can mend minor wounds. It just speeds up the healing process, so no reverting damage or anything like that," Lance said honestly, knowing it would be better to be as open about his Skill set as possible. These three had known each other for a long time, and every member was at a higher Level than he was.

Claudia chuckled before nudging Noel in the ribs. "See, Noel? We care about you. I told you we'd get you someone to help you out, you old fossil. This is almost as good as a private nurse, right?" Claudia said with a teasing grin. Noel and Myles chuckled at that, with the former trying to look upset but failing to do so.

Lance then slowly raised his hand, drawing their attention and halting their mirth. "Actually . . . I'm a registered nurse," he told them before Myles fell off his seat, laughing, while Claudia's face lit up like a Christmas tree.

Over the course of their meeting, Lance had gradually gotten to know each of them. From what he had learned from the broker, these three were the core members and had been working with one another for many years. Myles and Noel knew each other the longest, with Claudia joining the group a few months after that. Since then, the group had cleared an impressive number of lesser Rifts but spread over years rather than months.

"Are you ready?" Noel asked several hours later, watching Lance with a calm expression.

Lance nodded as he finished putting on his gear, looking hopelessly out of place compared to his three companions. He lacked protective clothes and armor and only had basic tools to defend himself with, but even then, he looked quite calm. "Yeah, I guess I am. No doubt that will change when we go in," Lance added, flashing Noel a reassuring grin.

The other three members of the party were all ready and armed to the teeth. Myles carried a large duffel bag and Noel had a big backpack strapped to his back with large rods sticking out from the side. The four of them had done all they could to prepare, going over the information that was known about the Rifts and reports of the previous Rifters who had cleared it, and discussing the strategy that the four of them would use in the beginning and throughout the Rift itself.

"It's a Level Two Rift. Just stick by my side and you'll be fine. Myles and Claudia will hold the front," Noel said reassuringly, his eyes focused.

Lance nodded to the man. He didn't feel the need to explain that he wouldn't hide in the back. He wanted to take the fight to the monsters. He had to. The whole reason he wanted to go back in a Rift was to Level Up. He watched Myles finish with the GRRO employee and the reporter that he was talking to.

"Go time!" Myles said with a grin as he slapped his cheeks a few times to get himself ready. Then, as if they'd practiced, the three of them grabbed folded cloaks from their table and slung them around their shoulders. The cloak was a perfect green fabric with a dyed white clover in the middle. "You mind wearing one, Lance?" Myles asked calmly, trying not to sound too pushy.

"Sure, it will help hide my pajama-like outfit," Lance replied, as he watched the man grin at the comment.

Claudia walked up to Lance and handed him a spare one, smiling when he accepted it. "They made me promise not to comment about your gear, but your current outfit is horrendous," she said as she helped him put on the cloak.

"It isn't Rift material, so don't get attached to it. We usually have it bulk-made for a few hundred pounds and wear them when we head to the Rift itself.

It helps with our public image, seeing our logo. That and it displays unity," Myles commented as he did his finishing touches on his own cloak.

"And it makes us seem badass when the cloak disintegrates as we enter the Rift," Claudia blurted out, slapping Lance's shoulders before she led the way outside.

Lance and the others followed her, moving next to one another as several local reporters began taking pictures, others asking them to comment on the Rift. Like they had rehearsed, the party members kept walking, turning the corner, and making their way toward the Rift with the GRRO barricades and safety net surrounding it. With all the pictures being taken, Lance was glad that he was wearing the cloak, since it allowed him to cover his face and his basic equipment.

Although Myles had already spoken with the GRRO representative, each party member still had to provide their Rifter IDs before they could go inside. One reporter with proper clearance followed them inside with a camera. Although this Rift was insignificant and wouldn't get any attention nationwide, on a local level, this was a momentous occasion. These Rifters weren't there for a quick clearing to prevent the Rift from spilling open or growing out of hand. No, these Rifters were here to get rid of this blight on their town once and for all.

The Rifters stood next to one another, facing the large pulsating black sphere of energy. It was quite large compared to the Rifts Lance had encountered before. The size of a Rift meant nothing in terms of the dangers that lay within. Still, it was impressive and intimidating to look at.

[You have retrieved an Item 2x]

A steel hand axe suddenly appeared in his right hand while a sturdy entrenching tool appeared in his left. He slammed them together to feel the weight of the material and psych himself up. The start of a Rift was always hectic, with nearby monsters being drawn by the sudden presence of Rifters. Lance had been inside of a few Rifts but never as the vanguard. Even weaker Rifts contained dozens, if not hundreds, of monsters.

"We go in as a team," Myles said as he pointed his sword at the Rift, his face devoid of any emotion.

"And return as one, in victory," Claudia and Noel said as one, each of them gripping their weapons tightly as they waited for the GRRO to start the timer. A nearby screen displayed a number, slowly counting down from ten.

Then, at the zero mark, the four Rifters rushed toward the Rift, as the unnatural black energy swallowed them up. The last thing the cameras managed to record were four green capes being torn apart when they touched the Rift. Bits of the cape fell on the ground, partially displaying a white clover symbol.

CHAPTER EIGHT

Rift 8

Mere Minutes Later
March, 14 AR
Inside Rift 8

LANCE

In a sudden flash of black energy, Lance arrived inside the Rift. Momentum kept him going as he crashed into a nearby wall, banging his nose badly. The throbbing sensation and the taste of blood were enough of a reminder to get his bearings. He forced himself to adapt to his environment, holding out his weapons defensively. The air here felt thin and had a chill to it, as if winter had suddenly embraced him.

He could hear the others call out their names one by one. They had adapted far more easily because of their higher Levels and Experience. "Lance!" he shouted, letting them know he was in one piece and conscious. From what he could tell, the others had all landed in different locations inside of the apartment complex but were still nearby. Firmly holding the axe and entrenching tool, he made his way toward the nearby door, slowly opening it. He held out the shovel and used the still, reflective surface to peer inside the other room, only for something to ram into the tool with great speed.

Lance let go of the tool and grabbed his axe with both hands. He waited near the partially opened door, just to the side, with his axe at the ready. Seconds went by as Lance kept silent, maintaining his ambush. Then the door slammed open, and a three-legged monster rushed in. It was the size of a large ram, a single jagged horn jutting from its head. Coarse gray fur, matted with filth and dirt, covered its body.

It barely registered Lance or tried to halt its movements when he brought the axe head down, slamming into the creature's back and shattering its spine. He then slammed the axe down three more times, biting into bone and severing tendons, muscles, and bundles of nerves.

Focus. Secure the kill and your surroundings, Lance thought as he remembered Daniel's advice. He held the axe at the ready as he moved toward the fallen monster, quickly checking its vitals before he looked to the door again. He didn't want a second monster charging in and attacking him. Having confirmed it was dead, Lance was about to leave when he spotted the notification above the monster's corpse.

[Would you like to store this Item?]
[Yes] [No]

For a split second, it reminded him of his last Rift when he noticed the same notification hover above the body of his best friend. Lance felt rage flow up to the surface before he managed to suppress it. Instead, he grabbed a nearby broken lamp and threw it near the doorway, creating a loud sound.

Moments later, another ram-like monster rushed at the lamp, its horn digging into the object as its two front legs trampled it. It stopped when it felt an axe bite into its side, crushing and tearing apart ribs and vital organs. As it fell to the ground, Lance placed his right leg on the monster's side and yanked out the axe. Afterwards, he checked to see if the creature was dead or not. This time, he didn't see the notification appearing right away. It only popped up when the monster had bled out.

So, something has to be dead for my Class to treat it as an Item, Lance pondered. It was something that he had never heard of before, but he figured it could speed things up, since he could assess whether a monster was truly dead. *Why check for a pulse or breathing when a notification would work?* It was one of the many mysteries that came with his Class as a Death Smith. His status screen listed two traits that barely hinted at what the pros and cons were. Still, the ability to know when a monster had died would be helpful in preventing any surprises and speed up his work.

He searched around for a moment before he found his entrenching tool. He grabbed it and went to the next door. From its design, it was clearly the front door, or what remained of it. The door appeared damaged and rotten, either by time or monsters. Lance opened it completely and peered outside, seeing a large hallway that was filled with a dozen more monster corpses, every one of them sliced apart, frozen and shattered into pieces, or their heads smashed in.

"You all right, boy?" Noel asked as he made his way over to him, his spear at the ready.

"Yeah, sorry. Smashed my face into a wall when I entered the Rift," Lance said with a red smile as he tried to reassure Noel and the others that he was fine. Claudia chuckled when she noticed Lance's red grin.

Mend Wounds
[You have used Mend Wounds Lvl 2 at the cost of 15 Mana]
[Current Mana 120/135]

Lance felt the healing energy flow through his body, mending the bloody nose and restoring a bit of the Stamina he had used up during his fight. When the blue light faded, he made his way over to Myles.

Myles nodded when everyone had met up. The man's blood-covered sword had the same hue as his bloody shield, which now had a few more scratches on it. "Perfect. The party is all here with no major injuries. Take a minute to catch your breath and secure your gear," he told them as he continued to examine his surroundings.

The four of them were in the middle of a hallway. From what Lance could discern from the faded signs on the wall, they were now on the fifth floor. This could either be factual, or the building could've lost several floors when it materialized here.

At Myles's command, the party closed all the apartment doors on this floor before checking out the staircase. They placed several traps near the stairs. It had taken Noel a few minutes to set it up properly. Arranged there were a mixture of bear traps, and a basic tripwire device that would lead to a shrapnel-filled explosion. It wouldn't be enough to kill a powerful monster, but it would make a lot of noise. That noise would allow the party to prepare for an unknown threat.

Then, with the hallway somewhat secure, the Rifters cleared each apartment one by one. The strategy was to always make a distracting noise from the outside to lure the monsters out. If the threat stayed inside, two Rifters would go in, backing one another up.

Safe and effective, but slow, Lance thought as he watched Claudia and Noel return from Flat 5-C. At their Levels, they would have no problem dealing with these monsters on their own. Even Claudia, their weakest member, could probably clear this entire floor on her own. That they went in as pairs was because of safety, or it hinted at what Lance had suspected—that they feared these monsters.

Lance went into the next room with Myles, having thrown in a handful of rubble to cause a commotion inside. Myles led the way, holding his shield out in front of him as he charged into the nearest monster while hacking at another one with his sword. Lance rushed past Myles and noticed that there were three horned monsters in total. Myles had already bloodied one with his sword and had disoriented the second one with a shield bash.

Wasting no time, Lance threw his axe at the third monster, hitting it in the rear leg with enough force to send him back a few paces. Then, Lance jumped toward the monster Myles had stunned while pointing the entrenching tool downwards. The shovel-like tool sank in violently because of the sheer momentum and Lance's weight behind it.

He then shifted his gaze toward Myles, seeing the man slice apart a monster's front legs and pin it down. No doubt Myles would go in for the kill next. With two of the three monsters down, Lance moved toward the third one. He had partially crippled it after having thrown his axe into it, but it still had some fight left. The monster's two powerful front legs dragged itself toward him. The monster aimed the tip of its horn at him as it charged forwards. It ran with all its might, but the creature was slower than he was. It had an impressive strength behind its charge, but this time it only collided with a brick wall instead of a soft human flesh.

Not all that intelligent, but capable of ignoring great pain, Lance thought as he swapped out the shovelhead for the pickaxe setting. Lance and Ash had trained to switch between the pickaxe and the shovel in their spare time. Both could change the head of the tool within a few seconds. By the time the beast came in for its second charge, Lance met it with a hardened steel pickaxe, smashing into its skull, killing it instantly.

[You have been awarded with a Level Up]
[You are now Level 12]
[You have 3 unspent Attribute points]

Lance was aware of the notification but ignored it for now. Instead, he inspected the slain monsters and saw the notifications hover above the corpses. "Are you all right?" he asked Myles, watching the man finish up with his kill and make his way over to him.

"That was supposed to be my line," Myles said, his tone neutral. He was no doubt revaluating the young man right there and then. "The broker said you just received your Veteran status. Was he wrong?" Myles asked him, his gaze shifting between Lance and the two dead monsters behind him.

"No. But I've had extensive training from several Rifters," Lance said honestly. He had figured that this conversation would pop up eventually, although this was too soon. He hoped he'd be able to build up a bit of a rapport with them first. "I'm here to learn and find myself again," Lance added, each word true.

Myles paused for a moment before he nodded. He threw one last glance at the slain monsters before he led Lance to the other rooms in the flat on the way back to the others. "The pup has fangs," Myles said to them before explaining what had happened inside. "We'll talk about it later, all right?" Myles asked Lance, waiting for his nod before the group went back to clear the apartments one room at a time.

Several hours later, they had cleared two entire floors, room by room. They had blocked off the staircases by placing a few large steel shelves and wooden tables to form a barricade. It was easy to remove, but it made a lot of noise to do so. The group had turned one flat into a temporary base, having picked the one with the sturdiest front door. Beyond that, Noel had placed a lot of makeshift traps on the other levels, all marked with obvious signs so no Rifter would fall prey to them. The older man had taken Lance with him, showing him how to prepare and place them. Afterwards the party had decided to have a meal together.

Lance felt silly for having purchased some of the items he had bought in the Workshop. He was contemplating this as he was dragging a dirty mattress closer to their base, hoping to use it as his sleeping spot for the next few days. Myles and Noel had started a small fire outside of the apartment, near an open window.

"Lance . . . your . . . well, I was going to say that your meat was ready, but I'd rather not call it that out of respect for actual decent meat," Noel said as he held up a fork that had bits of Rankling meat on it.

"Is that even edible?" Claudia asked with a shudder, while Myles simply watched it from a safe distance.

"I bloody hope so," Lance said as he sat down on a dented steel chair next to the others. It felt weird to "camp" in a Rift while it was still inside an apartment complex. Sure, there was no electricity or running water, but many of the sturdier chairs and tables were still intact. Beyond that, they also had plates, cups, and even a spoon they could use. Myles and the others all had their rations, cooking supplies, and tools, but they preferred local things like this.

The first bite Lance took was as if biting into an old, tattered shoe. The second bite was even worse. "Delicious," he said as he suppressed his need to gag and vomit. A part of him wanted to cry out, knowing that there were several more kilos of the stuff in his Inventory.

"Are you sure you don't want to try eating the monsters we killed?" Claudia asked, feeling sorry for Lance.

"Didn't you say it might be poisonous?" Lance asked before forcing himself to swallow his third bite.

"At this rate, wouldn't that be a mercy?" she replied, suppressing a snicker before explaining to the others that she was going to the bathroom and would use her mace on anyone who dared to walk in on her. The other men, wisely, didn't respond, instead focusing their attention on their meals.

"Does it bother you, being back in a Rift?" Noel asked finally, placing his empty plate on the ground before leaning forward, curious to hear the young man's thoughts.

"A bit," Lance said honestly. He had told the others a bit about his background after they had cleared the floors and secured the place. Although he was a lower Level, he had shown an affinity for combat and hadn't hesitated when fighting the monsters. Lance had explained about his experience within his first Rift and the training he had received from Daniel in the months after that.

Beyond that, Lance had told them about his time with R.A.M. and how he lost his best friend there. The latter he only explained in a few sentences, clearly not feeling comfortable with the subject. The others hadn't pried into the matter afterwards. Judging by their reactions, they had suffered losses as well.

"It feels weird being inside of a Rift on my own, you know? Without my friend here," Lance explained. He noticed how Noel and Myles nodded at that. They had talked for a long while, with them sharing a bit more about their previous lives, their first Rift encounters, and what they had lost.

"I understand. I wish I could tell you it will get better, but sometimes loss never does. You just learn to live with it," Noel said, patting Lance's knee once before he got up again. "More meat . . . or whatever you call it. Want some more?" Noel asked him as he got up and went back to the cooking fire.

"No, I'm fine, thanks," Lance said. Instead, he shifted his focus to his status screen and saw the notifications that he had Leveled Up twice since entering the Rift, resulting in him having reached Level Thirteen. It also meant that he now had six Attribute points to spend.

[Agility:] [28] (+6)

Lance figured the additional points in Agility would help him out here. The monsters—or "Trihorns," as Claudia demanded they call them—were strong, but quite linear in their attack patterns. Lance figured his best course of action while facing them was to outflank or outmaneuver them. The additional six points in Agility would increase his reaction time and boost his speed further. He could've improved his speed by increasing Strength, but that would limit his range of motion. Similar to the Trihorns, too much Strength would make it harder to turn and maneuver.

Accepting the upgrades, he could feel the changes to his body, with his chest tightening for a few moments before it all settled down again. Agility would also improve the handling of his weapons and help with coordination and other things. He had managed the two Levels due to his taking on several of the monsters, but there were diminishing returns. Lance had Leveled Up the first time by killing two of their numbers, but the second Level Up had only happened after Lance had killed seven more.

The others had explained that lower-Level Rifts and monsters gave less Experience, with higher-leveled Rifters such as Noel and Myles barely noticed the increase. Instead, they relied on clearing these Rifts and getting the Level Up after surviving a Rift-event. It made sense to Lance, but it also showed that he couldn't just do this repeatedly and hope that he could get as strong as Connor, Kira, or Louis. It meant that he had to, eventually, clear stronger Rifts and battle stronger monsters.

[You have retrieved an Item]

Lance retrieved the stack of red bark fruit from his Inventory as he grabbed a few pieces of it before storing the rest of it and the Rirkling meat. The fruit, at least, was sweeter and more manageable compared to the meat. It still tasted like an apple that had gone bad, but it didn't make him want to puke right from the start.

He sat there for a few more minutes before he and Noel went to bed. Myles and Claudia would take the first shift that evening, allowing the others a whole four hours of sleep before they would have to take over. After bidding the others a relaxing shift, Lance made himself comfortable on the old worn mattress he had found. His camp blanket would serve as a decent insulator against the icy wind that occasionally blew in through cracks in the building.

I think the others are warming up to me, he thought as he recalled the contrast between the first few hours in this Rift and how they had all interacted with one another when they had dinner. He wanted to learn from them and for them to trust him. His other reason for being here he kept to himself, keeping it hidden within his Inventory.

Status Compendium

Name:	Lance Turner
Level:	13
Class:	Death Smith

Attributes

Endurance:	37	**Agility:**	34	**Wisdom:**	22
Strength:	28	**Perception:**	25	**Luck:**	25
Health:	750	**Mana:**	155		
Stamina:	245	**Inventory:**	29		

Traits

Taint of death:	Able to use Rift corpses as items	Prolonged use results . . . ~ERROR UNREADABLE!~
Shard instability:	Prolonged use results . . . ~ERROR UNREADABLE!~	Prolonged use results . . . ~ERROR UNREADABLE!~

Skills

Mend Wounds	Lvl 2	Restores minor wounds	+20 Health +8 Stamina	−15 Mana
Death Forge	Lvl 1	Allows (re)forging of death related items	+1 Item	−Raw materials −Black-shards −50% Stamina regeneration −50% Mana regeneration
Repair Item	Lvl 1	Restores durability on items	+1 durability per 1 item per 1 minute	−Raw materials −Black-shards −25% Stamina regeneration −25% Mana regeneration

Retainers

Ash	1x	Human

CHAPTER NINE

Experiencing Traps

Three Days Later
March, 14 AR
Inside Rift 8

LANCE

Several days had passed since the party had entered the Rift, although back on Earth, far less time had gone by. Claudia, Myles, Noel, and Lance had cleared out most of the apartments, sweeping every room, staircase, or supply closet. The Rifters looted every slain monster, both for their black-shards or valuable items, afterwards dragging their corpses to a single room on the lower floor. Although they would only stay a few more days inside this Rift, one couldn't underestimate what rotting corpses could do to one's physical and mental health.

"There. See?" Noel asked as he pointed down the elevator shaft. Lance had to squint his eyes a bit but could see a dozen of the three-legged monsters down there. All the monsters had plummeted to their death or ended up crippled and unable to move at the bottom. "These monsters rely mostly on sound and smell," Noel continued, pulling on a rope that was previously lowered down the elevator shaft. At the end of the rope was a tin can filled with a small amount of human blood to act as a lure. The blood had dried up, however, and was losing its effectiveness as bait.

Lance had learned much about being a Rifter from his new companions. In terms of prowess, Lance knew they weren't all that imposing or skilled. Despite their decent equipment, all three of them frequently hesitated or were missing vital spots when engaging the monsters. Lance figured that even Myles, their strongest member, wouldn't even be able to hold a candle to Dieter or Daniel had they all been on the same Level. Still, the White Clovers had some other skills that Lance had learned to appreciate. Traps, fortifications, and defensive tactics. Lance would remember all of it and take with him on future Rifts.

Myles had grown up hunting with his father when he was a child and knew a lot about tracking and setting up basic snares. Noel had been an engineer before he became a Rifter, and Claudia had studied to become a chemist. The three of them combined resulted in quite effective traps, improvised explosives, and other gadgets. Not factoring in Lance's contribution, most of the kills lately stemmed from traps the four of them had placed.

He watched Noel grab his blade, placing it against the palm of his hand, but hesitated. Noel didn't like getting hurt. It was the reason he disliked fighting up close and why the spear and the Class of Mage suited him so well. "Here, let me," Lance said as he grabbed the blade and nicked a spot on his hand that he knew would produce a steady flow of blood. He would've rather used a needle to collect blood, but circumstances were never really accommodating.

Lance let a fair amount of his blood pour into the can before he moved away from the lift, dripping blood as he made his way down the hallway. He made sure the route was the same as before. It was a straight line to the eastern stairwell. The damaged walls there opened to the landscape of the Rift itself. Climbing outside, Lance let his blood pour onto the rocky soil, forming a small pool before he swung his hand sideways, propelling droplets far in different directions, carrying his scent with him. Afterwards, his whole body lit up like a blue flare as he activated his healing Skill to quickly close the cut on his hand.

"This place is enormous," he said out loud as Noel slowly caught up with him. Everywhere he looked was rock and endless snow. There were deep valleys on one side and large peaks on the other. The mountainous terrain showed little signs of life or vegetation. The four of them had performed short expeditions on the outside, to inspect the state of the apartment complex that was rammed into the side of a cliff, as well as locate the spot where the Rift-event would be.

"It sure is. Still, I prefer these types of Rifts compared to a boiling desert or an active volcano," Noel offered, shuddering as he remembered the temperature in those Rifts. "It's easier to heat yourself up than it is to cool yourself down most of the time."

"Thanks again for taking the time to teach me, Noel. Too bad the GRRO didn't offer many courses in this field," Lance commented, remembering the days when Daniel had given him a tour through one of the GRRO facilities, explaining what types of courses were being taught and what sort of personal trainers one could book for a private session.

Noel laughed at that as he ran a dark hand through his graying hair. "Well, I hardly think the government would approve of the GRRO teaching people how to make homemade pipe bombs or how to mix bathroom supplies into corrosive elements," the older man explained.

"But they are fine with the GRRO overseeing the buying and selling of swords, rifles, and rocket launches?" Lance countered with an amused expression.

Noel laughed as he patted Lance on the back. The two of them were making their way back to the open elevator shaft. "I never said their rules make any sense, right?"

Upon reaching the shaft, Lance moved slowly, peering over the edge to see if there were any monsters alive. If so, they would either bleed out in a little while, or one of the Rifters would throw heavy or sharp things down the shaft and end the threat there and then. They would come and collect their black-shards after a day had passed. "How many are still out there, in the mountains?" he asked Noel, wanting to hear the man's thoughts.

"Tough to say. From what we learned from the previous Rifters that cleared this Rift, there were a few hundred of them last time. But that was a Level Three Rift. So, I'd say a hundred at the very least at this Rift Level?" Noel mused as he scratched his beard and shrugged his shoulders afterwards. "I think we killed most of the roamers, the ones that actively search for Rifters. Myles figures it'll be safe for us to make a push for the Rift-event soon," the older man added as he retrieved a flask of oil from his backpack and poured a generous amount of it on the floor near the shaft. Doing so would ensure that any monster that rushed toward the scent of fresh blood would have no choice but to fall in.

"Come, let's get some lunch. Since you donated the blood, I'll let you have some of the proper meat and vegetables I brought with me. That will stave off any atrophy in your tastebuds," the graying man said with a chuckle as he led the ecstatic Lance up to the higher floors again, passing several barricades, rows of bear traps, and other improvised devices.

Lance had guard duty later that evening with Claudia. At the beginning of their stay in the Rift, that meant guarding a single floor, back-to-back. But with them establishing dozens of traps and barricades, and having gotten a general familiarity of this place, guarding was now more relaxed. Often that meant that one of them did the rounds while the other could chill out near a fire, and catch up on reading, repairing tools, or salvaging in the apartments for any valuable loot.

For Lance, this was a chance to train. When he was done with his rounds, he made his way down to the lower levels, past the destroyed stairs, and finally into a section where they had placed a few of the bear traps. Most nights, they would trap four or five monsters like that, with large steel rods hammered in the floor to keep the bear traps firmly in place.

Using his axe, Lance then killed the creatures that would be too difficult to handle outside of the traps, thinning their numbers until he felt comfortable in getting close to a wounded monster. It wasn't hard to subdue one at that point. He used large strips of bed sheets he had bundled together to make restraints.

Once he had secured one of them, he then dragged it into an empty apartment, closing the door behind it.

[You have combined and retrieved four Items]

Ash suddenly appeared, dressed in the R.A.M. outfit. The pale man quickly took up a defensive position, holding the shield out in front of him with the smaller knife at the ready. Like he'd practiced.

"Ready?" Lance asked him, waiting for a single nod before he undid the bindings of the Trihorn. The monster had many wounds caused by the bear traps and Lance's rough handling of it. Even wounded, however, it could prove a tough enemy to face. It was stronger than Lance, but currently had no real chance at matching him in speed or evasion. After clearing most of the flats with the other Rifters, Lance had Leveled Up once more. He had spent every Attribute point that he had gotten on Agility, preferring more speed and swiftness on his side now. He felt comfortable handling two or three monsters on his own if he had room to move. In a smaller room such as this apartment, he'd prefer to only fight one or two at a time.

For Ash, it would be a far more challenging task since he was basically a normal human in terms of his physical qualities. The shield and weapons would give him a decent edge, but Lance had already spent the previous night repairing Ash when he had attempted to train him. He had seen Ash get impaled by a Trihorn's nasty horn and trampled during his second attempt. Still, each time it happened was a learning experience for Ash and he seemed to be getting better.

Unlike the last time, Ash now took the fight to the monster as he sprinted as fast as he could. The man slammed his shield into the charging monster but hadn't put his weight behind it. Instead, he let the shield serve as a distraction while he slid to the side. In a split second, he seized the opening he had made as he rammed his knife into the monster's hind leg and started cutting like a madman. It was clear to see that he was aiming for essential tendons rather than more durable muscles and bones.

Clever move, Lance thought, having witnessed this first exchange between the two combatants. The monster was faster, stronger, and far more durable than Ash, but the man had rendered the monster's hind leg useless now that he had cut apart the tendons. In one move, Ash had leveled the playing field by reversing the advantage of speed.

As the second and third exchange happened, Lance already knew what the result would be. Ash was constantly on the offensive as he slashed and stabbed into the creature. With mobility and speed now favoring him, Ash managed to circumvent most of the damage dealt to him and used the shield to block the occasional blow. Ash was fine, save for some bruises and perhaps a few hairline fractures in his arms.

The monster was bleeding out as it slowed down, not to mention occasionally slipping on the red liquid with its hooves. Ash didn't have that problem since blood loss wouldn't lessen his combat prowess that much. The only thing the man had to monitor was the loss of function to his body and his overall durability.

After the fifth exchange, Ash blinded the monster on the left side and hid in the blind spot afterwards. By the time the monster had found the man again, it felt a sharp slab of steel slam into its throat as Ash rammed his shield into it with both arms. This happened again and again until he neutralized the threat.

"Is it dealt with?" Lance asked his pale companion, wanting to see if he had remembered to inspect the body of a fallen monster. He wanted Ash to always be aware whether a monster was dead or simply incapacitated. With the creature's throat cut open and neck crushed, Ash nodded confidently. "Good, cut out the black-shard and hand it to me," Lance instructed as he made his way over to Ash and placed a hand on his back while activating his Skill.

Repair Item
[You have used Repair Item Lvl 1. Reducing Stamina and Mana regeneration by 25% until completion]

Lance felt the shift internally as he became aware something was off balance. It was hard to put into words how Stamina and Mana felt beyond some innate feeling, almost instinctual. The sudden shift in his regeneration was noticeable, but it didn't cause any discomfort. The Repair Skill wasn't something that worried him because he usually repaired his companion when he was training him in private, or when Ash was inside the Inventory. It could prove more challenging in the future when Lance had more Skills that required Stamina or Mana.

[You have repaired an Item. "Ash" is now at 100% durability]

"Good job. I saw nothing wrong during this fight. Are you up for another round?" Lance asked. He smiled when Ash gave a determined nod. He then stored the man in his Inventory before retrieving the discarded makeshift restraints, determined to fetch another unfortunate monster or two.

Several hours later, Lance had finished his shift and was on his mattress, staring at the dark ceiling as if it might hold some sort of answer. Today had been an eventful day. Noel had shown him how to make more complex traps. Claudia had explained what Items to look for in apartments in terms of worth or usefulness, while Myles had taught him more about tracking and how to cover one's tracks or scent. This knowledge alone was exactly what he needed to survive a Rift on his own, provided he had some more tools and basic equipment. But all of that seemed trivial compared to the notification he had on his status screen.

[You have been awarded with a Level Up]
[You are now Level 15]
[You have 3 unspent Attribute points]

It wasn't the fact that he had Leveled Up again that made him so excited; it was *how*. He was slowly getting less and less bang for his buck in terms of Experience for each monster he killed. It took more kills to Level Up, with Level Fourteen taking him several days' worth of killing monsters. The other Rifters had allowed him to kill the monsters in the elevator shaft, letting him drop heavy things on them to kill them and gain their Experience. The amounts the others would get from it would barely make a dent in their own required Experience.

After having killed dozens of monsters in the lift or during his patrols, he knew he had been getting closer to Level Fifteen. He had figured he'd hit the mark when he killed the occasional monster that Ash couldn't take down on his own. What he hadn't expected was to see a Level-Up notification while Ash stood triumphant in front of a fallen monster.

This changes everything, Lance thought as he held up his hand in the dark, forcing it into a fist as he felt his mood taking a turn for the better. Getting Experience could happen in a lot of ways, but it had to involve Rift-related creatures or Items. Some could gain Experience from creating high-quality Items, or when healing or buffing others with support Skills. But a Rifter gained the most amount of Experience when killing a monster. It didn't matter if a Rifter killed something using a Skill, a sword to the brain, or a thrown javelin. Even traps worked, if someone had made it out of Rift-materials and a Rifter had placed it.

That Lance's Level Up came right after Ash's victory meant that he was gaining Experience through his companion's kills. It meant that this Rift, and the rules that governed it all, were truly treating Ash like an Item wielded by him. Suddenly, his goal of increasing his Level to where he could confront Connor, Kira, and Louis seemed a lot closer.

[Strength:] [30] (+3)

Lance deposited the three Attribute points into Strength, deciding it was fitting considering the moment. As expected, the surge of power overwhelmed him as his clenched fist suddenly felt more painful. He could feel the increased strain on his bones, tendons, and the muscles in his hand as he adjusted to how much stronger he had gotten. He finally relaxed as he placed his hand back on his chest, feeling his excited, rapid pulse.

After a minute, Lance opened his Inventory and let his gaze fall on Ash's name and icon. He was now fully aware of the true value of what his companion could offer him beyond an extra set of hands in combat or to carry things. It was almost fitting that Thomas's sacrifice had now given birth to the tool that he needed to get justice for his friend. And at that moment, just for a little while, Lance had let go of the shame and self-loathing he felt at what he had done to his friend's body.

I promise you, Thomas, I'll catch up to them.

CHAPTER TEN

Tools of War

Mere Hours Before Exiting the Rift
March, 14 AR.
Inside Rift 8

LANCE

Lance, on your left!" Myles shouted, ordering him to guard their left flank and protect Noel, who was busy channeling his Mana. "Claudia, hurry it up," Myles continued as Lance felt another monster slam into his shield, pushing him back a step.

The air was thinner this far up the mountain, with the Rifters having to exert themselves more and more. Out of all of them, Lance had the hardest time catching his breath, with Myles the least because of his higher Endurance. Non-Rifters would have passed out long ago or needed specialized gear to breathe properly.

With labored breath, Lance slammed his axe into a monster's neck before kicking it down the mountainous ridge. The Trihorn skirted down the path, slamming into several of its kind before it plummeted to his death. *Just a few more*, he thought, seeing the next wave of monsters climb up the ridge and charge toward them.

The party was standing on the top of a large mountainous peak with an ancient floor chiseled out of stone. It looked both captivating and decrepit, with signs of forgotten battles adorning the floors. Someone had at one point carved intricate lines and strange symbols into the floor, but it had faded over time, now only hinting at their former purpose.

[You have repaired an Item. "Bone javelin" is now at 100% durability]

Right on time! Lance thought, seeing the notification pop up. He switched hands with the axe and held his right hand above his head, seconds later retrieving an Item.

[You have retrieved an Item]

A slender javelin appeared in his right hand, already positioned so that he could throw it immediately. He timed it right, forcing every bit of power he could muster into his throw. He twisted his body as he threw the javelin. It impacted a monster with an incredible speed and force rivaling that of an Olympic athlete.

Lance's javelin was part horn, fastened on a thin bone shaft. It was all glued together and further fastened in place with cloth and sinew. In terms of reliability, it was a shoddy weapon that broke after a few throws. But it did a lot of damage during that time.

Myles had taught him how to use plant and animal fibers to make improvised sinew or cordage. Although the process took time to improve its quality, Lance had learned that by using animal sinew, he could speed up the process at the cost of lowering the quality of the binding. Beyond that, Claudia had shown him how to make glue from bones by boiling them and removing any impurities.

He watched the javelin embed itself into the skull of the charging Trihorn. The force of the impact was enough to kill the monster instantly. Lance then rushed to the next monster, sidestepping its dangerous horn as he began hacking at its limbs and neck, either destroying its mobility or killing it outright. Lance could feel the sting of minor cuts and large bruises on his side, slowly sapping his energy.

"Claudia, is it ready?" Myles shouted as he separated a creature's head before grabbing his pistol with his offhand and sinking two rounds into another beast. Both monsters dropped dead in their tracks at the same time.

"Done!" Claudia screamed, each hand holding a propane tank that had been jerry rigged to serve as an explosive device. Both Noel and Claudia had been working on them the last few days, ensuring that they were both volatile enough to do a lot of damage, but remain stable enough to not go off in their hands. Claudia had gone the extra step by taping jars filled with screws, spoons, forks, and bits of rubble on the side of her bomb, ensuring that the explosive would contain as much shrapnel as possible. "Hold on to your panties, boys!" Claudia screamed as she waited for Lance and Myles to rush back to her and Noel.

"I hope it's more stable than the ones you guys made in our last Rift," Myles said, his voice betraying his uneasiness at the fact that they were about to set off two explosions to introduce an avalanche to kill most of the monsters.

"It will be fine," Noel said, his eyes glowing bright blue as he activated the Skill he had been preparing. Lines of blue energy appeared around them, forming a circular shape as the thin air became dense with Mana. They could feel the surrounding temperature decreasing rapidly, even atop the mountainous region they were in.

"Now!" Myles said as he emptied his pistol at the monsters that had gotten too close to them. Claudia then activated both bombs as she threw the devices into the growing wave climbing up toward them.

Lance wasn't looking forward to the explosion of glass and shrapnel. He had never endured something like it, but he had a healthy fear of what speeding glass and metal could do to the human body. Luckily, he didn't have to find out because the lines of Mana solidified as they transformed into layers of ice. A moment later, crude, thick walls encased the party, forming an improvised bunker.

"Five . . . four . . ." Claudia counted down as Myles reloaded his pistol. Only a second later, two explosions furiously rattled the air, assaulting their icy fortress with stone, ice, and shrapnel. The protective ice cracked in several places, and a deep groaning sound grew around them. The very earth underneath trembled as the rumbling increased. This continued for several minutes as Noel continued maintaining his Skill and holding the barrier up.

The Rifters rested and readied themselves as best as they could. During this time, Lance activated his "Mend Wounds" Skill a few times, healing the others whenever he touched them. None of them had any major wounds besides a few cuts or bruises, but the Stamina recovery would no doubt help. Lance himself had taken most of the damage and had the least amount of protection to prevent it.

Mend Wounds
[You have used Mend Wounds Lvl 2 at the cost of 15 Mana]
[Current Mana 49/175]

Lance felt the ache and sting of his many bruises and cuts lessen, only leaving a dull ache behind. As the blinding blue light faded from his body, he could see the others more clearly. They all had determined looks in their eyes. Despite the many monsters that had charged them, they were doing rather well.

"Is everyone all right?" Myles asked, his gaze scanning his companions to assess any damage. When everyone had nodded and Claudia simply grinned, Myles then gave the order to Noel. "Blast them."

"Get ready," the older man warned them as he stopped his "Ice construct" Skill while activating another one. The Skill he was using now could create blasts of air pressure around him. Lance and the others bundled up next to Noel, holding onto each other to prevent them from getting swept up by the blast as well. The pressure in the ice bunker increased bit by bit as Noel held the Skill at the ready, waiting for the ice walls to show even more cracks.

They could hear the remaining monsters on the outside ram into the walls, desperate to breach the ice fortress and slaughter the Rifters inside. Cracks

turned into larger scars until chunks of ice fell apart. Noel then activated his
Skill, turning the ice fortress into a 360-degree artillery barrage. The walls
shattered in hundreds of individual pieces that were propelled outwards in a
violent fury.

Heavy ice chunks slammed into the surrounding landscape and monsters,
ripping some apart while ramming others off the mountain with a tremendous
force. The sudden ice barrage unleashed indescribable fury of biblical proportion.

"I still say I did the most damage," Noel said a few hours later as he stood on the
newly formed ledge next to Lance.

Lance stayed silent. He didn't want any part in Noel and Claudia's contest.
Ever since the battle, the two of them had been at odds with one another. Both
had claimed that their explosive device had dealt the crucial blow that had caused
the avalanche to trigger. It had swept dozens of monsters off the cliff, plunging
them down the mountain and entombing them in ice and snow.

"I mean, I taught her how to build those contraptions," the man continued,
with Lance nodding once or twice, knowing it was better to do so, lest he'd get
even more involved.

Lance moved a little closer to the edge to peer down, seeing the steep drop
where rock and snow had formed a torrent and swept downwards. From what his
acute Perception could make out, he spotted a few monsters half-buried, their
limbs sticking out of the snow in a mangled mess. *That's a bad way to go*, he thought
as he stepped backwards, not trusting the structural integrity of the ledge he was
standing on.

Looking back, he noticed the splattered remnants of the monsters they had
been fighting. Dozens of them hacked apart or impaled by one of his javelins. A
few others had bullet holes in their skulls or sides, or even whole limbs shot off
from Claudia's shotgun. But most of them Noel had reduced to red smears of gore
and crystal when his ice barrage had hit them. The blocks of ice had been akin to
cannonballs in terms of size and speed.

"You guys made the right call. The plan worked perfectly," Lance commented,
remembering how they had started this day off. Myles and Claudia had set up
some lures near the base of the mountain, reeking of fresh human blood, while
Lance and Noel had made some large fires on the other side by burning bits of
wood and plastic that they had scavenged from the apartment buildings.

Most of the remaining monsters had rushed down the mountain to investi-
gate the blood and fire while the Rifters had climbed the unguarded sides of the
mountain. By the time the monsters had realized what had happened and rushed
back upwards, layers of traps, ice barricades, and four determined Rifters had met
them. Rifters who were eager to make the monsters bleed for every bit of ground
that they wanted to reclaim.

"That it did. Myles has a knack for that sort of thing. The monsters themselves weren't all that dangerous, and we culled their numbers enough to remove their biggest advantage. The tactics and barricades were simply there to remove any chance of failure," Noel commented as he stepped backwards before he taking a seat on one of the monstrous corpses that was missing its head. "Why leave things to chance? That's our motto."

"I can't argue with that."

"Ha! It's impossible to do so," Noel countered while grinning.

"Do you think the others will be back shortly?" Lance asked, rubbing his arms to stave off the bite of the freezing wind.

Noel scratched his gray beard once, his mind working out how much time had passed. "A few minutes or so? We might've damaged the path up because of the avalanche, but I reckon it won't take them much longer." Noel then activated his Inventory and retrieved two tin cups that he placed on the stone floor. After that, he produced a steel flask that contained some warm tea he had made last night. It had stayed warm in his Inventory, despite them having been in the cold for hours. "There we go," he said as he handed the young man a cup as well.

Lance eagerly accepted the drink while offering a smile as currency. He then sat down on the stone surface across from Noel. "Remind me next time to only accept Rifts that lead to warm and exotic places," he joked as he accessed his own Inventory to retrieve his thick camp blanket and leather raincoat. He wrapped both tightly around him. Although it didn't provide as much heat as he would've liked, it still lessened the sting of the icy wind.

The older man laughed at that, taking a few generous sips of his tea before cocking his head to the side, making out the clear signs of snow being trampled by feet.

"Friendlies," Myles stated, hiking his way through the snow until he came into view of the two men. Myles looked almost regal in his armor, a thick fur cloak draped around his form. He was pulling on a thick rope, dragging a tied-up monster behind him. The monster was larger than the other Trihorns, with bulkier layers of muscles. It would've proven a tougher opponent to fight, had Claudia not shot it off the edge of the mountain at the start of the battle with her shotgun. It was moments like these that made Rifters appreciate just how potent a modern gun could be in lower-Level Rifts.

They found the Rift-guardian, Lance thought as he spotted the guardian-shard embedded in the monster's chest. It was black, but it had a red hue to it, marking it as the Rift-guardian. "Nice. Did it put up a fight?" he asked Myles and Claudia as they joined them, dropping the wounded Rift-guardian next to them.

"No. We found our buddy passed out and half-broken on a boulder at the base of the mountain. I think if we waited a while longer, it would've died on its own," Myles said as he also accepted a warm cup of tea from Noel. "Good man."

"Really?" Noel said to Claudia, watching her drop four bundles of Items on the floor belonging to each of them. The Rifters had safely stowed them at a lower area of the mountain before they had made their defensive stand. Over her shoulder, Claudia had slung a bicycle she had found in an apartment. Time had rusted some of its bolts, but it was otherwise still in good condition.

"What? You know the dorks over at the Workshop are going to love this one. If not, we could always hit up the 'Little Market' near Dublin," Claudia said as she placed the bicycle next to her and rang the bell a few times. She smiled eagerly as it produced a lovely sharp sound.

Lance finished his drink and handed his cup over to Noel before grabbing his sack of items and double-checking if everything was still there. Inside were several dozens of Items he might need in a new Rift or were valuable enough to sell. The larger and more impractical items Lance had wanted to take with him were now stored in his Inventory. He had filled his backpack with a lot of black-shards he had retrieved from the dead monsters, along with several of the horns, hooves, and teeth.

This should do nicely, Lance thought, having tied up the cloth again. He'd made the sack out of bedsheets he had tied together. It looked ugly, but it would do for now. Inside the sack were strips of copper and tin he had looted from the flat. Beyond that, he had grabbed cables and electrical devices, as well as silverware. Your average person might have viewed it all as junk, but the people in the Workshop would pay good money for it, especially any electronic device that was still intact. "This should at least get me some decent shoes," Lance said with a smile. The others agreed.

The four of them then went over the last things they needed to do before they left this Rift. Myles did a last-minute shave; Claudia swapped some things around in her Inventory to not have to carry the bicycle around; Noel double-checked his sack full of Items as Lance had done.

The young man had kept himself busy with his Items. He had hoped the others would discuss the 'Little Market' some more but hadn't brought it up himself. He had heard Claudia and Noel mention it a few times, with Myles usually putting a stop to these types of discussions when they knew he might overhear them.

Perhaps some sort of black market? he thought as he strapped his rucksack on, securing his weapons before flinging the sack of items over his shoulders. Then, one by one, the rest of them got up and neared the center of the Rift. They all stepped close to a spot in the air where reality felt wrong, and you could see dark, unnatural black energy swirling.

As they had discussed before, Noel would be the one to kill the Rift-guardian, since he had the highest Luck stat of the entire party. They had explained to Lance that the higher a Rifter's Luck, the more chance there was that the Rift-guardian's shard would contain a Skill-shard. This item alone would be worth more than whatever else the four of them could loot from this Rift *and* the one after that. A Skill-shard contained a tremendous amount of energy. It was useless to mere humans, but a Rifter could break it up in his Inventory and absorb the energy as a new Skill. A weak common Skill could be worth hundreds of thousands of pounds. A rare one could be worth millions, even billions.

"Here we go," Noel said as he activated a Skill, shooting a sharp shard of ice from his hand. The ice easily pierced the inside of the Rift-guardian's cranium. Mere moments after Noel killed it, the very ground trembled as the Rift became unstable. Not wanting to waste any time, Noel grabbed a knife and began cutting out the shard. He clicked his tongue before showing the Guardian-shard to the others with a disappointed expression. "I'll have better luck next time," he said.

They all prepared for the closing of the Rift-event. Each person moved as close to each other as they could, pressing against the impassable dense flow of energy that was now becoming more visible. It was getting even darker, with black energy surging, until it became a pillar of impenetrable blackness. *Here we go*, Lance thought as he held onto his salvage bundle while his body tensed up with the muscle memory of how he had left his last Rift. Sweat ran down his back as his heart rate increased, his mind conjuring up every painful memory of that moment.

Then, the Rift-event collapsed in on itself and this world as it enveloped the Rifters in pure black energy.

CHAPTER ELEVEN

The Cost of Victory

Mere Seconds Before Exiting the Rift
March, 14 AR
Ipswich, England

LANCE

As the violent mass of black energy lessened, it shrank in size and violent behavior. Four figures suddenly appeared. Motion sensitive cameras recorded and transmitted the footage as GRRO personnel rushed toward the Rift itself. Protocol demanded they check for any wounded Rifters and take care of immediate threats such as fire or falling debris. It took little training for a GRRO employee to realize the Rift clearing had gone successfully at the sight of three Rifters calmly walking toward them with smiles on their faces while a fourth conjured a bicycle out of thin air and started riding it.

"Still alive," Lance said, an unusual instinct taking over again as he patted Myles's shoulder and flashed him a warm smile.

"You've got guts, Lance, I'll give you that. Bloody hell! That was a solid run. And ahead of schedule," Myles said just before the GRRO personnel reached them, inquiring how they all were doing and asking the team leader for a debriefing.

Although not required, it was the norm for a party to give rough sketches on how the Rift had gone. This to help better prepare any other Rifters going in after them, or to let the GRRO know if they had encountered anything that required investigation. Most of the time, it was about losses they might've incurred or severe injuries that might need treatment. In a successful run like this, however, the debriefing usually only took a few minutes.

Placing the sack down on the ground, Lance closed his eyes. He lifted his chin upwards and momentarily basked in the heat of the afternoon sun. It wasn't all that warm, but after all, he'd just spent several days in a colder climate, and the last few hours atop a freezing mountainous plateau. He stood there for a few minutes, letting the fact that he had just survived his first Rift without Thomas and had gotten stronger in the process sink in. At that moment, Lance was blissfully unaware of the cameras focusing on him, capturing the sight of this young Rifter who had done his duty to help the people of Ipswich remove this blight upon their town.

"Come on, you need to buy an old man a drink," Noel said as he nudged him in the side before collecting Claudia. The three of them made their way over toward the exit. They walked past the GRRO installations, including the private booths that held dressing rooms and showers. They briefly stopped to collect the personal things they had stored there.

Lance knew that the White Clovers preferred to stay in more public places before and after a Rift. Myles had explained that it helped them remember why they were out there, risking their lives. Lance wanted to believe that, but he couldn't help but shake that there also was a PR element behind it all. *Either way, these three did something great for the people of Ipswich*, he thought, remembering the information the broker had provided. The White Clovers had accepted the job of completely eradicating the Rift.

Myles joined the group moments later, handing each of them a cloak with the White Clover symbol on it. Lance could feel the man's gaze on him as he accepted it. He didn't have any problems wearing it. He knew Myles wanted them to go out like that, united. It would send a powerful message, as well as strengthen their name.

When they exited the GRRO security post and stepped out into the open, nearly a hundred people greeted them, with more of them rushing over to join them. There were reporters, townspeople, officials, and children of all ages. All of them began cheering as soon as the White Clovers stepped outside. Myles, Claudia, and Noel smiled, holding up their right hands as a sign of victory. Decked out in imposing armor, they even impressed Lance in that moment. Ice, dirt, and blood still adorned their equipment, adding to their mysterious nature as Rifters. Only three days had passed on Earth, yet a lot more had passed within the Rift, and the Rifters were now starved for human interaction, decent food, and relaxation.

"People of Ipswich, within a few weeks, we will remove this Rift from your town. This we swear!" Myles said, letting his strong voice boom out the last part so that those in the back could hear it as well. Then, as one, the people exploded into an orchestra of excitement, hope, and tears, as some remembered lost loved ones. It didn't take long after that for them to give the Rifters a hero's escort to the nearest pub.

"Three more pints for my comrades in arms!" Claudia said as she stood on top of the bar. She still had all her armor on as she showed off one of her weapons. She had been retelling their adventures in great detail when she'd spotted that the other Rifters' glasses were empty. Wanting to hear more of her incredible stories, the patrons quickly began slamming on the bar to get the older bartender to hurry. One patron had even climbed over the bar to help speed things up, only to get kicked out again by the elderly bartender. "So, there I was! Holding what I can only describe as DaVinci's wet dream in terms of homemade explosives . . ."

Lance smiled as he watched her go on, with people hanging onto her every word. Noel had found a cozy spot in the corner and stuffed himself with the dishes that locals had brought him. Afterwards, the older man had sunk into a blissful state of nothingness. Myles was chatting with the locals, occasionally explaining elements of the Rift or when they would come back to finish it. There were more than a few women by him, no doubt drawn to the appeal of this charismatic leader who'd promised to liberate their town.

I'm no better than Claudia and Myles, Lance thought as he accepted the next beer shoved in his hand by a local man with shaky hands, acting as if he was meeting a celebrity. Lance brought the glass to his lips and took generous sips, doing his best to ignore the exposed Rift-shard in his chest. He was all too aware of the fact that this was his sixth beer since they had entered the pub, ignoring the shots Noel had forced them to take due to it "putting hair on your chest" like a proper man ought to have. *The increase in Endurance must've boosted our tolerance*, he thought, remembering that a mere year ago he would've already been hammered at this point.

He finished the drink and placed it on the table, telling the surrounding people that he would return in a moment. He knew what they wanted to see and hear, so, with a grin, Lance made his way past them, touching the occasional shoulder.

Mend Wounds
Mend Wounds
Mend Wounds
Mend Wounds

One by one, random patrons erupted in bright blue lights, drawing the attention of the rest of the pub. Loud cheering followed immediately, with Claudia shouting at the top of her voice that it was a sign to drink more. No doubt the people who Lance had touched would feel the immediate effect of the magical energy flowing through them, restoring their energies as if they had just gotten a few hours of rest. The ones that might've had a headache or a stiff joint that day would've felt a sense of relief as well.

And I'm not one bit better than Thomas, he thought as he made his way over to the bathroom and located the nearest sink with a mirror. He let the cold water flow through his hands for a few seconds before he splashed his face several times.

When he finally forced himself to look into the mirror, he saw his unshaven reflection staring back at him. He noticed the way his shirt was hugging him and that it felt tighter than before. His Rift-shard was visible due to him having opened the top buttons.

"Why the hell did I do that?" he wondered out loud as he stared at himself. He wouldn't normally want to stand out so much, not even when under the influence of several pints. He had done so when he had changed into his civilian clothes, having used a private room in the back to have some privacy as he changed. Just before he had gone out, he had felt an ache in his chest for a moment, before he had opened his shirt a bit, feeling a surge of confidence as he did so. "It must've been the alcohol," Lance lied to himself as he shifted his attention to the notification on his status screen, demanding his attention.

[You have cleared this Rift]
[You have been awarded with a Level Up]
[You are now Level 16]
[You have 3 unspent Attribute points]

There were several things that demanded his attention after he had survived the last Rift. Lance had hoped that he would've gained another one from all the fighting in the end. Sadly, he was losing momentum in terms of Experience. He didn't doubt that he could level up further in a Level Two Rift, but it would take even more time and Experience. Still, the additional Level gained upon completing the Rift was a welcome sight.

He briefly contemplated where he'd put the points. Agility had truly been effective inside the Rift, but it might be less important in others, such as a narrow cave passage. His Strength, Agility, and Endurance were his top three Attributes and were somewhat balanced. *Should I stick to spreading out my points evenly, or should I specialize in a specific way?* On the one hand, he would do a lot of the heavy lifting himself if he wanted to solo a Rift, but on the other, he also had Ash with him.

Perhaps I should make that decision when I'm not several pints in? Decision made, he splashed some more water on his face before buttoning up his shirt again and heading out of the loo. For now, he allowed himself the night off. After all, the four of them had just done a good thing for this town and its people. He joined up with the others, seeing the euphoric state everyone was in.

I could get used to this.

The following day, Lance had caught a late train back home to London. He had spent the night and the following day in Ipswich with the Rifters, hanging out and having lunch and dinner together. After that, he had said his farewells to

Myles, Noel, and Claudia, thanking them for their guidance and companionship in the Rift. It was strange, really, to have spent so many days with one another, sharing hardships and triumphs, only to have the calendar back on Earth reveal that just three days had passed.

The White Clovers had invited him to join them again in a few weeks to clear the Rift in Ipswich. He was certainly tempted, since he'd enjoyed working with them and knew what to expect. Lance told them he'd give it some thought and that he wouldn't mind working with them again in the future. A big part of him wanted to accept, to belong to a group again, perhaps even learn to call them friends. No matter how big that part of him was, however, he knew his oath to Thomas—an oath drenched in blood and anger—dwarfed that feeling.

Still, over the course of this Rift, Lance had gone up from Level Eleven to Level Sixteen, resulting in quite the decent increase. *It's nearly incomparable to what I experienced when I was working for R.A.M. both in terms of profit and experience*, he thought, remembering how happy he had been back then. In those days, he and Thomas were eager to earn a few thousand pounds and a Level Up just from participating as porters. Still, there had been far more risks in this last Rift compared to the average one he'd had with R.A.M. With the latter, there were a dozen other porters who had your back, as well as skilled fighters to keep them all safe, so the pay-out was far less.

The White Clovers had gotten a bigger cut, as per their agreement, but Lance was still more than happy about it. He had recovered most of the money he had spent in the Workshop. Just to be sure he had read the amount correctly, he opened his banking app and read the most recent deposit he had received out loud. "£45,000."

That money alone will help me gear up for the next Rift and restock on supplies. And who knows how much money I will have after selling these? He shifted his gaze to the bundle in the seat next to him. The dirt- and blood-stained sack contained a lot of the Items he had salvaged from the Rift. Some, he figured he might keep and take with him, such as a knife, fork, mug, and a pot. But the rest he had no use for at this stage, so he would sell them.

Lance closed the app on his phone, seeing nearly thirty missed calls and several text message notifications on the start screen. Most of the missed calls had been from Daniel, while the text messages had been more varied and included his brother, Marcus, Dieter, Daniel, and Kate. As per usual, he felt conflicted with all things related to his brother. Out of habit, he wanted to ignore but forced himself to read them, since he had promised Thomas that he'd give him a chance.

Of the two messages Marcus left, the first one was him asking how he was doing and if he was taking care of himself, and the second was a photo of Marcus and his family, with some kind words attached about how his son and daughter wanted to meet their uncle. Not sure what to make of it, for now, Lance marked the text as "read" and went to check out the other ones.

There were many texts from Daniel asking how he was doing and if he wanted to go train at the GRRO facility as they had done before, or to go out for a cup of coffee. Dieter's text was blunter, asking Lance in German if he wanted to grab something to eat this week, not even bothering to translate into English.

He was unsure how to respond to Daniel and Dieter, especially the former. Lance had texted them before he left for the Rift, telling them he was going to travel for a few days and see the country to get some fresh air. He felt confident that he could deal with Dieter, but Daniel had a way of knowing when someone was lying. Lance wasn't sure if it was Daniel's natural gift for reading people, or if it was his absurdly high Perception stat. Either way, both would no doubt freak out if they learned he had gone to another Rift, mere weeks after surviving and experiencing a traumatizing event and losing his best friend.

I'll send them a text tonight and offer to grab a bite in a few days. He hoped that would sufficiently appease these men's overly protective natures. He would come clean with them at that point, because it was only a matter of time before they would find out. Lance then began reading Kate's message as he entered his apartment complex, making his way up the flight of stairs. He felt the heavy bag full of Rift-items jiggle occasionally, a reminder that there was plenty of salvage inside.

His smile faded as he reached his door. His sensitive ears could pick up wood groaning on the other side, hinting that someone was moving inside. After spending the last several days fighting monsters, his survival training and experience quickly kicked in.

[You have stored an Item in your Inventory]
[You have retrieved an Item]

The phone vanished from his hand as the steel axe flickered into existence. He flung the sack of items over his shoulders as he opened the door and rushed inside, the axe ready to strike. He heard a deep, roaring laugh as he entered his room, finding not a potential threat, but around ten people who were busily decorating his living room.

Most of them looked shocked or confused at the sight of him brandishing his axe. Dieter, however, clutched his sides, nearly falling to the floor with laughter. Besides the amused German, there were several other Rifters who belonged to Dieter's guild. On their right stood Kate, Jacob, and Oliver Walker, with Kate holding a homemade cake in her hands. Suddenly, it dawned on Lance. The missed calls, the weird text message from his brother . . . His gaze shifted to the side as he found the digital clock next to the television mark today as the 28th. It was his birthday.

Hearing a small cough, the young man shifted his gaze to the side, seeing Daniel standing there with a blank expression. Daniel made eye contact with him before he shifted downwards to the sack of items that Lance had dropped in the confusion. A sack that had spilt all sorts of Rift-items out in the open.

I'm so dead, he thought as he closed the door behind him, the room eerily silent save for Dieter's constant laughter.

CHAPTER TWELVE

Fiery Mark

One Hour Later
March, 14 AR
Lance's Flat
London, England

LANCE

S ee? Zhe dog loves it," Dieter said in a thick German accent as he handed Oliver Walker another horn. It had belonged to one of the Trihorns Lance had defeated and looted.

Lance watched Oliver give the treat to Little Hans, who sniffed it before carefully grabbing the treat. He was still amazed by how intelligent Little Hans was. He was playful with the boy but calm enough as to not frighten him. Dieter had explained to Oliver that Little Hans could recognize the similarity between him and his brother, Thomas. Therefore, Little Hans would also see Oliver as a friend. That gesture alone had been enough to put a permanent smile on the thirteen-year-old's face.

Oliver is doing well, Lance thought as he pulled out another horn from his pack and handed it to Dieter. Internally he winced, realizing that each chewed-up horn would lessen his spending power by hundreds of pounds. Still, he was desperate to placate the people in his apartment at this point.

His axe-wielding entrance had startled most of the people in the room, although most of the Rifters had quickly joined Dieter in laughing at the absurdity of it all. The Rifters were Dieter's guild members. Lance had met quite a few of them during his brief career as a Rifter.

This is a nightmare. He refilled several bowls with crisps and other salty snacks. He flashed a grin when a Rifter made fun of his entrance, calling the scene "cute."

Lance had no choice but to laugh along with them to play it off. That, or throw himself out of his window to end it all.

Basically, everyone in the room had figured out that he had just returned from a Rift. While Dieter's laughter and comments had lightened the overall mood in the apartment, Lance could still occasionally feel Daniel's stare burn holes into him. There were going to be words later. He was sure of that.

Working up the courage, he stepped toward Daniel, who was talking with Thomas's father. Daniel and Jacob got along rather well, with both having frequently spoken with one another ever since Daniel had saved Thomas and Lance back in the hospital. "Do you guys need anything else? Beer, coffee?" Lance asked, showing a calm exterior, although inwardly he was anything but. Jacob had been the closest thing to a father figure throughout Lance's life, and Dieter had taken up the mantle of a mentor. Their opinions mattered to him.

"Already have one. My lovely Kate beat you to it," Jacob said as he placed a hand on Lance's shoulder and patted him playfully. "Why don't you take it easy for a while? It's your birthday, after all. Besides, you have been busy the last few days, right?" he asked, his hand still patting Lance's shoulder, although the mental weight of that touch suddenly increased tenfold.

"Quite busy," Daniel added, his eyes fixed on Lance as if he were already visualizing the sparring match he was practically inviting Lance to.

"Daniel was telling me about his new job within the GRRO. Suit and everything," Jacob said, removing his hand from Lance's shoulder as he made some room. The mere mention of the GRRO was enough to change the mood of the room, with every Rifter with a decent Perception number fully aware of what Jacob had said.

Daniel seemed troubled by the comment. He smiled awkwardly before adding his take on the matter. "It's just a temporary consultant job for now. The London branch needs more hands-on and general Rift experience. Nothing glamorous. Mostly improving personnel training, helping to better equip the facility for new Rifters, and possibly working with the occasional investigation if I show the aptitude for it."

"That's great news. Right?" Lance asked, his mind searching for dozens of ways in which he could thank Jacob for bringing up this topic. He wasn't sure whether Jacob had done it to make small talk or if he wanted to spare Lance on his birthday. Either way, Lance was willing to swear a life debt at that point.

"Yes, it's a suitable position for a former Rifter. But it's only temporary," Daniel said, his eyes moving away from the conversation toward Dieter, seeing the large German approaching them.

"A beer?" Lance asked as he tactfully backed off. The last thing he heard was Daniel asking for something stronger, as Dieter complimented Oliver's father for having such a wonderful son and stressing the value of family and loyalty. The latter he said while flashing his former guild member a dirty look.

Lance then grabbed a few of the empty beer bottles and cleaned bits of the broken horn Little Hans had discarded before he went toward the kitchen. He noticed Kate sitting there on the countertop with an amused expression.

"Still alive? I figured your mothers would've torn you a new one by now," Kate said as she handed him a beer while patting the spot next to her, noting that it was free.

Grabbing the beer, Lance moved next to her, but leaned against the countertop instead. "Mothers? And your dad bailed me out by dropping a bigger bomb in the apartment."

"Yeah, mothers. As in, I can smell the estrogen and their overprotective musk from here. They'd make a cute couple. And what might be a bigger bomb than a fool who lost his marbles and fell into another Rift?" Kate teased, with a coy smile both reassuring and taunting.

"I never said I had marbles," Lance argued.

Kate nodded once in approval. "You're friends with Thomas. I assumed as much."

"Touché. But Dieter is tearing Daniel a new one for leaving the guild and joining the GRRO," he explained as he downed a few mouthfuls of beer to collect his thoughts. He was grateful that she spoke about Thomas in present tense, emphasizing that their friendship was still intact. He wasn't sure if she did so on purpose, but he loved her for it.

"So, my dad just casually dropped this hot potato on Daniel's lap, while most of his former guild members are all in the same room?" Kate asked. Lance nodded and she broke out into a giggle. "Absolute legend," she finally offered, her gaze shifting toward her father as her eyes softened.

"How's the old soldier holding up?" Lance asked carefully, still conflicted and guilt-ridden.

"A stone pillar, but crumbling here and there. Oliver is doing great. His friends are over nearly every day, dragging him off to get into trouble. Pesky lads, but filled with love and healing," Kate explained as she finished her beer and placed it next to Lance's. "I think seeing Oliver doing all right is helping dad as well. Mom is . . ."

Lance kept silent. Both knew that neither had any answers. Besides, he didn't want to ask any more questions. He feared by doing so, he'd lose himself once more in that dark place inside of his heart. So, Lance simply stood there next to her, feeling both bad and strangely alive in that moment.

"Do you think you can spare a moment in a few days? I wanted to talk with you about something important to me," Kate explained before she stopped talking and jumped off the countertop when her father walked in.

"Discussing your wedding?" Jacob asked with a smile before Kate playfully nudged her father in the ribs, leaving the kitchen afterwards to grab a seat next to Oliver.

"Thanks for tonight . . . for this," Lance said to Jacob. He watched the man clean up a few of the empty bottles before taking a spot next to Lance.

"No need to thank us. We needed a reason for a drink just as much as you did. Besides, a family takes care of one another, right?" Jacob asked, although it sounded more like a statement.

"Right." The words unsettled Lance, but he also needed to hear them.

Jacob watched the young man for a moment before he continued. "So, how are you holding up, lad?"

"Good. The Rift went well. The other Rifters took good care of me and the job itself was a straightforward one," Lance said quickly.

"You know I wasn't talking about the Rift," Jacob said as he placed his hand on Lance's shoulder again, squeezing gently. "I won't tell you what you should and shouldn't do. Had the roles been reversed, Thomas would have done exactly what you're doing. Perhaps even more so to channel his loss and feelings into something he could punch. Perhaps I would too, had I been younger."

The two men kept quiet at that, both remembering Thomas in the way they wanted to. Lance didn't need his elevated Perception to feel the pain that Jacob was carrying inside. The man's hand slid off his shoulder and tapped him on the chest, near his heart.

"Lad, I don't know what's driving you at this moment, nor do I want to know what it is. Wield it, for now. Use it as fuel. But take care not to cling to it too long. A fire that sustains a person can also burn them up to where only ash remains." At that, Jacob grabbed another beer and steered Lance and himself back to the living room.

"Ein schöner Mann," Dieter said proudly as he pointed his phone toward Lance and the tailor. They were busy helping the young man out with the finishing touches. Daniel, who was on the other end of the call, was smiling from behind his desk, clad in his GRRO outfit. Today was the 30th of March, two days after Lance's birthday. Although it was a Saturday, there were few people in this shop within the Workshop.

Lance felt a bit embarrassed at being called good-looking in German, but even he couldn't refute the fact that his new outfit was a thousand times better than the horrible one he had used in his previous Rift. Most of his body was now covered in a protective steel mail shirt, with leather armor placed over it to better secure, and to lessen the reflective nature of the steel.

Protective fingerless Sap gloves offered protection to his hands and increased his damage output in hand-to-hand combat. The steel knuckles made sure of that. Protective combat boots and steel shin and knee guards protected his lower body, reducing as little mobility as possible, while allowing Lance to shrug off minor blows. The tailor had fastened a steel pauldron on Lance's left shoulder, adding more defense while leaving Lance's right side as flexible as possible.

"So, how does it feel?" the tailor asked, watching Lance move left and right, jump, and make a few jabs to test out the equipment.

"Light, not too restrictive," Lance said, looking at his gloved hands and making a fist, feeling the protective fabric caress his hands. "Fantastic."

"You've a Strength rank of twenty-something, right? A bit of leather and steel won't slow you down," Dieter said, aiming the camera at Lance as he moved closer to him. "It's machine-made, not Rifter-made. So don't expect it to stop a dragon."

"Rifter-made?" Lance asked.

"He means that a Rifter with a specific Class made the item. They're typically more durable and incredibly expensive," Daniel said, his voice flowing out of the speaker.

"But the upgradable slots are well worth it. Speaking of upgrades . . ." Dieter said with a smile while he held up his hand to silence Lance for a moment. Moments later, he retrieved a large mace from his Inventory and handed it to the young man. "There we go. A proper birthday present."

[Item transfer complete]

Lance struggled with the weight of the mace. Although it was a one-handed weapon, it was far heavier than most two-handed weapons he had practiced with in the past. *What the hell is this thing made of?* he thought as he ran a hand over the black steel material and traced a line over the many dents and ridges at the side.

"An older weapon of mine, back when I only had a dozen Rifts under my belt. Now, don't get too attached to your gear. You'll outgrow them in no time," Dieter said with a smile as he pointed at the weapon. "I bought it for £200,000, give or take. Expensive back then, but you'll see why. Check out the slots."

It took Lance a few minutes to figure out what Dieter meant. He had to open several additional screens of information about the weapon until he found what he was looking for. *A crafter filled three out of the three slots. A Mana crystal core, Red-stone casing, and a black wood handle,* Lance noted, going over each of the upgrades to see what their uses were.

The black wood offered more flexibility to the handle, allowing more kinetic force to be produced while protecting the Rifter's hand upon impact. The Red-stone amplified heat while the Mana crystal could store Mana or transfer it to the Red-stone, increasing the heat of the weapon. Compared to a regular person making a mace out of the materials, a crafter could imbue the item with far more beneficial traits.

Sort of like a boiling mace? Lance wondered as he forced more Mana into the weapon. He watched the core grow hotter as the metal turned a red hue. He held his hand above it and could feel the heat coming off it, like a small bonfire. He had no doubts that it would hurt when pressed against exposed flesh, allowing the wielder to burn someone after smashing a mace in their ribs. *This lacks any sort of finesse. I can see why Dieter purchased it*, Lance concluded as he noticed his Mana dwindling, showing that the weapon drained a lot during use.

Does this mean that Ash has slots as well? Lance thought for a minute before he noticed Dieter staring at him. "This is way too much. I mean . . . a birthday present is a few pounds or more, not something equivalent to buying an expensive car," Lance said, his mind finally wrapping itself around the price tag of the weapon. He knew that more expensive gear could be worth hundreds of thousands of pounds or more, but to get one as a gift was something else.

"Don't be like that. It's a gift. Besides, it was only worth a lot when I bought it years ago. Back when there were fewer resources and even fewer Rifters classed as Smiths or Crafters. The weapon is quite Mana hungry, and the damage output isn't worth it at higher Levels. Still, it's a boon at your current stage. That and you can turn it into a heater in an emergency," the man said with a grin as he pointed the camera toward Lance, showing Daniel's face.

"My present will be more modest and practical. But I must get back to work. We'll talk later, all right?" Daniel asked Lance and waited for him to nod before closing the call.

Lance then moved back toward the mirrors, inspecting his new outfit while he did his best to ignore Dieter, who was buttering up the tailor, asking for a discount for the "light of Ipswich." Lance hated that bit, since Dieter was referring to the article that a local journalist had published after the White Clovers had cleared the Rift in Ipswich for the first time. Attached to that article was a picture of Lance basking in the light after returning to Earth, with his gaze toward the sun.

I'll never live this down, he thought before he shifted his attention back toward his new outfit and weapon.

[You have retrieved an Item]

A satisfied grin appeared on his face as he stood there with a shield and mace in his hands. He felt the heat coming from the mace as he charged it with more and more Mana until it became almost too hot to handle. Filled with renewed purpose, he then joined Dieter in the negotiations, for once not feeling bad about spending most of his earned profits.

Things are looking up!

At the same time, in a different country, a woman answered an incoming call. "What do you have for me?" she asked, her voice calm and composed. A stark contrast to what the blade she had wielded had just done.

"Information about the three marks. Two of them have been active. Uploading the data now," a distorted voice conveyed to her through her earpiece, hidden by black hair that matched her dark features.

A device materialized in her grasp as she settled down, heedless of her macabre seat—the lifeless body of a man someone had contracted her to dispatch. Slipping the blade back into its temporary flesh scabbard, she brushed off the unsettling sound it made. Her gaze swept across the received information, weighing her alternatives.

Target One hasn't moved. The older brother knows better than to let him off the leash now, the woman thought, as she looked at the photo of the man, irritated to see his attractive features again.

Two has made some irregular moves, working closely with the GRRO branch in France. Atonement? He's become a liability, she decided, not bothering to look at his picture again.

She took her time reading the information about the third target, seeing several medical documents suggesting trauma, information regarding his social circle, and a recent article about him clearing a Rift in Ipswich. *A shame. Three could've had a peaceful life, had it not been for those eyes*, she thought, seeing past the article's lofty words and the young man's shoddy equipment. *Those eyes contain not the coldness of loss or the joy of renewed purpose. A fire burns within those eyes.*

"What do you want to do?" the distorted voice asked without a hint of emotion.

"Two and Three need to be addressed if we're to have a chance at salvaging negotiations with my one's older brother." Pausing for a brief moment, her thoughts raced, weaving a plan within her mind. "Offer the twins the contract for Two and Three. Assure them they'll receive a payment comparable to what they got in Madrid," she decided, aware of the weight her words carried as they sealed the fate of two people.

"Someone employed the twins elsewhere at the moment," the voice stated calmly.

The woman clicked her tongue once before she replied. "Tell them that Kira will owe them a favor, each."

"Understood," the voice said before the line disconnected.

Her fingers curled around the blade's handle, gripping it with a firmness that echoed her irritation. With a controlled motion, she twisted the blade within the corpse, cutting and rending. It frustrated her that the situation had escalated to this point. *A billion-dollar deal on the brink of collapse . . . All because of a spoiled brat's desperate need for validation from his older brother.*

"The twins will take care of these loose ends," Kira finally said, retrieving her blade as she stood up and finished her own bloody task that day.

Status Compendium

Name:	Lance Turner
Level:	16
Class:	Death Smith

Attributes

Endurance:	40	**Agility:**	40	**Wisdom:**	25
Strength:	34	**Perception:**	28	**Luck:**	28
Health:	900	**Mana:**	185		
Stamina:	290	**Inventory:**	35		

Traits

| **Taint of death:** | Able to use Rift corpses as items | Prolonged use results . . . ~ERROR UNREADABLE!~ |
| **Shard instability:** | Prolonged use results . . . ~ERROR UNREADABLE!~ | Prolonged use results . . . ~ERROR UNREADABLE!~ |

Skills

Mend Wounds	Lvl 2	Restores minor wounds	+20 Health +8 Stamina	−15 Mana
Death Forge	Lvl 1	Allows (re)forging of death related items	+1 Item	−Raw materials −Black-shards −50% Stamina regeneration −50% Mana regeneration
Repair Item	Lvl 1	Restores durability on items	+1 durability per 1 item per 1 minute	−Raw materials −Black-shards −25% Stamina regeneration −25% Mana regeneration

Retainers

| **Ash** | 1x | Human |

CHAPTER THIRTEEN

Loose Ends

Three Weeks Later
April, 14 AR
The Walker Residence
London, England

KATE

Kate closed her violin's protective casing, casting a dark shadow over the instrument as she did so. Long, slender fingers with calloused fingertips found their way over to the edges of the case and zipped it up. *Your new life is starting, girl. No way out but forwards*, she thought, remembering her grandmother's advice and feeling strengthened by it.

"I could make you stay. I'm your father, you know," Jacob Walker said to his daughter as he sat on the bed next to her bag and suitcase.

"And I would love you for it, but I'd still go," she said with a smile, placing the violin case on her father's lap as she folded a few more clothes that she would need. Although her father was making a show of her leaving the country, she knew he'd be the first one to carry her bags to the airport.

"I could beg. Tears and everything. It would be a heart-wrenching sight," Jacob teased as he helped his daughter by folding a T-shirt.

Her smile widened playfully as she nudged him in the side. "Wouldn't work. Redheads don't have a soul. It would be a waste of tears."

They had been at it for the better part of an hour already, her father continuously offering ways or reasons why she should remain home, even though she had already been living on her own for several years, with her staying over only now and again. They both knew why she was leaving for Italy to work as a violinist.

Music had been her passion ever since she had been old enough to pick up an instrument. While Thomas had gotten trophies for sports, Kate had been entering music competitions and even winning a few of them that culminated in her getting a scholarship several years ago. To see more of the world, to meet people and experience music from other places—that was her dream, her passion.

"Besides, you'd like Italy. Food, wine, warm weather," she said as she closed her bag and gave him a peck on the cheek. "And far fewer redheads."

"The last part sounds perfect. When can I move in?" he said with a chuckle as he got up and pulled her in for a warm hug. "And when you break through and become wealthy and famous over there, never forget the most important thing."

"I know. Be safe and happy," Kate said, her features softening a bit as she planted herself deeper into the hug.

"No, sweetie. The most important thing is that your old man wants his Ferrari in red or black," he said, quickly backing off while his daughter began nudging him in the ribs again. The man had spent years in the military, so he knew when to retreat before he got shelled by a dozen folded socks. "I love Mum the most," his daughter yelled after him, only to grin when he exclaimed that he did so as well.

I'm going to miss that sense of humor of his, Kate thought as she picked up the thrown socks and placed them back in her suitcase. Her gaze shifted toward her plane tickets, her passport, and the stack of papers concerning her position with an orchestra in Italy. It had always been a dream of hers to do so, but she had been hesitant about taking the leap. After losing her brother and seeing her mother drown herself in grief, she had decided she needed to do something different with her life. In her mind, she felt like she owed it to Thomas to broaden her horizons and give the Walker family a pleasant development for a change.

She still felt bad about leaving, since her father was shouldering the world, her younger brother would be on his own, and her mother still struggled with the loss of a child. But she knew her father would drive her to Italy himself if she didn't take this chance.

"No way out but forwards," she said several times. Each time her tone grew louder as if she were convincing herself. She paused when she spotted her younger brother standing in the doorway, holding onto a sandwich and a glass of orange juice.

"Dad! Kate is talking to herself again. Is she off her meds?" her brother said, flashing her one of his trademark mischievous grins before he backing off and retreating to his room, with Kate in hot pursuit.

She stepped into his room and noticed the many posters of famous Rifters on his walls. Oliver had a Mana stone on his desk, next to a picture of Thomas and Lance inside a Rift. The entire room shouted Rifter fanboy, with several newspaper articles about Lance pinned to the wall, including an article from Ipswich.

"Are you going to be all right when I'm away?" Kate asked, moving over to him and putting her hands on his shoulders, squeezing gently. The young lad was growing taller and wider by the day. She had worried that he'd end up a musclehead like Thomas, but fortunately, his grades were far more promising.

"I'll be fine. Really," Oliver stated.

"And you can call whenever you need to talk, all right?" Kate asked, a hand moving a dirty towel up from the desk, revealing a half-eaten horn underneath it. *No doubt one of the monster horns that Rift-dog had been chewing on*, she mused. "You are the biggest nerd I know. Never change."

"I'm too stubborn for that. Besides, it's a collector's item. When Lance joins a major guild, I can sell this bad boy for fat stacks," the youth exclaimed, placing the towel back on the horn to hide it from his parents. His father probably wouldn't mind the item, save for the smell, but the young man was smart enough to know that it would startle their mother.

Kate squeezed his shoulders playfully before she took a seat down on his bed. "Fat stacks?"

"It beats fingering a few strings on a piece of wood for months on end. Seeing as we were talking about your boyfriend, have you told him about your change of scenery already?" he asked, although he probably knew the answer already.

"Boyfriend, huh? Big words from his personal stalker. But no. I hear the reception in a Rift is terrible, so unfortunately, I couldn't speak to him face-to-face. I'll send him a text when I arrive in Rome tomorrow morning."

"Or you could . . . you know . . . tell him in a few hours when he finishes up with a Rift?" Oliver said, as his eyes met Kate's.

"How?"

"Well, being a personal stalker has its benefits. I know where he'll be in a few hours . . . roughly. I just found an article about Lance and the Rift he might clear today. And this information can be yours, provided my favorite sister does something for me in return," Oliver negotiated with a sly expression on his face.

His sister slowly leaned closer. "I take it you like your ribs intact and not broken?" she asked calmly, countering Oliver with a smile of her own—one that was disarming enough to turn the boy's expression into one of fear and uncertainty.

No way out but forwards, Kate told herself once more as she stepped out of the pizzeria, clutching a pizza box that was pleasantly warm to the touch. She could smell the cheese, tomatoes, and the spices wafting from the container. Kate felt tense, having driven from London to Ipswich as fast as she could, hoping she would get there on time. She made her way toward the Rift itself, near the center of town. The whole place was alive, hundreds of people gathered near the Rift.

There were street vendors selling small trinkets, drinks, and food. Beyond that, there was also a small stage where a live band was performing to keep the crowd entertained until the big moment. They had erected large screens that played live footage of the Rift itself. The pulsating mass of black energy was absolutely alien to

Kate. *I can't believe my brother and Lance actually walked through these things*, she thought, remembering the footage she had seen of Lance and the White Clovers.

She did her best to get as close as possible to the Rift itself, nearing the GRRO barricade and the control post behind it. People were eager to enter, but the GRRO was adamant in maintaining the barrier until the White Clovers had fully destroyed the Rift. The GRRO would only allow people entry again when there wasn't a chance of Rift-materials or a Rifter exiting the Rift at a high speed.

That thing is huge, Kate mused, observing the massive barrier and safety net constructed around the hulking black mass of energy. She felt silly standing there, holding a pizza box and waiting for a Rifter to appear. It could be a matter of seconds, or it could take hours. According to Oliver's information, the White Clovers had agreed with the GRRO and the officials of the town to aim for a set date and a rough estimate in terms of time. It wasn't an exact science, but these Rifters had a good idea of how long they needed to clear the Rift and at what time they would exit. She was about to go to a stand to buy herself a coffee when the world itself screamed. Her gaze instantly shot toward one of the screens.

The massive black energy was erratic, bits of it imploding or exploding as the core destabilized. Even from where Kate was standing, she could feel the unnatural amount of energy as it dissipated in the surrounding air. Then, in a last violent roar, the Rift exploded outwards in a tidal wave, knocking back the GRRO personnel on the site and masking the entire area in a thick cloud of dust.

Please be all right, Kate begged, her fingers digging into the cardboard box as memories of Thomas and Lance stormed in her mind. All around her she could see people behaving similarly, with some praying that it would be all right, others mumbling to themselves. Then, when the dust cleared, four armored figures stood where the Rift had once been.

The crowd went mad at that point, cheering for the Rifters and celebrating that the Rift was truly gone. The camera showed the Rifters making their way toward the exit, talking amongst themselves, and patting each other on the back. By the time they left the GRRO barricades and met the townspeople, they were given a heroes' welcome. People nearly threw themselves at them, showering the Rifters with praise, flowers, food, and drinks.

Fearing she might have lost her moment, Kate moved forwards, elbowing her way closer and closer, ignoring the angry comments she received in return. Finally, she broke past her last obstacle and planted herself directly in front of Lance as she shoved the pizza in his hands. "I figured you could use a meal," Kate said as she gave him a bright and knowing smile.

"More?" Kate asked as she pulled off another slice of pizza and held it out behind her, allowing Lance to grab it. She could hear the water splattering as he took his warm shower in his private GRRO cubicle.

"Yes, please. God, I missed good food," he commented, tearing into the pizza while taking his shower. Dirt, grease, and dried-up blood from days of living in the Rift flowed down the drain. Eventually, the shower transformed him from a Rift-hobo into a person who resembled Lance.

Kate glanced over her shoulder at Lance's back as he ran a hand through his hair. She could see the scars adorning his body, ranging from older cuts, claw marks, and even a bite mark. *How are you able to deal with all this?* she thought as she remembered a younger, more innocent version of. The longer her gaze lingered, the more she noticed the difference in his physique. His muscles were far more defined and hinted at a strength beyond what was normal. "What the hell have they been feeding you?" she thought out loud.

"Sorry?" Lance asked as he turned off the shower.

Kate blushed but managed to hide her face from him as she replied. "Nothing, I was just asking you when you lost your marbles? Oliver told me that in the last three weeks you've thrown yourself into three Rifts. Excessive, don't you think?"

Lance paused at that. No doubt he was searching for the right words to say or to conjure up a decent excuse. She scolded herself for putting him in that situation. This wasn't why she had wanted to visit him. "New hairstyle?" she asked, offering him a way out. She had last seen him on his birthday three weeks ago, and his hair had been much shorter back then. Now it reached his neck, far longer than what was possible in a mere three weeks. *How much time passed for him inside of these Rifts?*

"Yeah. Remind me to take a barber with me the next time I throw myself in another Rift," he countered, laughing. Then he put on a pair of trousers and a shirt.

"Noted," she said as her gaze shifted toward Lance's bag next to her, which was filled to the brim with Items from the Rift. It was different than the bag she'd seen in his flat. Instead of a makeshift bundle of cloth, this was sturdy and made of woven plastic. Besides it, she noticed a large steel mace that was dented in several places and a partially broken steel shield. She knew the latter had belonged to Thomas, her brother having shown it to the entire family after he bought it at the Workshop. It pained her to see it, but she was also glad that it was with Lance, protecting him from whatever he faced inside a Rift.

"Ready?" Kate asked, turning around as she heard Lance put on his shoes. "Do you know a place where we can grab a drink? I wanted to discuss something with you."

"That's great," Lance said, his smile widening at the news.

Idiot, that isn't what I wanted to hear. Kate nodded. "Yeah, it is." The two of them had found a small bar away from Ipswich's busy city center. They had shared a few drinks and Lance had another bite to eat as she told him about her job in

Italy, how her mother and father were doing, and how Oliver had turned into his number one fanboy. She told Lance about the "Rift shrine" Oliver had made, with Rift Items, pictures of Thomas and Lance, and printed-out news articles. "So, what do you do inside a Rift when you have time off? Count stones?" Kate asked, attempting to lighten the mood.

"Honestly? I read a book or watch a movie on my phone. Beyond that, salvaging for things can be quite time-consuming," Lance said, his gaze shifting over toward his bag before returning his focus to Kate. "But Italy. That's great. Imagine all the things you'll see over there."

Kate smiled. "You're one to talk. Mister I-jump-from-one-realm-to-another."

"Touché, but the places I visit tend to not have a lot of culture, Italian cuisine, or ice cream," Lance said, his smile oddly infectious. "I'm sure Oliver will miss you."

"He'd better," Kate said quickly, her tongue proving to be as quick as her wit. "But speaking of the little brat, he made me promise to ask you for a favor. Apparently, he wants you to get him autographs from the White Clovers," Kate continued, rolling her eyes.

"That seems reasonable."

Come on, girl. You've liked him for years. You've flirted with him, and you know that there is something there. Just say it, Kate told herself, forcing herself to look him in the eyes despite the way it made her feel. "I bloody hope so. I only have a few more hours to tie up loose ends before I go, and I wasn't looking forward to begging you for some nerdy autograph." She smiled as she brushed a few hairs behind her ear. *Just say it, Kate. No way out but forwards. Just like Grandma always said. God, no! That just makes it sound weird,* she thought as her mind turned chaotic.

"Kate? Are you all right?" Lance asked, slightly concerned.

"Yeah, sorry. I got side-tracked there for a minute," she admitted, her cheeks slowly matching the fierceness of her hair. "I'll be in another country tomorrow, so I wanted to make sure I didn't have any regrets."

"Regrets? Is there something you need help with?" Lance asked, blissfully unaware of Kate's internal conflict.

Kate closed her eyes at that, her right hand running through her red strands. "Well, you're the one who threw me into this ugly mess," she said. She forced herself to look him in the eyes. A moment later, she unleashed all the chaotic feelings she felt as she let them drive her forwards, out of her seat and toward Lance's.

"Kate—" was the last thing Lance could say before their lips found one another in a sudden passionate embrace. All the while, Kate kept moving forwards.

CHAPTER FOURTEEN

Bloody VIP

Four Days Later
April, 14 AR
London

LANCE

Lance shook his head as he got his bearings again, tasting blood in his mouth, directing his gaze at the man in front of him. Although he himself was well above average in terms of height, the man facing him was even taller. The man looked like a younger, meaner version of Dieter, with thick, cable-like muscles on his limbs and a broad, developed back that looked intimidating even to Lance.

"Did your sister teach you that punch?" Lance asked the man. The words felt unnatural to him as they left his mouth. Still, they proved effective, because the tall fighter rushed at him again just as he got back up.

Lance evaded the furious blows, ducking underneath several of them as he retaliated with three jabs of his own. He forced a bit more power and speed into them to startle the man. The last one hit him in the nose, causing a small trickle of blood to flow from one nostril. *That felt right*, he thought as he circled the big man and saw the other fighters watching them from the sidelines. Lance had bloodied and bruised quite a few of those onlookers during earlier sparring matches.

Forcing himself to keep his power and speed to more realistic levels, Lance tried to keep up with the large fighter and his punches. No matter how he looked at it, the man had far better technique and rhythm, and years of experience. Lance wasn't sure what his name was again—Michal? Mitch? The trainer had told Lance his name before they had gotten in the ring. The large man had been a heavyweight fighter who had been doing well, but the legal boxing circuit had banned him due to his less-than-legal activities. Not to mention his many altercations with the police. Not a pleasant person to interact with, but people like him were perfect for Lance.

He'd gone to this gym for the past three days in a row after striking a deal with the trainer who ran the place: Lance could fight several of their toughest fighters, while they made sure his sessions didn't become public knowledge. In return, Lance had to sign several waivers and spend a bit of his hard-earned money. In the past, the amount might've startled him, but after having completed four Rifts with other independent Rifters, he had gotten used to having a larger cash flow. To keep the fighters motivated and committed, he had also offered them £3000 if they could knock him out.

Lance rushed forwards again, keeping low and evading a few of the taller man's jabs and enduring those that eventually reached him. He felt the area around his Rift-shard throb and ache again, as a gut feeling manifested itself. *Left!* He wasn't sure if it was a feeling or an actual thought, but it crashed into him, his chest aching even more while tasting fresh blood in his mouth. The moment this happened, Lance spotted the fighter's left elbow going for his face. He could barely dodge in time as it grazed his cheek. *He is really going for it*, Lance thought as he backed off to collect himself. The fighter smiled, unashamed by resorting to such foul play.

Anyone else might've been furious, but Lance was glad the man had done that. He wanted the experience of facing a technical threat who would even cheat in order to win. If he wanted to have a chance at subduing Kira, Louis, or Connor, he would have to grow in Level and combat experience. Fighting a monster wouldn't be the same as fighting an actual human who knew how to fight back.

Still, the discomfort around his shard was increasing. Not to mention the strange dreams, behavior, and thoughts he was having. He realized that something was off, as if there was someone or something else inside of him, fighting to get to the surface. To be noticed. *What the hell is wrong with me*, he thought as he tried to focus and send out a few fast jabs, keeping the large fighter at a distance.

At first, he thought it might've been fatigue or symptoms of damage he had sustained to his head when Thomas had thrown them both off a cliff or when the Rift had spat him out afterwards. More often, he felt like something inside of him was trying to become a part of him, sharing behavioral traits, knowledge, or insight.

The fighter blocked Lance's next jab and stepped in to deliver a painful body blow right where his liver was. Although Lance was faster, the fighter's experience allowed him to adjust to Lance's rhythm and patterns. The fighter rushed at him, hammering lefts and rights into him as he closed the distance.

Lance kept restricting his power and speed, despite wanting to lash out. He had to endure the onslaught. His increased Endurance meant that he could take one hell of a beating, but the fighter was clearly intent on chipping away at him. No Rifter at his Level could sustain a constant barrage of blows to vital organs.

Left.

Again, Lance felt the strange sensation echo in his mind, demanding him to move. As predicted, Lance noticed the tall fighter shoot forwards while another elbow made a beeline toward his face. *Now!* The sensation became louder and louder, screaming in his mind until something snapped.

It was as if someone else placed a hand on the steering wheel. Lance's body moved on pure instinct, leaning to his right as a large elbow grazed his ear. Before he realized, he had already moved his right hand, launching it straight up as it connected with the fighter's chin. At Lance's uppercut, the fighter flew backwards into the ropes with enough force to topple him over it and out of the ring.

Thomas? Lance thought, taken aback at what had happened. *Thomas!* he howled inside his mind but got no response. There was no way to describe what had just happened. Lance knew what a counter was and what an uppercut looked like, Daniel having trained him well. But he had never landed a counter like this. It was as if Lance could suddenly rely on years of boxing experience to judge when an opponent would strike and how to take advantage of an opening in a split second. The movements and style reminded him of Thomas.

As he noticed the other fighters' stares, Lance made his way over to the trainer, handing the man back the gloves he had borrowed. "Thanks again for letting me train here. It has really helped me," he said as he tried to compose himself and not escalate the situation.

"I'll say. You just knocked out Mathew. I've never seen anyone do that before," the man said with a smile as he moved closer to Lance.

Mathew! I knew it, Lance lied to himself and nodded to the trainer. "Sorry about that. I'll help him out with the pain before I go."

"No, no. You did great, lad. You've got my number. Now, if you ever want to do something beyond clearing a Rift, you call me and I'll set something up for us," the trainer said, patting Lance on the back as if they were childhood friends.

"I will," Lance lied as he grabbed his things and shoved them in his rucksack before placing a hand on his face and activating his healing Skill. It illuminated his body in a bright blue light. Normally he'd feel self-conscious about drawing attention to himself, but the fighters there knew he was a Rifter, and he had healed himself a few times already. He grabbed his bag as he then made his way over to the unconscious fighter. He placed a hand on the fighter.

Mend Wounds
Mend Wounds

Twice he forced healing energy into the man, knitting damage and lessening fatigue. The muscular fighter would probably be all right after a few minutes, but the former nurse didn't want to risk leaving someone with a concussion. He walked out shortly after that, leaving the bewildered fighters behind as Mathew suddenly woke up with only a minor bruise to show for it.

It would be the last time Lance went to this gym since he had fought their strongest fighters already. He would switch to a different combat sport next time. He wanted to experience a lot of unique styles of combat to further his growth. But only after he had made sense of what the hell had just happened to him. Still, all of that had to wait until tomorrow, since he had an appointment with a member of the Walker family in a few hours.

"But you're a Rifter . . ." Oliver asked Lance two hours later. The boy's left eyebrow was raised as high as it could.

Lance nodded once, wondering why all the redheads in the Walker family were so confrontational and direct. "Yes, shard and all."

"So, why are we taking a bus?" the thirteen-year-old asked.

Lance was thankful that the subject was about transportation and not about his meeting with Kate. He was still very much unsure what to make of it all beyond feeling strangely excited by the encounter, but Lance wasn't in the mood to explain it to her little brother.

"Did you prefer to walk then? I don't have a spare car lying around," he answered young Oliver, doing his best to keep the irritation out of his voice. He wasn't upset with him, and he knew why Oliver had asked it. Most Rifters had fancy cars or even personal drivers. Some even had personal helicopters or jets to take them from place to place.

Lance was upset because his jaw was still sore from the punches he had taken, as well as still feeling unsettled at what was going on inside of his mind. To make matters worse, he had nearly snapped his phone in half upon reading the news article about a massive expansion and acquisition move from an American guild.

At the start of the article, he'd seen a photograph of Ryan Moore, one of the most influential Rifters in America, and the owner of said guild. He was similar in appearance to his younger brother, if not more physically developed. The man's appearance and fancy clothes drew the eye to him. To Lance, the man barely existed. He had instead focused on Ryan's younger brother, standing next to him in the picture. Connor Moore had a warm and charismatic smile, seemingly happy to be in the spotlight with his brother.

The only reason Lance's phone was still intact, beyond it being expensive, was the fact that Oliver was sitting right next to him. Thomas would've torn Lance a new one if he'd learned that his friend had thrown a tantrum in front of his baby brother. So, Lance forced it all down. He pushed those thoughts and feelings about Connor back down, letting them smolder along with the rest of those feelings.

"Right?" Oliver asked as he tapped Lance's shoulder to get his attention again. "You will eventually get a car, right?"

"Perhaps. Or a moped. A pink one," he said jokingly. He knew the lad was optimistic about his prospects as a Rifter. "Here, this will get your mind off me owning a car." He handed Oliver a folded piece of paper that Noel, Claudia, and Myles, had autographed, along with a few kind words to Oliver.

The way boy's jaw dropped was priceless and more than enough to remove Lance's unpleasant mood. Besides that, he had also agreed to let Oliver "help" him by mailing articles about interesting Rift-related things or sending some inspirational music to him. *He is like Thomas's clone. It is only a matter of time before he condemns my music choices.*

"This is our stop. Grab your things," Lance said as the lad sprang into action. The two of them got out of the bus and made their way over to the museum in the distance. Large banners showing Rift-shards, monsters, strange weaponry, and photos of famous Rifters were on display. "Are you ready for a treat?" he asked Oliver as they reached the entrance and passed a line of people who were waiting to buy their tickets. Instead, Lance made his way over to the side and went straight toward an employee who was on a smoke break outside.

"Hey there. Mind fetching your supervisor?" he asked before he materialized a monster horn out of thin air and threw it in an arc so that the man could catch it in time. "I'd like to make a donation."

"Thank you so much for your contribution to the museum . . . and for your service to this country," the supervisor said, although Lance figured the man was more pleased with the former. "I hope you and your brother have a pleasant experience with us. I'll be back after a while, but ask the aide here for any help, should you need something!"

"We will," Lance said, glad to be freed of the man's presence. He had figured the donation would allow his "younger brother" and him quick access to the museum along with VIP status. What he had failed to calculate was the time he had lost because of the supervisor's chatty nature. Still, seeing Oliver's excited face and the VIP lanyard around his neck was worth it. They had allowed Oliver to touch and hold certain items, even lift a rare red Mana stone, and take a picture together in front of a large monster claw.

"Lance! They have Ogre teeth here . . . and white-shards! Come check it out," the boy exclaimed as Lance moved toward him with the aide in tow.

"You're right, that's neat," Lance said as he looked at several white-shards in a row, their sizes increasing the further along you went. From what Lance could read, they belonged to mice, birds, a human, and even a cow.

What amazed him was the description on the plaque underneath the mouse's white-shard. It explained where they had found it and that the mouse had lived for three years, nearly double their normal lifespan. *I wonder what that means for us humans?* Lance pondered, deciding he should read more about it when he had the time.

"Look, that one is even bigger than yours," Oliver said with a grin.

Lifting his T-shirt, Lance tapped against his own shard. "Well, it isn't the size of the shard, you know."

"Can we touch them? Please?" Oliver asked the aide, even going as far as to flash his innocent bright green eyes.

"Err . . . fine. I guess it's fine. It is one of the strongest materials known to man. Just don't drop it, all right? Or tell my supervisor."

"We won't," Oliver said, his fingers eagerly moving toward the first shard once the protective glass was gone.

Curious himself, Lance touched the white-shard that had belonged to a human. From what he read, the family of a Rifter had donated it when the Rifter had died of their injuries. They kept the donor anonymous, as per the family's instruction. The moment that Lance touched the shard, however, he noticed his status screen showing a new notification.

[Item can be forged. Templates available: 1]
[Required Shards: 100. Do you wish to continue?]
[Yes] [No]

Lance removed his hands from the shard, as if burned by it. He remembered the way he had felt back when he had seen that notification, thinking he could save Thomas with it. Knowing he'd drown himself in self-loathing later that evening when he was alone, he instead focused on what the notification meant. *Does that mean I can make more companions like Ash?*

He touched it once more, just to be sure. Again, the notification popped up. Curious what the other would do, Lance touched the smaller and larger white-shards but didn't notice any notification pop up. *I think that means that I can only use this template on fallen humans.*

He continued touching a white-shard that had belonged to a pigeon at one point. He opened several menus until he got to a notification that displayed the item's weight and durability. Nearly closing it, Lance noticed a small icon before pressing it.

[Unknown template. Base 5% chance of discovery
when destroying this item]
[Do you wish to destroy this item?]
[Yes] [No]

Lance suddenly stopped touching the white-shard as his eyes widened. *I never had that choice before!* he thought. He remembered the hours he had spent with Thomas in the hospital when they had become Rifters. They had explored all the menus of their system to learn as much about it as they could. After that, Daniel and Dieter had filled in the rest.

Is this a Class-specific thing? he asked himself, his thoughts racing chaotically. Lance opened his own Inventory and focused on a certain item, trying to see if this was indeed the case. He chose a javelin he had made from bone and a horn. He shifted through the menus until he reached the option.

[Unknown template. Base 25% chance of discovery
when destroying this Item]
[Do you wish to destroy this Item?]
[Yes] [No]

This is amazing! he thought as he tried to act normal, since Oliver and the aide were staring at him. *The chance of discovery is much higher this time. Is it because I made the item myself?* Lance mused. After opening the same option on a bunch of things, such as his steel axe, knife, and his phone, he learned a few things.

Some things I can't get a template from, such as my phone. And the chance of discovery starts at five percent, with it being higher if I made an item by hand myself. So, familiarity plays a significant factor, Lance thought as he ran a hand through Oliver's hair to let him know he was all right. "Sorry, it just felt surreal to me, touching other shards. I'm going to get us some drinks, okay?" he asked Oliver before moving away from the displays.

As he did so, he grabbed his phone and texted Daniel, asking him for a favor. As he finished, Lance reached the small kiosk and flashed his VIP badge. He asked for two drinks and some snacks. As the woman behind the register asked if he wanted straws for the drinks, Lance's reply was the same as the choice he had just made within his status screen.

[Yes]

CHAPTER FIFTEEN

Icarus

Several Days Later
April, 14 AR
London, England

LANCE

I mean, I'm not going into the Rifts, per se. But the job I do here is vital, you know?" Stefan said, his voice loud enough to carry the distance.

Lance nodded as he pulled on the hood of his GRRO-issued raincoat, hoping it would lessen the chance that the man would continue his boasting. More than once, the conversation had tempted him to reveal his status as a Veteran and a Level Twenty-Three Rifter compared to Stefan's single digit. Luckily for Stefan, Lance had suppressed that urge as he pretended the hood was mostly for the constant downpour.

Lance had asked Daniel for a favor in hooking him up with a job as a "debris collector." Although GRRO personnel did most of the collecting after Rifters had cleared a Rift, they occasionally hired Rift survivors to help in finding or identifying objects. For many survivors who never wanted to enter a Rift again, this occupation would offer a decent income, not to mention getting similar benefits to those of actual Rifters. These collectors were quite a boon for the GRRO, but also a liability. They could easily store valuable Items in their Inventory without the GRRO finding out. Quite a few shards, Mana stones, and weapons had been "lost" in the hands of debris collectors, only to end up in underground auctions somewhere.

As expected of a typical British day, the weather was atrocious. He had started his shift as a collector four hours ago in the rain, and it hadn't lessened one bit. He wasn't enjoying working in this weather, but the rain couldn't have happened at a more fortunate time. "Got something!" Lance barked. He then pressed the button on the radio device fastened to his shoulder to alert the GRRO personnel huddling near a heater underneath a tent. A moment later, a woman, Amira, approached him. The rank on her uniform listed her as a senior, marking her as someone who had some weight and authority on the site, albeit still a rank lower than a site overseer.

"I think it used to be a weapon," Lance said as he placed both hands underneath a small rock and sliding it to the side. With the rock now gone, Lance could see the dented weapon. It surprised him it had traveled this far when the Rifters had exited the Rift. Still, remembering how far a Rift had propelled him at one point, he let that thought rest.

"It's definitely made of Rift material," Lance said as he placed a hand on the Item, seeing the notification on his screen asking him if he wanted to store the it. He did so before he brought it out again, clean of rocks and dirt.

[You have retrieved an Item]

Lance suppressed his grin at the startled expression on Amira's face due to the sudden materialization of a weapon in his hand. No doubt the woman had seen it before but doing so up-close was another thing. "The system lists it as just damaged, so I think the owner can still have it repaired," Lance said as he handed her the weapon. "Probably a spare weapon that wasn't properly secured when the Rift-event closed."

"Great find. We'll contact the owner once we figure out who it belongs to. Do you want a break and some coffee?"

"Coffee would be good. But I don't need the rest for now. Where do I need to go next?" Lance asked as he stepped closer, allowing him a better look at the digital map she had on her handheld device. He watched her fingers trace the lines marked on it, away from the location of the Rift. Cameras had recorded the Rifters, debris, and other Items that had been expelled from the Rift, so it made tracking them easier, though still labor-intensive.

It had been a tough one to deal with, according to the Rifters. Due to it being an initial Rift, there had been some loss of life. The Rift had spawned in a park, so thankfully the incident had only claimed three people, alongside a lot of wildlife.

"Grid 23-A. Analysis shows a high grouping of projectiles going in that area. Do you want Stefan to help you out?" Amira asked, a knowing smile forming on her face.

"No! No, no. I'm sure Stefan is busy at his own grid, saving the world," Lance replied, desperate to put some distance between Stefan and himself. Although the man was a Rifter like him, Lance was fairly sure the man had never stepped foot in a Rift after his initial one. He didn't devalue the man for not doing so. Plenty of survivors were struggling with trauma or injuries, or simply felt unsuited for the Rifter life. But Stefan elevated his position as a debris collector to be at the same Level of Rifters like Dieter.

Amira chuckled at that as she stored the device. "Noted. You head on over to the next grid while I fetch you a cup of coffee."

Lance nodded as he made his way over to the next grid and began searching for more expelled material, be it equipment, rubble, or the bodies of animals. Although the GRRO would no doubt rate them in that line-up, Lance was more interested in the latter. An animal that had survived a Rift was a rare sight, with dogs such as Little Hans being incredible finds.

There were plenty of cases of Rifters reporting that they found animals inside of an initial Rift that had come from Earth, such as rabbits or birds, but because of their wild nature, they would stay away from Rifters. Sadly, this meant that they would end up getting shot out of the Rift when the Rift-event closed. Often, the GRRO would find red smears of animal carcasses around the Rift site.

Another one, Lance thought as he jumped down a small boulder and noticed another smear of gore and feathers. *Could be a pigeon?* He picked up a feather and rolled it between his fingers. A moment later, he noticed the small white shard in the bloody pulp that had once been its body. The pigeon had survived the inside of the Rift because of its ability to fly, and the Rift had rewarded the animal with a white-shard, only for it to die upon arriving back on Earth. Luckily for Lance, he didn't need the animal, just the shard. And a white-shard was one of the strongest materials known to man.

[You have stored an Item in your Inventory]

He added the shard to his growing collection. "Got something," Lance said when Amira returned to him with a warm cup of coffee. "Thanks. I found this little fellow. I'm not sure about the shard. It could've bounced off a rock or buried itself in the ground. Want me to dig here?" Lance asked as he took a sip.

"No, we're paying you too much for that. Best we mark it with a flag and let the interns do it. That or Stefan," Amira said with a smile as she grabbed her device again and explained to Lance that there should be at least three more projectiles in the area.

Finishing his coffee, Lance continued his work, feeling bad for taking advantage of the trust she had shown him.

A few hours after his shift as a collector, Lance was back at home, drinking some warm tea in an attempt at heating his rain-soaked body. He took another generous sip as he looked to his side, seeing Ash sitting in a seat and watching TV.

The man was wearing some old clothes Lance had given him. He could've simply equipped Ash with the R.A.M. uniform, but he wanted the man to learn as much as possible, including being able to dress himself properly. Seeing his companion so intently watching a children's program that was teaching him how to count could have been endearing, had it not been for the fact that Ash was also sharpening the edges of a bear trap at the same time.

That's so messed up, Lance thought as he wondered why he had thought it was all right for Ash to combine both activities. He had bought four bear traps in the Workshop from someone Noel had recommended. They looked like your average bear traps, with thick metal teeth but obviously thicker and more durable. Each trap contained far more compressed force hidden behind a sensitive trigger. Each had set Lance back at least £2000, but he had seen first-hand how effective they could be during his runs with the White Clovers. The best part was Lance could reset and retrieve them as often as needed. Although Ash still lacked the strength to arm them without using a tool.

"Ash, what is five?" he asked as he placed the cup down and made his way over toward Ash, doing his best to ignore the children's program. He smiled when Ash held up five fingers. "Good. Seven?" Lance asked, grinning when Ash again held up the correct number of fingers. He was teaching Ash to count, write simple things, and communicate using hand signs. He figured it would help long-term. "Keep up the good work," he said as he made his way over to the table where he had an assortment of white-shards on display.

"Sorry, Amira," Lance muttered as he picked up the first white-shard that had belonged to a small goldcrest. The shard was tiny compared to his own, but even then, it was incredibly tough. Lance had tried destroying it with a hammer, only for the hammer to crack after several minutes of intense striking.

He had gained Amira's trust because he worked hard, had returned every expensive item he had found, and had come with Daniel's recommendation. Lance figured the loss of a few white-shards that had belonged to some unfortunate animals wouldn't be a major loss for the GRRO. Still, he felt bad about it.

[Unknown template. Base 5% chance of discovery
when destroying this Item]
[Do you wish to destroy this Item?]
[Yes] [No]

Lance watched the notification pop up when he opened the additional screens and pressed a small icon at the bottom. *Like I feared.* He had seen a similar event back in the museum, where an unfamiliar Item had a far smaller chance of resulting in a template. Items he was familiar with had a much higher chance, such as the javelins he had made. Even then, it had cost Lance several javelins before he had gained the "Crude javelin" template. He had named it himself, figuring it would help him keep track of what was what.

Here goes nothing, he thought as he clutched the shard tightly.

[Yes]

He waited a few minutes as a timer ran out. When it was finally done and the Item destroyed, Lance felt it disintegrate in his hands. But his mood soured when he spotted the failure notification. *Dammit! Let's try it again.*

[Failure]
[Failure]
[Failure]
[Failure]
[Success]

Lance was about to throw his hands up in the air out of frustration when he finally realized it had worked. *It worked?* he thought as he suddenly jumped to his feet. "Ash, it bloody worked!" Lance got up and rushed toward his pale companion, clapping him on the shoulder as if they both had been just as eager for it to succeed. Ash watched him with a confused look before he returned to sharpening the bear trap's teeth.

"Alright, so . . . What was it again? One gold crest, three pigeons, one crow . . . the last one was the crow, right?" Lance asked out loud as he went over his notes on how he had organized the shards. He had started with eight and now had three left. He then grabbed the next shard and waited for the notification.

[Item can be forged. Templates available: 1]
[Required black-shards: 50. Do you wish to proceed?]
[Yes] [No]

Lance pressed "yes" and agreed to the forging process, every fiber of his being bursting with excitement. He absolutely lost it when the notification turned into an active countdown, exploding into an ecstatic state. He even jumped over toward Ash, nearly setting off the bear trap as he lifted the man off the ground and forced him into a confusing victory embrace.

A few hours had passed since then. Several empty energy drinks lay discarded on the table in front of Lance and Ash as the two of them watched TV. Lance was half dozing off but had instructed his companion to nudge him in the ribs whenever he fell asleep.

Next to the discarded bottles were several pieces of paper covered with strange, erratic sentences, although they made perfect sense to Lance. Some were notes about his javelins. He could now make them from within his Inventory instead of crafting them by hand, and they were identical to one another. He could also choose what materials to use for them. This included the head, the binding material, and the shaft. Lance had also marked down that he could only use materials made of dead things, be it bone, horn, leather, etc. He had added a question mark to this due to him not being one hundred percent sure of this.

"Ash, our friend Bravo is in the way again," Lance commented as he rubbed his eyes, noting the gray crow on the table blocking his line of sight. The animal, like Ash, was devoid of every color except gray. It behaved similarly to how Ash had acted in the beginning, falling frequently or staring at random things in the room as if they might hold some answer to its existence. "Just put him next to Alpha," he said. In response, Ash picked up the crow and placed it next to a similar crow that was on its back on the floor, struggling to get back up. "Thanks, buddy," Lance said as his companion sat back down next to him.

While they were waiting for the timer in Lance's Inventory to tick down, the two of them were watching an action movie. It was about a trio of heroic Rifters trying to save the president of the United States by clearing a Rift that had opened up in the White House. It wasn't Lance's natural choice of viewing material, but he had once again felt a strange pull inside of him, as if some memory of Thomas demanded to be heard. That feeling had subsided when he had given in and picked that movie.

The two created crows had entertained Lance the first few hours, thus him calling the first one Alpha and the second one Bravo. He had decided at first that they were placeholders until he found better names for them, but the names were growing on him. It felt amazing to see create something out of white-shards. Although they differed from Ash, they had surprising similarities. They were essentially blank slates that looked to him for guidance. Lance had done this as a test, to see if Ash was simply a one-off, or if his Class as a Death Smith allowed him to create more. The price of each crow had been fifty black-shards, putting quite the dent in his reserves.

He checked the timer on his latest forge, seeing it nearing completion. He was particularly curious about this one because it wasn't a crow but rather a peregrine falcon, or so Lance thought. He had taken a few photos of the carcass he'd pulled the white-shard from, but he was convinced that he was right. Upon using this shard, he had the ability to use the crow template, or risk a five percent chance of getting another template. Seeing as Lance only had one chance, he used the crow template.

Lance paused the movie as he got up, seeing the timer dwindle to double digits. "Almost done, buddy," Lance said. At that, his companion get up and fetched

Alpha and Bravo, placing them on the table in front of him. Both Ash and the crows appeared quite calm around one another, as if they had a sort of kinship.

"People say the peregrine falcon is the fastest bird on the planet. It can reach speeds between three and 400 kilometers per hour when it dives," he said, entertaining Ash while trying to keep himself busy. It wasn't just that he wanted this bird as an ally, although he figured it would be an amazing boon. He was using a different template on this white-shard, something he had never done before, or had the chance to before. *Please work!* he thought repeatedly.

[You have finished forging an Item]

"It worked? It bloody worked!" he exclaimed as he placed his hand above the table between the two crows.

[You have retrieved an Item]

Mere moments later, a gray bird sprung into existence. It wobbled on its feet before falling over to its side. As Ash picked it up and placed it on its feet again, Lance looked at one of his peregrine falcon photos and compared it to the one on the table. Despite the lack of color, it appeared to be the same bird. "I think it's bigger?" he said out loud as he guessed their sizes. The crows were still bigger than the falcon, but the crow template had mixed some of its traits with the falcon, resulting in a sort of hybrid in terms of size and wingspan. *Would that be the case with humans as well?* Lance thought as he watched Ash place the falcon back on the table.

"Now, what to call you?" he asked as he inspected the bird closer, seeing its streamlined features. He recalled the state he had found the original bird in as he carefully picked it up and activated the option to rename the Item.

[You have named this item "Icarus"]

CHAPTER SIXTEEN

Gore and Spices

Three Days Later
April, 14 AR
Above the Irish Sea

LANCE

W e would once again like to thank you for choosing our airline and trusting us with your care," the flight attendant said, giving Lance a warm, inviting smile. Her co-worker wasn't far behind with a cart filled with beverages and snacks. Although the flight to Dublin was a short one, Lance was getting pampered in first class due to being a Rifter. "Are you sure we can't help you with anything else? Champagne, whiskey, conversation?" she asked, sounding both professional and slightly suggestive at the end.

Naturally, the latter confused Lance. His life had changed so much, going from being a nurse to suddenly someone receiving preferential treatment on a flight. The pilot himself had even greeted him as he'd boarded the plane. *Her number! I should ask her for her number*, the foreign, intrusive echo of Thomas reverberated in his mind, growing in intensity until he had to willfully suppress it.

After struggling for a moment, he finally felt the echoes of his friend suddenly recede, leaving him in charge of his own mind again. The last few days had been hard on Lance, more and more feelings and memories of Thomas continuously bubbling to the surface, occasionally polluting Lance's thoughts and steering his actions.

"No, thank you, I'm fine. Thank you for taking such good care of me," he said, giving them both a warm smile as he slowly reached for his headphones again, letting them know, in a friendly way, that he was done with the conversation. He switched on his phone and pressed play, drowning out the rest of the world as he lost himself in his music . . . or rather Thomas's music. He wasn't sure if this was due to honoring his friend's memory, or if Thomas's presence lingering in his mind was affecting him in a more profound way.

He opened his banking app and double-checked his cash reserves. He noticed the payment the GRRO had made for the debris collector job he'd done. Since losing Thomas, he had gone through four more Rifts, netting him quite a hefty pay cheque each time. He had spent a lot on upgrading his equipment, getting a ranged weapon and supplies. But after all of that, he still had plenty of cash left in reserve.

He had spent some of his reserves renting a large van and a private place just outside of Dublin. He figured it would serve as his little "personal lair" while he rested, trained Ash, or did other things he didn't want the public to find out about.

Lance felt the plane shake again and he instinctively gripped the sides of his seat. It turned out he hated flying. The last time he had flown anywhere was when his mum had taken him from the Netherlands to move to London. He had remembered it as this marvelous adventure and an experience of a lifetime. Looking back, he might have suppressed certain elements of it. There was something worrying about sitting high in the sky in a steel death trap filled with flammable fuel. *I prefer a Rift to this. At least there I have some control over my fate.* Luckily for him, the flight from London to Dublin was quite short. He could see on the screen in front of him they would arrive in a few minutes.

Instead of looking outside and getting even more nervous, Lance reminded himself that he had his own place, car, and plenty of spending power at his disposal in Ireland. And although his plan was to find the black market there and get his hands on items that might bridge the gap between him and Connor, Kira, and Louis, it didn't mean that he couldn't enjoy himself while he was there. He had already tasked a broker to line him up with a job in Ireland to get his feet wet. With that in mind, he opened one of Thomas's emails and clicked on a music file in the attachment, smiling as he noticed the title: "Make a Little Money" by Royal Deluxe.

[You have retrieved an Item]

"And done!" Lance said a few hours later, an old mattress now dumped in the corner of the dirty room. He glanced around at the horrible state the place was in. Now he could tell why the rent was so low.

At one point, this place had been a butcher's shop, but it had seen no activity in quite some time. Lance had agreed to rent it for a few weeks and the owner had allowed him to make some minor modifications on the inside if it didn't cause structural damage. Lance had painted over the windows to give him more privacy and boarded them up, just to be sure. The best thing about this place was that the meat hooks were still there, and the drains still worked.

[You have retrieved an Item]

A moment later, the body of a Trihorn appeared. It materialized and dropped to the floor like a sack of potatoes. It was strange to see a monster here on Earth. After watching it for some time, he nodded to Ash and pointed to the meat hook at the end of the room. "Just ram it on there," he told him as he judged the distance from here to there, wondering how far it might be.

The Trihorn was still in a decent state, having no visible wounds on the outside, beyond the bent neck that Lance had snapped. As he had suspected, the creature had not rotted, even though it had been some time since he had joined the White Clovers on their second run and destroyed the Rift in Ipswich. *The Inventory system halts all forms of decay after all*, Lance thought as he remembered how hot or cold beverages stayed that way inside of his Inventory.

[You have retrieved an Item 5x]

One by one, Lance summoned his other companions, letting Alpha, Bravo, and Icarus spring into existence. Afterwards, Lance summoned a bow and several arrows, placing them on a dirty table next to him. "Are you ready, Ash?" he asked his companion, and waited for his nod and hand signal they had practiced for the affirmative. "Good job. Now, try using words."

Ash paused for a moment before he spoke. "Y-es . . ." The word came out twisted and deeper than what was normal. It had improved a lot, but it was still strange to hear.

"It's . . . Well, it's good enough for now," Lance said as he gave Ash an encouraging smile.

Lance figured that the biggest reason for his companion's speech problem was the fact that the man didn't need to breathe, meaning that for him to produce words, he would first need to inhale. That and Ash's throat produced far deeper tones. The words uttered sounded strange and somewhat alarming. Still, Ash had come a long way and already had a decent grasp of simple words such as yes, no, monster, and danger.

"Ready," Lance said as he grabbed his bow and nocked a single arrow. He recalled the lessons Daniel had given him. Over the last few days, he'd read all he could about archery, after buying a bow in the Workshop. But nothing he read could even come close to Daniel's teaching. It made sense, since the man had been an archer for years and even had a Class tailored for it.

Remembering the proper stance and breathing, Lance aimed for a weak spot on the monster's corpse. He missed and hit the wall behind it, shattering a ceramic tile in the process. "That didn't count. It was just a warmup," he said, as he picked up the next arrow and nocked it. He could feel Ash and the birds staring at him. Although they were devoid of emotion, his own mind interpreted it as judgement.

The second and third shots all reached their targets, hitting the monster's chest and shoulder. "That should do for now," Lance said as he handed the bow over to Ash and helped him get into the proper stance. The bow itself was a normal one, suitable for non-Rifters. It had enough strength to kill weaker monsters, so it would suit both men for now.

Lance figured that training his companion to use the bow would allow more versatility in their tactics. To encourage Ash a bit more, he let him stand much closer to his target. He did so to get Ash used to hitting the target and to build up more trust and familiarity with the weapon. It didn't take Ash long for his accuracy to increase. Soon he was hitting the monster in more vital spots.

"Keep it up," Lance said as he made his way over to a table with three rusty chairs. The place smelled and was in a horrible state, but it still felt somewhat luxurious to him. He had spent a lot of time in Rifts and had gotten used to the rougher lifestyle. He could still appreciate the cleanliness of his own apartment, but dirty environments didn't seem to bother him as much anymore.

Lance leaned backwards and propped his feet on the table, considering what he should bring with him to the next Rift and how to prepare until that time. He had a bunch of empty crates stacked in a corner that he would hopefully fill with parts harvested from monsters. It was the reason he had rented this place.

Instead of harvesting a few monster items and bringing them with me, I'll spend the next few Rifts collecting monsters and harvesting their parts here, he thought as he imagined just how much more profitable it would all be. He would have to be careful and remove any traces of his activity here afterwards, but he was optimistic.

Still, a low-Level Rifter suddenly having hundreds of monster items would be suspicious, hence why he needed to find the black market. As soon as he did, he could find a fence to take some of those items off his hands. The only lead he had was that the "Little Market" was supposed to be near Dublin. There were probably hundreds of these black markets across the world, but for now, Lance only had this lead to follow.

He spent the next few minutes watching Ash line a dozen more shots before he told the man to take a few more steps backwards and increase the difficulty. As Ash did so, Lance turned his head to stare at the birds, seeing them observe with curious expressions on their faces.

"Who gave you guys permission to slack?" Lance asked them as he pushed a chair hard enough to let it slide toward the other end of the room. "You know you need practices as well. So, fly from this chair to the one in the back, land, and walk backwards. Do this until I tell you otherwise."

Lance had to suppress his laughter at seeing the birds clumsily try to fly to the chair, only to walk in a wobbly manner back to the chair next to him. It was still far too humanlike, and his gray feathered companions would need all the nature documentaries Lance could offer them. Still, the fact that they could already fly for a few seconds without dropping like bricks was a vast improvement.

Provided Lance could deploy them in a Rift without getting caught, the uses he could get out of them would be unimaginable. Perhaps they wouldn't be the greatest fighters; they could still scout, distract, or back Ash up. Lance had read up about how crows have extremely wide vision, reaching an astonishing sixty-degree angle. The peregrine falcon could spot a threat or prey from an incredible distance and maintain sharp vision despite traveling at immense speeds. Just imagining their future uses was getting Lance fired up.

"Alright, Ash. You can put the bow back on the table and retrieve the arrows. I'll teach you how to harvest the monster parts next," he said, reassuring him. "Step one, find a knife."

[You have retrieved an Item]

"God, I needed that," Lance said, brushing away some crumbs from his lips and leaning backwards. He savored the aftertaste of the chicken lahmacun. A strange mixture of garlic, onion, tomatoes, and red peppers hung in the air, along with the unmistakable stench of monster blood and gore.

Both Lance and Ash had spent an hour cutting a monster apart, carefully removing its pelt, bones, tendons, and muscles without ruining too much of it. They had failed previous attempts at this process, and Ash had even lost a finger at one point. But they were getting better at it. To celebrate their first day in Ireland, Lance had ordered Middle-Eastern food as a special treat. He knew his companion didn't need to eat, drink, or sleep, but he occasionally tempted the man into trying new things. Partially because of boredom and curiosity.

"Good, right?" Lance asked him, seeing the blood-covered man sniff at the bit of food drenched in garlic sauce. Whatever Ash thought of it, he didn't share his thoughts with Lance. Instead, the man chewed a few times before placing the fork back down again. "Whatever. You'll learn to appreciate the finer things in life," Lance said, a hint of irony in his voice.

"Well, if you're done, you can help the feathery trio over there." Lance pointed at the crows and the falcon. The birds were busy dragging the bits of monster Items into separate containers. Lance had sorted the Items into separate piles, one for the freshly harvested parts and the other for those that he had stored in his Inventory and retrieved again. Doing so removed any other bits from the monster parts. If he didn't, a keen observer might notice bits of tissue still sticking to a bone, horn, or organ, which would give away that he'd harvested it outside of a Rift. Still, if he were careful, no one would ever find out.

Lance watched the birds drag monster bits toward Ash while the pale man grabbed them. Ash placed the monster parts in Ziplock bags to separate and preserve them. He then efficiently stacked them inside a sturdy metal crate. His spatial awareness was clearly improving.

Even without a proper Rifter's combat abilities, he's proving himself more and more, Lance thought as he cleaned up the table and threw away the rubbish. Afterwards, he helped Ash and the others finish packing up the remaining Items and wash away all the blood and gore that had pooled up on the floor. The built-in floor drain made this a simple task. Lance almost enjoyed the straightforward nature of it.

When it was done, he grabbed a small tablet and placed it against the wall. He had purchased the device in London for a few pounds, without any specific purpose other than playing movies and documentaries. Lance had taught Ash how to operate it, allowing him to play different bird documentaries and train the birds how to behave more like actual birds and improve their techniques, while he grabbed some rest.

"You kids have fun," Lance said as he lay down on the mattress. His camp blanket would offer some warmth that evening. He recalled the information the broker had provided for the Rift and the team he would be joining. The GRRO had marked the Rift as a Level Three, with other Rifters having cleared it a few times already.

It would be his first Rift at that difficulty, besides what he had experienced with R.A.M. He wasn't that worried, because survivors could still clear a Level Three Rift, provided they had decent equipment and a large group of people. With Lance now a veteran and at Level Twenty-Three, he was more than qualified to take on such a Rift.

From what the broker had provided, the other Rifters were at his Level or lower. The GRRO had organized a ragtag group for this Rift, with little experience in working with one another. But their higher Levels would make up for that. The reason Lance was taking on this Rift was to get used to how the Irish branch of the GRRO did things and see how the Rifters there operated in the field.

Lance opened his status screen and saw a notification telling him that he had three unspent Attribute points. He had made it a habit to save those three points and spend them the night before his next Rift. This allowed him to spend them more wisely, since he would know what Attributes would play the biggest role in the next Rift.

Jungle environment. Several types of monsters. Lance read, going over the information he had on hand.

[Perception:] [39] (+3)

Lance figured the additional points to Perception would help in this Rift, allowing him to spot ambushes better, not to mention serve him well in field testing the basic bow he had purchased. He went over his Attributes once more, seeing the impressive number that each of them now contained. He had Leveled Up seven times during the last three Rifts. Three Levels through clearing the Rifts, and another four from slaughtering the monsters. He had distributed his Attributes evenly, trying to be as well-rounded as possible, for now.

The amount of Experience he'd gain from Level One and Two Rifts had ground to a halt. He'd still be able to Level Up, but he had essentially run into the same problems that the members of the White Clovers had. A Level Three Rift would be just what he needed to keep the momentum going.

Just a little longer, Thomas, Lance thought as he closed his status screen and then his eyes.

Status Compendium

Name:	Lance Turner
Level:	23
Class:	Death Smith

Attributes

Endurance:	47	Agility:	47	Wisdom:	39
Strength:	47	Perception:	42	Luck:	39
Health:	1250	Mana:	255		
Stamina:	395	Inventory:	49		

Traits

Taint of death:	Able to use Rift corpses as items	Prolonged use results . . . ~ERROR UNREADABLE!~
Shard instability:	Prolonged use results . . . ~ERROR UNREADABLE!~	Prolonged use results . . . ~ERROR UNREADABLE!~

Skills

Mend Wounds	Lvl 2	Restores minor wounds	+20 Health +8 Stamina	−15 Mana
Death Forge	Lvl 1	Allows (re)forging of death-related items	+1 Item	−Raw materials −Black-shards −50% Stamina regeneration −50% Mana regeneration
Repair Item	Lvl 1	Restores durability on items	+1 durability per 1 item per 1 minute	−Raw materials −Black-shards −25% Stamina regeneration −25% Mana regeneration

Retainers

Ash	1x	Human
Icarus	1x	Falcon (hybrid*)
Alpha	1x	Crow
Bravo	1x	Crow

CHAPTER SEVENTEEN

Rift Twelve

The Next Day
April, 14 AR
Outside Rift Twelve
Galway, Ireland

LANCE

Lance slid on his gloves as he prepared himself. He could feel his hands straining against the fabric, hinting at how much stronger he had gotten. Today was a special day. Not only was this his twelfth Rift, and the fifth one he would try to clear without Thomas at his side, but he would be trying something new. That something was hovering in the sky and hidden underneath his scarf.

The scarf was a birthday present from Daniel. It resembled a kaffiyeh, a piece of cloth people in the Middle East frequently wore. Beyond that, it was also popular among military personnel. A talented crafter had made the scarf out of durable fabric. Beyond being sturdy and easy to use, it had two slots that someone had filled with a steel-like material, to offer more protection, and a plant-like fiber that had filtering properties. With it, Lance had more defense around his neck, while also being able to use the kaffiyeh as an improvised gas mask in case he needed to prevent smoke inhalation.

The gift from Daniel was the opposite of the mace Dieter had given him, and it spoke volumes about how these men thought.

Lance had stuffed Alpha, one of his crows, underneath his kaffiyeh in such a way that no one else could see the bird. Lance's neck was directly touching the animal, maintaining contact. He did this because he wanted to find out if he could bring one of his companions through the Rift outside of his Inventory. While he had hidden Alpha underneath his kaffiyeh, Bravo was circling above the Rift itself, waiting for the signal from Lance. Although the bird was still struggling in the air, it maintained enough altitude to only appear as a tiny dot in the sky.

I hope this works. He knew he was in uncharted territory today. Alpha would test entry with direct skin contact while Bravo would test entry without. He hoped both crows would make it to the other side of the Rift without a problem. In the worst-case scenario, Lance would still have Ash and Icarus. He figured a crow would be easier to replace compared to the body of his best friend or a skilled falcon.

"Are you guys ready?" the site overseer asked as she walked up to the Rifters and inspected each of them. Her heavy build struggled to make it up to the small hill that the Rifters had picked as a staging ground. Once she had received confirmations, either verbally or through simple nods, she radioed another staff member to start the countdown. "Good luck."

Lance watched the woman leave as he did the last check of his gear. He felt the weight of his mace in his right hand and the emotional weight of the shield in his left. Around him he could see other Rifters do the same. Some had decent equipment, while most of them had lower-quality gear. *Lots of beginners. The majority are still without a Class, or have just gotten it*, he mused. He tried to measure them by how they behaved and from the state of their gear.

A fair few looked uncertain and even fearful. A young woman at the back seemed outright terrified, her hands running over the prosthetic leg she had on her left side, as if she were trying to calm her nerves. Besides Lance, there were only two others who appeared calm and composed, hinting at the experience they had under their belts.

"Alright, just follow my lead," a larger man said, slamming a two-handed hammer into the ground as he activated a Skill that caused his weapon to glow. "I'm a Level Thirty warrior. Just stick with me and you'll do fine," the man said as he inspected his troops one by one, pausing when he noticed the quality of Lance and another person's gear. No doubt the man realized that they could handle themselves just fine. "Here we go!" he barked as he made his way toward the Rift, even though the countdown was still ticking.

Sighing, Lance then slammed his shield and mace together, signaling to Bravo that it was time to dive into the Rift. Although there were plenty of protective cables and nets fastened around this Rift, Bravo's smaller size could still pass through the gaps. A moment later, the Rift swallowed the crow up as it flickered once. One by one, the Rifters then entered, with their loudmouth leader spearheading the charge.

Lance took a last look around the Rift-site here on Earth. He observed the old shed and fields for farming. It hinted that they would have little protection when they entered the Rift in terms of usable structures. *Here we go, Alpha*, he thought. He felt the crow rest against his neck as he walked forward, stepping through the Rift with a clear goal.

Lance arrived at the other side. Several other Rifters were already there and some continued to arrive right after him. Some were several paces away from one another, while the majority had landed close by. Although this was a Level Three Rift, there were quite a few types of monsters lurking in this world. *Alright, first things first*, he thought as he scanned his surroundings for immediate threats.

Around them were the remnants of a farmhouse, damaged by conflict and decayed further by the passing of time. Vegetation had overgrown much of the house. Beyond that, Lance noticed trees and bushes in every direction. It felt as if someone had dropped them right in the middle of a jungle, although the trees looked far thicker and taller than he had ever seen on Earth.

As he looked upwards, he could see two large orange suns in the sky. *Think about your immediate threat*, he reminded himself, not wanting to waste time on the astronomy side of things. Lance spotted a dot in the sky, circling slowly in a number eight pattern, revealing that it was Bravo and that the crow had survived entry. He freed up a hand and slid it underneath the scarf. He could feel Alpha nestled there.

[You have stored an Item in your Inventory]

Lance felt satisfied with the outcome of his experiment now that Alpha was safely back in his Inventory. He could hear the hammer-wielding Rifter issue commands, pushing the inexperienced Rifters into action as the large man assumed the role of leader. *Scott, was it?* Lance thought, seeing the smile on the man's face widening as he got more underlings. That smile faded when Scott noticed one of the Rifters hoist herself on top of the ruined house. The prosthetic leg made that feat quite difficult for her.

"What're you doing up there? Get down and help the others," Scott ordered as he walked closer to her, fuming as the young woman argued the need for a lookout.

Lance heard a horrible metallic sound in the sky as Bravo produced a warning cry, changing the number eight pattern into a circle moving toward the sun. It indicated that there was an enemy in that direction. Quickly, Lance opened his Inventory as he climbed onto a nearby rock to get a height advantage.

[You have stored an Item in your Inventory 2x]
[You have retrieved an Item 2x]

Lance swapped the mace and shield for his bow and arrows. He nocked one of them as he peered in the sun's direction, doing his best to ignore the brightness.

Is it just a random chance the monsters are attacking us from that direction or are they intelligent enough to use tactics? he thought as he held his breath and waited for a moment. His eyes scanned the treeline for movement. When he noticed a bush twitch, he let the arrow fly, speeding past several Rifters. A few of them looked confused.

Lance barely had his second arrow ready when he heard a sudden rumble and a dozen enormous monsters crashed through the treeline. Thick, bark-like skin covered their bodies, their bright yellow eyes fixed on the startled Rifters.

"Defensive formation!" Scott barked frantically, as if he miraculously expected every Rifter there to understand what specific one he was referring to. A hail of Skills, bolts, and arrows met the charging monsters, as the Rifters used every ranged attack at their disposal as the chaos of melee began.

Within minutes the site had turned into a pitched battle, the Rifters holding the enormous monsters at bay and occasionally retreating to more favorable terrain. The monsters were slower than the Rifters, but they had proven to be quite tenacious. Large limbs slammed apart brickwork, trees, and the very ground itself, as they destroyed everything in their path.

Thirteen of these monsters had arrived to meet the Rifters, but the Rifters had already killed seven of them. The Rifters found that fire and blunt weapons worked best because of the treelike properties of the monsters' skin. While the fire would burn and consume them, the blunt weapons could bypass the sturdy wood layers by causing trauma further into the body, hitting vital organs.

[You have retrieved an Item 3x]

Lance rushed forwards as fast as he could. In his hands, three bone javelins appeared, his right arm already in a firing position. He waited until a monster faced him before releasing the first javelin. The weapon embedded itself in the monster's face but didn't manage to penetrate the thick wood layer despite the strong Trihorn tip Lance had crafted the javelins from.

That's right, keep your eyes on me, Lance thought as he tried to distract the monster. He could see another spear-wielding Rifter who was getting ready to throw a torch at the creature. Clenching his jaw, Lance then threw a second javelin, hitting its chest with little result. *Come on, one more,* he thought as he lined up the third throw, waiting for the beast to get closer to him in a frenzied rush. Just before he threw his javelin, he heard a high-pressure air rifle go off and hit the monster in the left eye. It roared out in pain.

Now, Lance thought as he threw his last javelin into the monster's mouth while the other Rifter quickly set fire to the monster's limbs. In minutes, the creature had turned into a living bonfire while still clawing at its own throat.

Lance nodded to the spear wielder before glancing over his shoulder. He spotted the young woman who had helped him out with her rifle. From what he could see, it wasn't a typical Rifter's weapon. *Is that an air rifle? Something she had with her when she became a Rifter?* The weapon itself didn't seem to have the same penetrative ability as a traditional rifle, but it was quiet, and she seemed skilled enough to hit the monsters in the eyes or other soft targets.

Lance watched her pull out the empty magazine and grab a new one, clutching it for a moment as the pellets inside began glowing. *A Skill?* Lance thought as she slid the magazine into the spring rifle and lined up the next shot. Then, in quick succession, she shot seven glowing pellets one by one, quickly cocking the spring between each shot.

Lance watched her strike multiple monsters in the eyes and visible wounds, causing great irritation but not inflicting significant damage. Just when Lance doubted their effectiveness, a series of seven minor explosions echoed through the air. The tiny pellets transformed into explosive bursts, ripping apart bits of flesh. While the monsters' resilient wood-like skin minimized the impact, the explosions proved devastating within their vulnerable innards or eyes.

Some sort of detonation Skill? he thought as he watched her reload another magazine, this time not making them glow. *No doubt a heavy drain on Mana.*

[You have retrieved an Item 2x]

Lance brought out his shield and mace again, having recovered a bit of his own Mana. He rushed toward the remaining two monsters, seeing Scott deal with the one on the right while other Rifters were peppering the one on the left.

"Cover me!" Lance shouted as he rushed forward, pushing his Mana into Dieter's mace. It was still warm from before since he had kept the weapon inside his Inventory to prevent any loss of heat while he recovered his Mana. By now, the tip was already glowing a horrible bright red. It was like holding an entire bonfire on a stick.

Lance ducked underneath one of the monster's large limbs as he slid closer, moments later slamming the mace into its chest, just below its black-shard. Instead of continuously smashing into it, Lance instead forced the mace into the monster's tough exterior, the weapon's heat increasing the damage.

He poured every bit of his Mana into the weapon. He could hear the monster hiss and scream as its protective exterior caught fire. Lance could feel it sink deeper into the creature's wound. A horrible, foul burning smell filled his nostrils while doing so. With his Mana now depleted, Lance pushed the weapon in as deep as he could before releasing it and grabbing the monster's black-shard.

He twisted the shard left and right, as if undoing a stubborn rusty bolt. In doing so, he ripped apart flesh, organs, and vital veins before it finally came loose in a torrent of blood. The monster fell not long afterwards. Lance then retrieved his mace from the hole he had burned inside of the monster.

Then he cast a quick glance over his shoulder, his attention drawn to how ruthlessly Scott finished off the last monster. The imposing figure pummeled the monster's face with his weapon, reducing it to a macabre canvas of oozing fluid and scattered fragments.

Like Lance, monster blood and gore covered him from head to toe. When the rest of the fighting finally died down, Scott greeted the other Rifters with a wide smile. Then, with no concern for his appearance, he addressed the others.

"Now that was a proper fight. Who's ready for lunch?"

Hours later, the Rifters had established a safe base of operations. They'd dug up rows of minor trenches and filled them with sharpened stakes, using the excess dirt to create temporary earthen walls. They'd strengthened as much of the farmhouse as possible before leaving it alone, knowing it would serve other Rifters who would come in the future. It was just common courtesy.

With their temporary base now secured, the group would try to find traces of previous Rifters, be they markings carved in stone or other clues pointing to places of interest such as fresh water or good scouting positions. Because of the difference in the flow of time between Earth and this Rift, those markings could've already faded by now.

Fires dotted the camp, with improvised shelters close by. Compared to the R.A.M. camps, there wasn't a large stockpile here where everyone placed what they had gathered. Here, everyone kept their own loot and black-shards. The general rule was the Rifter who had killed the monster could lay claim to its corpse, with the exception for when team effort had been required to bring it down.

Fortunately, during their first battle, there had been no casualties and the biggest injury had been a few broken ribs and a nasty cut across the face. Most of the Rifters had bonded during dinner, having shared blood and peril with one another. Some preferred their own space, and lingered at the edges of the camp with Lance, another experienced Rifter, and the air-rifle-wielding woman falling into that category.

At one point, it had seemed like Scott might've clashed with Lance and the spear-wielding Rifter after the battle, Scott having seen just how capable the two men were. Luckily for Scott, however, Lance preferred to mind his own business, and only really interacted with people when he helped with his minor healing Skill. The spear wielder also mostly kept a low profile.

[You have been awarded with a Level Up]
[You are now Level 24]
[You have 3 unspent Attribute points]

Going for a Level Three Rift was the right choice, Lance thought. He noticed the difference in experience he was getting. The last Rift he had been in was the second run in Ipswich. That Rift had been a Level One. It had barely given him any experience from killing monsters. The monsters here were indeed a fair bit stronger, but he had significantly increased his defensive and offensive capabilities. Beyond that, he now also had Alpha, Bravo, and Icarus up in the air. He had brought the birds out when he had secluded himself in the forest for a few moments, pretending that he needed to go to the bathroom.

Both crows would look out for monsters while Icarus would scan the surroundings to look for any points of interest. At least, Lance hoped they would do that, since all three of them were very much still learning the ropes.

Lance finished his meal and leaned back into his mattress. He looked up at the sky, which was still bright thanks to the second sun. He was glad he could now buy decent food for a change as he remembered the horrible meat he had eaten in the past.

[Strength:] [48] (+3)

He finished spending his points as he closed his eyes. He knew a bit of extra power would help him deal with these larger foes. And although sleep would be difficult with all this extra sunlight, the presence of three avian sentry guards flying overhead provided a comforting sense of security, eventually guiding him into a fitful slumber.

CHAPTER EIGHTEEN

DIY Upgrades

Two Days Later
April, 14 AR
Inside Rift Twelve

LANCE

'*Three . . . two . . . one,*' Lance counted. Seconds later, he heard a soft popping sound. It signaled that a small pellet inside the batlike monster had exploded, taking out a small chunk of its flesh. The chunk being its entire throat.

These weren't difficult foes to fight, but they had a nasty habit of sneaking up on you and attacking from the rear. Lance had heard some Rifters speculate on whether these monsters had thermal vision, because they were quite skilled at locating Rifters. Compared to the massive tree-monsters they had fought in the beginning, these flying creatures were fairly weak.

"That's quite effective," Iyas, the spear wielder, said as the monster fell out of the tree it had been hiding in. Iyas was about as strong and experienced as Scott and Lance. Armed with an expensive-looking spear and decent equipment, he was easily one of the stronger Rifters in the group.

Like Lance, the man had not wanted to fight Scott over a leadership position. Iyas preferred the freedom that came with doing what he wanted. He was about as tall as Lance, only thinner and with healthy tanned skin, a product of his Moroccan heritage. His brown eyes matched his hair, although he kept the latter short and shaved at the sides.

Lance agreed with Iyas. The young woman wielding the spring rifle had made a perfect shot. Although the weapon used air pressure, the projectile could kill smaller monsters with ease. He had also seen just how brutally effective it could be on larger foes if the woman combined the pellet with her "Explode item" Skill.

"Thanks, guys," Mira said, running a hand through her blonde hair. She looked slightly embarrassed but proud of her contributions. She reloaded her spring rifle and armed it, pulling on the lever to build up pressure.

She got up from her sniping position and slid the rifle over her shoulders. Afterwards, she grabbed a short sword from her hip and nodded to the others. She wore basic leather wrist guards and a sturdy, thin gambeson of sorts. It was clearly less protective, compared to what Iyas and Lance were wearing, but anything would help in a Rift. She had also tied some cloth wraps around her prosthetic leg on her left side, making it less reflective.

"I still say you shouldn't hide that leg. Weaponize it! Perhaps some blades on the side?" Iyas offered with a confident nod as the three of them reached the fallen monster and saw the brown blood that covered it. "Well, that thing won't be moving anymore."

"I still think it's a stupid name," Lance said with a sigh as he ignored his status screen notification that he was gaining Experience. This despite not being in direct combat himself.

"What? Rift-glider is a good name for this type of monster," Mira said defensively while Iyas cleverly refused to comment while retrieving the black-shard for Mira. "Such a gentleman."

"Anyway, that should cover this side of the camp," Lance said as he closed his eyes. He could feel the pull of the Rift-event somewhere further to the north. Any Rifter would have felt it—that gut feeling that led Rifters to where unnatural energy was densest.

So far, the Rifters had been focusing on clearing out their immediate surroundings, improving defenses, and securing fresh water. Every few hours a small group of Rifters would patrol the area and take care of smaller groups of monsters. They had also dug ditches to prevent any potential fire from threatening the camp. There were trees everywhere and a small fire could quickly turn into something worse with all the trees surrounding them.

"Good enough for now. Let someone else take over, right? You two wasted enough ammunition," Iyas said as he stored his spear within his Inventory and grabbed a canteen to quench his thirst.

"Lance, perhaps! He missed two of his arrows. I traded ten pellets for ten kills. And they're cheap to replace," Mira said as she rubbed her left upper leg to ease some of the tension.

Iyas laughed at that while nodding. "True. You're a crack shot with that rifle. But remember, most Skills rarely work well with modern weapons and bullets. You having that 'Detonate' Skill and a pellet rifle is just a weird and overpowered combination."

Lance smiled. He was getting better with the bow, but against moving targets, he was clearly still an amateur. But even the others would have to admit that he was far better with throwing weapons.

"Are you coming with us, or do you want to check your traps again?" Iyas asked as he noticed Lance glancing in the direction away from camp.

Lance nodded. "You two kids go on ahead. I won't be long," Lance said with a smile as he ignored another Experience notification. He stayed there for a moment watching Iyas and Mira leave. It wasn't strange that he went on by himself. His higher Level made smaller monster groups less of a danger to him, and most of the Rifters had seen him sharpening his traps at the camp or placing them.

He placed them in the opposite direction of the Rift-event, making it less likely for people to run into them. He planted them out in the open so any Rifters could spot them, but they would still tempt monsters due the blood he had poured over them.

"Let's collect some shards," Lance said to himself as he started walking in the direction of his traps, spotting three smaller gray dots in the air, flying in unusual patterns before one of them dive-bombed downwards at an incredible speed.

"Mind your surroundings," Lance said as he watched his pale companion bash the monster he was facing with his shield. Lance had taken a seat on a nearby tree branch that allowed him to observe what was happening.

He watched Ash hack a few times with the steel axe, attempting to hit the six-limbed monster, which looked like a cross between a toad, a goblin, and a deer. It had greenish slimy skin and its four legs allowed it to cross the terrain with ease. It was also intelligent enough to use tools and crude bone armor and was carrying a long branch with sharpened bone tips tied on one end, forming an improvised spear.

Lance and the other Rifters had encountered this type of monster before, having fought off smaller raiding parties of them yesterday. He had caught a few of them in his traps as well.

After having brought back one of their corpses, the others had given Lance the honor of naming it. Luckily, the name "Centaur-toad" had been catchy enough for him to gain some respect from the other Rifters. Beyond the Rift-glider, the Centaur-toad, and the large, hulking tree creatures they had called "Bark-brains," the Rifters had encountered others as well. It was strange how some Rifts would only have one or two types of monsters, while others had more than a dozen.

"Remember, you aren't just facing him," Lance said. He watched as a second monster occasionally tried to hit Ash in the rear before flying off. *Those Rift-gliders are fast!* he thought. Although Ash's strength was comparable to that of a basic human, he was still stronger than the flying monster and the Centaur-toad but lacked the speed to hit either of them. *I guess two are still too much for him.* It was just a matter of time before Ash went down again.

Not wanting to waste more time and black-shards on repairing Ash, Lance snapped his fingers, signaling to his avian squad to go for the kill. As they had practiced, Alpha and Bravo moved toward the Rift-glider, driving the bat creature away from Ash and straight into a deadly trap. A moment later, Icarus broke the beast's neck in one violent dive-bomb very similar to how a peregrine falcon would normally hunt. *I made the right choice in letting the birds practice on their own ever since entering the Rift. They've gotten so much better.* He recalled just how often the three birds were able to pick off the occasional single Rift-glider by working as a team.

"Nice job." He watched the two crows secure the body so that he could find it later, while Icarus moved toward the Centaur-toad to distract it. *Now that the roles are reversed, what will you do?* Lance thought. Moments later, he dropped from his elevated position to make his way over toward Ash and the monster.

With Ash no longer fighting on two fronts, he was doing much better. The man circled the monster to position himself more advantageously. Then, as if he had been waiting for it, Ash threw his axe toward the monster as a distraction while closing the distance. The man tackled the creature and himself through a small bush.

Lance could hear twigs snap as the two combatants broke clear of it and slid down a small hill. They ended up in a murky pool at the bottom, Ash holding onto the monster's wrist to prevent it from using the spear.

Lance slid down the hill as well, seeing Ash drag the monster further down into the water with him, submerging the two of them completely. Lance could still see them in the water as air-bubbles escaped from the Centaur-toad's mouth. *Nice one*, he thought before instructing Icarus to help the crows in dragging the Rift-glider's corpse to him, giving them something to do.

Ash continued to drown the monster while Lance opened his Inventory and checked the timer on his forging process. He could see the next crude javelin would be ready in two minutes. He had been crafting a lot of them in his free time from the parts he had harvested from monsters. Although he had long since run out of the Trihorn bones, sinew, and horns, he had used other types of monster-bone to make the javelins. They lacked the penetrating power of the original ones and showed a massive decline in effectiveness. Lucky for him, however, they still worked like a charm in a lower-Level Rift like this one.

In his spare time, he also made crude javelins by hand in camp. It gave him a plausible reason for why he continued to have so many of these javelins on hand. He preferred people not knowing about his crafting Skill.

He watched Ash wade his way to him, dragging the drowned monster along with him. Ash then snapped the monster's neck as he dropped it next to Lance. "Axe . . ." Ash said, uttering a single word as he inhaled the air to do so, giving the word a deep and creepy tone.

"Sure, go on ahead. Can you help the others as well? I think the Rift-glider might be too heavy for them to carry," Lance said as he grabbed a knife and began cutting out the black-shard from the Centaur-toad. As it came loose, he could see the many arteries and nerves that were still attached to it, hinting at how his own white-shard would look inside his body.

[You have finished forging an Item]
[Death Forge has reached Lvl 2]

He was about to craft another bone javelin when he noticed the additional message on his status screen. Seeing that his forging Skill had increased, he smiled widely. Lance had been constantly using it ever since he figured out how to use a template. Still, compared to how long it had taken him to gain another Level in his healing Skill, this had been much faster. *Is it because of the associated black-shard cost?* Lance mused, knowing that each javelin required black-shards to craft, just like it had cost him to make the birds and Ash.

"Just in time!" He heard Ash slide back down the hill, carrying the corpse of the Rift-glider. Attached to it were three birds, desperately holding onto it with their beaks or talons, as if not understanding that Lance's earlier command had stopped. "You guys can let go now."

He watched the birds do so and assume a position near him while Ash sat down to his side. "I Leveled Up my crafting skill just now. Great, right?"

Ash paused at that. No doubt he was searching for the correct word to use. "Yes . . ."

"Again, way too deep and creepy. But yes, it's great," he explained as he handed his knife to Ash so that he could cut out the Rift-glider's black-shard. As he did so, Lance read up on what had changed for his skill.

[Additional −50% Stamina and Mana regeneration per Forge]
[Forging Capacity +1 item in total]
[Unlocked reforging option]
[Reforging slots available] [3 base slots]

That's a lot to take in. Slowly, he went over all the changes. He was especially interested in the reforging option, since it was something Dieter and Daniel had explained to him. It was how individuals with crafting Skills could upgrade items, like the mace he had gotten from Dieter.

"Let's test this out." He felt quite giddy with anticipation. He opened his Inventory and focused on a crude javelin but got no option to do so. Eventually, he retrieved both the javelin and a piece of bone before he got the choice to use the reforge option. *So, I can only reforge items that I physically touch?*

[Filled slots] [0/3]

So, three basic slots per item, Lance thought. He wondered if he could get more slots if he Leveled Up the Skill further. *Would it also work with my companions?*

He then began touching his companions, opening their menus, and seeing a similar number of open slots. Three was the base number of upgrades per Item. No reforge option became available for his companions, despite Lance retrieving and trying out a lot of materials from his Inventory.

Regarding his javelin, he had plenty of options from adding additional bone to strengthen the handle, or by adding a claw to the spearpoint to imbue the weapon with additional bleed-damage.

Lance accepted the reforge option for the javelin, strengthening the weapon with bone and claws. He watched the Items disappear the moment he accepted it. The first slot Lance filled set him back ten black-shards, while the second one cost one hundred. *If the cost of upgrading goes up per slot, I'll run out of black-shards in no time.* He had already been struggling with getting enough black-shards to repair his companion each time Ash lost a finger, while also have enough to make more javelins.

He could see a notification appear above the weapon displaying a timer. When he stored the javelin in his Inventory, he could still see the timer continuing to count down. He then shifted his gaze toward Ash. "Well, the weapon I can upgrade, but I'm not sure how it works for you guys." He felt disappointed for a moment before he suppressed those feelings. *Is it because of my Class as a Death Smith? Just like I can only make items from monster parts, perhaps I'm missing something here?*

Knowing that solving this mystery would take some time, Lance instead focused on the questions he could answer. He looked at the timer on the javelin upgrade and noticed how it drained half of his Mana and Stamina regeneration rate. Lance then pressed the forge button and started the crafting of another crude javelin.

He wasn't sure whether the second crafting process would cause a hundred percent decrease in his regeneration rate, or if the second process would halve his remaining, resulting in a seventy-five percent decrease. He breathed a sigh of relief when he found out it was the latter. It meant that he could always recover a sliver of Stamina and Mana while crafting, no matter how many items he was juggling.

Lance patted Ash on the knee, then snapped his fingers, sending the birds up in the air again. "How about we celebrate the good news by throwing javelins at monsters?" he asked, encouraged by the excited smile on his companion's face.

A few hours later, Lance pulled out his left earbud and cocked his head to the side. He had spotted Mira sitting there, peering over his shoulder to see the movie he was watching on his smartphone. She had done so for several minutes already but was getting bolder by the second. "Can I help you?"

"Sure, scoot over," she said as she moved forwards and even grabbed the free earbud. "What're we watching?"

"*Dirty Harry.* I was told it's the greatest movie ever made." Lance placed his phone between them so she could see better.

"Really? It's that good?"

"It's awful, but they filled it to the brim with guns, so you'll no doubt love it," Lance said with a grin.

[You have retrieved an Item]

He produced a small canteen in his hand and undid the lid, taking a few large sips of water before storing it again. Afterwards, Lance closed his eyes, letting his thoughts drift toward that quiet place in his mind where he liked to brood. He could feel Thomas's presence tug at him, wanting to watch the movie. But not even the remnants of Thomas could bother him right now.

He went over what he had accomplished these past few days inside the Rift. Both Alpha and Bravo had been a tremendous help in terms of sentry duty and offense. Their flying ability had improved rapidly, and Lance figured a few more weeks of practice would make them equal to normal crows, if not slightly better due to them not having to sleep, eat, or deal with fatigue.

Icarus was in a league of his own. Lance wasn't sure if it was just an affinity for flying that falcons instinctively had, or if it was something specific to Icarus, like boxing was for Ash. Either way, seeing the bird take out Rift-gliders was a remarkable sight, not to mention music to his ears. Lance's heightened Perception made it possible for him to hear the zipping sound as the falcon dived low, only to adjust its course at the last second.

Ash, like always, was constantly proving to Lance that he was more than just a tool. Ash was a companion, his friend in his quest for justice.

So, Lance rested with ease, knowing that his four companions were grinding Experience for him somewhere in the jungle.

CHAPTER NINETEEN

Heart of a Nation

April, 14 AR
GRRO Main Office
London, England

DANIEL

Daniel's two knives hit their marks perfectly: a piece of wood fastened to a wall, and a board in a corner. He frequently changed their position, allowing him to practice throwing with his left hand when he was at the office.

Just another minute, he thought as he got up from behind his desk and made his way over to a cabinet to grab some things. Moments later, he had placed a pillow on the floor with a bowl filled with water next to it. Having decided it was a worthy throne, he made his way over to the door. He could clearly hear commotion on the other side.

Opening the door, Daniel noticed Dieter leaning over the desk of his assistant. His friend was arguing vigorously that the Rift-hound wasn't "just an animal" but an emotional support dog and that Dieter had the right to take Little Hans with him. "And I'll have you know that this fine young man is a thoroughbred—"

"Clark, it's fine. I was expecting them," Daniel told his secretary as he stepped aside, letting the dog walk past him. Daniel smiled as he watched the hound claim his throne while giving him an approving look. "You look good, boy."

"He looks overweight. I caught the little devil digging through the rubbish last night. Chewed right through the steel bin," Dieter said as he stepped inside while giving Clark one last satisfied smile before closing the door and patting Daniel on the belly. "Speaking of overweight."

"The mirror is over there," Daniel rebutted as he made his way over to Little Hans, stroking the dog's fur a few times and scratching him behind the ears.

"You're still growing, aren't you, boy?" he asked, knowing full well that he was reinforcing bad behavior.

When Daniel got back behind his desk, he noticed his friend had grabbed and opened a few of the folders, looking at the classified documents and pictures. "So, Dieter, pray tell. What can I do to help, beyond breaking several laws and losing my job?"

"Bah, just tell them I overpowered you. What's this?" Dieter asked as he slid a picture of a Rift-site in Bulgaria toward his friend. "This looks wrong."

Daniel nodded, knowing what the man was referring to. "It's outside of GRRO's authority. Their government has classified it as an accident but has shared some of the information to foster cooperation."

The tall German snorted, offering his thoughts on politics in a single succinct exhalation. "They can call it what they want, but this is all wrong. Either they repositioned the bodies and did something with the blood spatters, or someone came out of that gate and killed all of these people."

"Why?" Daniel asked. He knew what Dieter was referring to, but he wanted to hear his friend confirm what he himself had concluded.

Dieter paused for a moment before he answered. "Looking at the damage, I would say an outbreak has happened . . . but then the Rift would've looked different, plus we would've heard it on the news by now." He narrowed his eyes at the next picture and read the rest of the information. "Perhaps something went bad inside the Rift and turned the Rifters mad, or they went rogue? It looks like they came out swinging."

Daniel smiled, impressed as always at how quickly his friend could put two and two together. In a few moments, the man's heightened Perception and Experience allowed him to spot quite a few inconsistencies in the information and the pictures. "All the Rifters have been located and identified. Forensic evidence places them on site when the attack happened, with them dying at the same time as the non-Rifter personnel on the site. All ten of them. Six veterans, three experts, and one Elite."

Dieter went quiet after that as he went over the pictures once more. No doubt he spotted more details now that he knew what he was looking for. "Well, something came out of that Rift. The signs of struggle point away from the Rift, and it looks beyond what mere civilians can do. Perhaps rival Rifters? Hidden amongst their numbers or near the site?"

"Perhaps," Daniel said, knowing there were plenty of reports concerning this "incident." It was one of the many "headache documents" the GRRO had, or cooperated on. Daniel had taken a crack at it. With Rifts and Rifters, one needed to expect the unexpected. Even stable Rifts could surprise humanity now and again.

"By the way, is this how you treat your best friend when he comes to visit you at Judas HQ? Make him do your work instead of offering him a drink?"

Dieter said as he placed the folder on the desk while propping his feet next to it.

Daniel chuckled as he slowly materialized several throwing daggers on the table and lined them up. "So, best friend. To what do I owe the pleasure?" he asked as a knife sped past Dieter's face only to hit the wooden board in the corner.

"Just checking up. Me and the lads are taking a job up in Scotland in a few days. Should be gone for a few weeks, a month at most. We still have a spot open for you. You have holiday days, right?" the man teased as he picked up a knife and hit one of the wooden boards with a loud noise, revealing the amount of power he had put behind it.

"I do. And no, I will not spend holiday days in a Rift with you and wade through rivers of blood. You know most people spend their holidays in comfort, right? I was thinking about Bali," he said while wondering if he even had the ability to relax like a normal civilian.

Dieter shrugged before grabbing another knife and throwing it against the other board, the force of the impact splitting it in two. "We'll see how long you can endure the civilian lifestyle. So, how's our lad doing? Up to his ears in Rifts and turning your hair gray? I assume that you've been keeping tabs on him like some creepy surrogate father?"

Daniel smiled as he grabbed a knife and threw it skillfully. It landed right next to Dieter's last knife. "I take offense at that slanderous suggestion, ignoring the fact that it is, in fact, a hundred percent correct." The two of them shared a laugh at that. Little Hans joined in with a single bark.

"Lance is . . . well, he's active. After his little stunt at his birthday, he went in three more Rifts, including a second run in Ipswich. The White Clovers and the lad fully destroyed the Rift there. After that, he contacted me for a favor. He wanted to take a temporary GRRO job to help clean up a Rift-site," Daniel said, cocking his head to the door when he heard some commotion. "I figured he wanted to take time off. Imagine my surprise when his ID registered for a Rift somewhere in Ireland, of all places. Still, it's a Level Three Rift, so he should be more than fine, although I can only guess what Level he's at himself now. Eighteen or something?"

Dieter took it all in as he listened. No doubt Daniel could see his expression soften a bit. "Well, whatever he's doing, he seems to have some sort of plan and he's sticking to a relatively safe route. You of all people know how a Rifter can lose himself in a singular purpose after losing a loved one."

Daniel felt a flash of anger at that. He never enjoyed talking about his past but knew why Dieter had brought it up. He felt the anger leave him as he thought about the loss of his wife and child. "Remind me to punch you later."

"No problem. I can think of a dozen other reasons you should hit—" Dieter said before being interrupted by Daniel's assistant barging into the room.

"Sir, apologies. It's about the situation in France. They're finally addressing it," the young man said as he turned on the television. He switched channels until it displayed a live broadcast, showing a large crowd of people that had gathered near the walled-off city of Paris. The French president and several Rifters were there addressing all of France and the rest of the world.

"And that's precisely why we're standing here, on the other side of this wall, shielded from the violence that has claimed the heart of this country. The outbreak in our beloved Paris has been unchallenged for years now," the president of France said to the dozens of journalists facing him.

Behind him stood a massive wall that encompassed nearly all of Paris. The military had built enormous towers, spacing them apart to allow overlapping fields of fire. Inside of these towers were large machine gun outposts, snipers, and artillery platforms. It was all designed to contain the monstrous horde that had overwhelmed the city when the Rift outbreak had occurred. Although the GRRO, the military, and the government had predicted it would happen and had evacuated most of the city, the damage was still beyond description.

"For too long have we cowered behind these walls, forced to witness how these monstrous creatures defile the heart of this nation . . . our capital . . . our home!" The microphone carried his words far and wide. In the background, you also could hear the occasional shot from a sniper picking off a monster that came too close to the wall.

"But we aren't alone in this horror, for these Rifts have been terrorizing our brothers and sisters across the world. Rifts have terrorized humanity with their sudden appearance. They have forced us into send good people into them just to hold back whatever is on the other side." The president paused at that. Large projectors behind him displayed exact numbers of how many Rifts had occurred in France, how many people had lost their lives because of them, and how many Rifters had died in the line of duty.

"And to make matters worse, these outbreaks have breached into our world, spewing forth horrors from other dimensions. Seven times this has occurred around the world. Even now, years later, all seven outbreaks have endured. Brave souls around the world have given their lives to contain and wall off these threats," the president said, the emotion clear in his voice. It was public knowledge that he had lost his own son to a Rift several years ago. It was the reason he had campaigned so hard to become president in the first place.

"But no more! We as a nation . . . as a people . . . as mothers and fathers . . . brothers and sisters . . . daughters and sons . . . we will not allow this to continue.

We will show the rest of the world that fire flows through the veins of every French man, woman, and child. That righteousness beats in our heart!" He paused, looking directly into the cameras as he prepared himself for what were the most important words he would ever utter.

"So, this year, on Bastille Day, on the fourteenth of July, we will hear the drums of war throughout the city of Paris as we take back our home . . . clearing it street by street . . . until the very Rift itself is no more!" he pronounced, his voice rising at the end as he slammed his fist on the small wooden stand in front of him.

A high-ranking general took his place after that and explained what they were calling Operation Bastille. There would be months of bombardments, airstrikes, and constant gas attacks as the military reclaimed the city street by street, forming newer defensive lines as they did so. Hundreds of French Rifters would supplement the military, serving as both specialist teams and universal support. They would also accept foreign Rifters in certain fields.

For months, the entire weight of the military would squeeze on the city of Paris, pushing back the monstrous hordes until the Rift was finally in sight. Then, an elite squad of Rifters, led by the best Rifter in France, would carve a path to the Rift. They would trigger an experimental weapon that would destabilize it, removing the outbreak, and cutting the remaining monsters off from reinforcements.

Several Rifters then stepped forward, including the number-one Rifter in France: Viviane "Newton" Beaumanoir. She and the other Rifters stood proudly in their highly specialized gear, which showed signs of past battles, being adorned with nicks and dents. As dozens of Rifters' names were called, all eyes were on Viviane. Although she was of average height and had a modest appearance, there was a brutal determination in her eyes. Every citizen knew of her achievements in the past, from her being the sole survivor in her first Rift, to her being the only Rifter in Europe to have cleared a Level Thirteen Rift on her own.

She hadn't been on the news in the last few months, and many speculated about whether she had retired or worse. People could now clearly see by her appearance that she had been constantly training, getting as much Experience and Levels as she could in the shortest amount of time. All this to get her ready for what was to come. When the names of the Rifters had all been called, she moved forward.

"My message isn't for the people of France, for I know we will all unite in this singular purpose. I direct my message here today to the Rifters around the world. I don't care if you fight because of civic pride, for status, or for wealth. What I care about is to see you stand with us when the time is right, to do what's required to free Paris. For if we can remove one outbreak, we can destroy the other six infestations upon this world as well." Although her message was in French, she knew that every Rifter around the world could understand her at that moment.

"So, take your place alongside us, or hide in the shadows while we . . . the brave . . . shoulder the mantle of responsibility."

"Well, that was something," Dieter said as he ran a hand across his jawline, feeling the stubble. "What kind of weapon can destabilize a Rift? I've never heard of anything like that."

"Indeed," Daniel said, nodding to his assistant that he could go. He stayed silent for a moment after that, listening as his friend went on about the sheer scale of the operation. The outbreak in Paris had happened a while back, thus there was no shortage of monsters inside the city, with more spilling out each day.

To fight against that monstrous horde, human ingenuity would see the implementation of artillery, aerial bombardment, gas attacks, and many other lethal options to level the playing field. They would thin out the enemy numbers as ground forces started their slow advance, street by street. And if the president could keep the country united and committed to this plan, then hopefully it would liberate their capital.

Dieter's face lit up with excitement. "I'm getting goosebumps. I mean, just how many Rifters will flood to that city? Usually, I dislike working with any form of government or bureaucracy, but can you imagine the sight of hundreds of cannons going off at once, seeing the air force concentrate all their effort in one place? Or the combined power of hundreds of Skills?"

Daniel nodded slowly. "You're right. But there are many variables at play here. The monsters have had a lot of time to make the city their own. There are countless types of beasts out there and we can only guess what their exact number is. Not even factoring the weapon itself. They called it experimental, so that brings with it even more layers of uncertainty," Daniel said, holding up his hand to cut his friend off.

"But, even just pushing back the hordes, say . . . several streets, setting up in more strategic areas to better protect the rest of the country. Even that would be a monumental achievement. That act alone will echo through the rest of the world, letting them know that there is hope." He smiled softly as his friend nodded in agreement.

"So, why the sour expression?" Dieter said, grabbing a small snack from his pocket and throwing it to Little Hans. The dog eagerly caught it in midair.

"The sour expression is because of what I noticed in the background while you were fantasizing over cannons and your Rifter dream team." Daniel grabbed his laptop and found the clip they had just watched. A moment later, he spun the laptop around so that it faced his friend.

Dieter watched the footage again, seeing the general and the president address the people. "I don't see . . ." He paused when he spotted a list displayed in the background. It contained all the names of Rifters who had already pledged themselves to Operation Bastille. One of the names suddenly stood out to him. "Louis Vidal," Dieter said slowly, feeling the weight of it.

"Correct," Daniel affirmed, leaning forward to grab the last knife from the table. He gripped it tightly, its weight comforting in his hand. "We're talking about Louis—the one who caught the GRRO's attention and investigation, along with two others," he said, his voice tinged with a mixture of certainty and resentment. "The same Louis who likely had a hand in Thomas's death," he murmured, his gaze momentarily captured by the knife's glinting reflection. Then, without warning, he unleashed it. The blade streaked through the air, propelled by a surge of raw power and electric energy. It crashed into the wooden surface, shattering it into pieces, and buried itself deep within the wall.

"And with the enormity of this undertaking in Paris, there's no doubt Louis's name on that list will attract considerable interest," Daniel asserted. "In the coming weeks, the list will become the center of attention for every major news agency worldwide, if not all of them." As he spoke, Daniel closed his eyes, attempting to envision the situation from Lance's perspective.

"Imagine what it will do to Lance when he finishes his current Rift and steps out and finds his world changed. A world that will now constantly remind him of a person who played a role in Thomas's death, who is still walking this world as a free man. And to compound the agony, that very person is hailed as a hero."

"We need a drink," Dieter said solemnly, his hands balled into fists. Daniel could only nod and agree with his friend.

CHAPTER TWENTY

Pyromaniacs Unite!

Ten Days Later
April, 14 AR
Inside Rift Twelve

LANCE

Lance rushed through the bushes when he spotted Alpha fly not that far above him. The bird kept him company and occasionally steered him in the right direction. The further Lance moved away from the Rift-event, the more uncomfortable it made him feel. *I wonder if all Rifters feel the same?* he thought as he jumped over a small rock formation and landed in a clearing. He noticed the markings on the nearby trees and knew that Ash would be close.

Peering backwards, Lance could feel where the Rift-event was. He had heard from Daniel how it worked, and the GRRO manual had gone into more detail. A Rift-event would draw Rifters to it, with the unnatural energy resonating within their white-shards. The further someone was away from it, the more uncomfortable that feeling would get. Lance figured it worked like a strange energy compass, allowing every Rifter to know exactly where he needed to go.

Lance moved carefully, not wanting to get stuck in traps that Ash made in the area. It didn't take long for him to see the bear traps. Two of them still contained dead monsters, while the third one held a gnawed-off leg. No doubt the monster had died not too far from here due to blood loss. Lance let Alpha steer him toward the last trap, seeing it untouched. At that point he had disarmed and stored all four of them before he moved on.

Lance had taught his companion how to dig small pit traps and place sharpened branches at the bottoms. He had instructed him to spread those pit traps around the forest to either kill or wound unsuspecting monsters. The two of them had gotten better at making these traps during the last few days. They still had a lot to learn to increase the lethality of the traps or camouflage them better, but the basics were there. It proved how helpful his time with the White Clovers had been, seeing as the traps were earning him a lot of Experience.

Alpha pointed out the pit traps they encountered, landing near them, and pointing its beak at them one by one. So far, Lance had found six of those traps, all dug over the last two days. "He's kept himself busy," Lance said when he reached the last pit, seeing two monsters at the bottom, their shards cut out and retrieved by the birds.

It didn't take Lance long after that to find Ash. The pale warrior climbed out of a murky pool he had been using as a base of operations. He was dirty but intact, save for some minor cuts on his arms and a rip in his uniform. The way he rose out from the water, javelins in each hand, was terrifying.

Lance could see three monster corpses near the edge. No doubt Ash had killed them by drowning or throwing a javelin or two. Lance had left Ash with ten javelins two days ago, so with only two of them left, he figured his companion had seen plenty of action. "Have you been picking on the local monsters again?" he asked as he walked up to Ash and patted him on the back before activating his skill.

Repair Item

He watched Ash's minor cuts repair as the man's durability restored to one hundred percent. His companion nodded before leading him to a small hole he had dug. Inside were dozens of black-shards Ash and the birds had collected. Bravo and Icarus joined them not long after that.

On their own, his companions would struggle when fighting a monster. When they worked as a team, however, their lethality was becoming formidable. The birds took care of the smaller flying monsters, while Ash dug pitfall traps or rearmed the bear traps to wreak havoc. Ash could also ambush the occasional Centaur-toad that was close to his hiding spot. It wasn't always perfect, seeing as Lance had repaired all his companions a few times over the last few days, but he was still gaining more black-shards than he was spending on repairs.

"You guys did great. Ash, I am going to let you watch all the *Rambo* movies you want back in Dublin. You'll love them," he said with a smile as he began counting all the black-shards before storing them in his Inventory.

"Let's pack up and return to camp. The other Rifters are going to push for the Rift-event in the morning. We've already cleared out most of the roaming bands of monsters, so we should leave this place tomorrow," Lance explained, allowing his companions to finish their assignments.

Ash retrieved the steel-entrenching tool from a nearby bush. Afterwards, he took up a position next to Lance while sliding a finger through the rip in his uniform. "Broken . . ." His voice was deep and unnatural.

"You're doing much better. It still sounds like all my childhood nightmares combined into one sound. But keep it up, buddy. I'll fix the uniform in my Inventory. Remind me to buy you proper gear when we get paid, all right?" Lance asked,. Ash nodded once before placing his pale hand on Lance's shoulder.

[You have stored an Item in your Inventory]

I've way too many items, Lance thought four hours later as he inspected his full Inventory. He had packed what he could inside his backpack, but even then, he was running out of options. He had Leveled Up four times within this Rift, going from Level Twenty-Four to Twenty-Eight. The speed of his growth was good, but his Inventory was the limiting factor here. At Level Twenty-Eight he had access to fifty-nine storage slots, but with three birds, Ash, provisions, blackshards, and his equipment, not to mention several monster corpses, he was hardpressed to store it all.

Life would be so much easier if I didn't have to store Ash and his gear. Hell, slapping a backpack on Ash and getting him to carry stuff in and out of the Rift would be amazing. He knew full well that the GRRO registered each Rifter before entering and exiting a Rift. With no proper documentation, and Ash being absurdly gray, not to mention lacking a proper white-shard, there was no way it wouldn't alert the authorities.

Some countries have less strict rules in place. It could be beneficial to go there. He prodded the little fire he had made a while ago. He had just finished his meal and was simply enjoying the heat and some time to himself. Although he was concerned about his growing Inventory need, it was also a good problem to have. That he had several monster corpses in his Inventory, instead of just their hides or claws, meant that his income would increase once again exponentially.

He leaned backwards and stared into the sky. Seeing just one sun meant that it was "evening." Although he had hardened himself through constantly clearing Rifts, he still got annoyed by the constant sunlight, since it was affecting his quality of sleep.

Now, where should I put these? he thought as he went over his status screen and noticed the three Attribute points he still had left. He had already spent the points he had gotten from his first three levels on Strength, Endurance, and Agility.

I feel like my physical Attributes are doing fine now. Perhaps even decent enough for a Level Four Rift. Perhaps more points in Perception? To help with my archery, Lance mused, wondering what the best pick would be. Wisdom was a stat mostly used for mages, but even he benefited from it. His Mana would regenerate faster, as well as squeeze out a better mental performance. It would also allow him to think faster in the heat of a moment and recall information more clearly. *Perhaps Luck? A few more points might help with the item drop rate, or with a critical hit?*

[Luck:] [44] (+3)

He finally decided to go with that, figuring it was always good to have a bit of it on hand. That and the increased drop rate might award him better resources in the future or even a Skill-shard. As he opened his status screen, he noticed that his Mana regeneration had already improved due to his decision, allowing him to heal more frequently. *That should do for now.*

Lance spotted Iyas and Scott getting up and making their way toward him. Nodding, Lance kicked out the fire with dirt and followed them. He heard Scott give orders to the other Rifters to watch out for monsters, fires, or other threats while they were away. Scott had discussed the plan with the other Rifters, outlining a strategy that involved turning the surroundings into a weapon against the monsters.

"Are you ready?" Lance asked Iyas, watching the man summon his spear and swirl it around several times to warm up his shoulders. Like him, Iyas wasn't particularly worried, not even as they were walking toward the Rift-event.

The Moroccan man nodded, exchanging his normal generous smile for a more determined expression. Although all three of them were the strongest Rifters in the party, the threat of an injury from an accident or trap could always happen. "Yeah. Igniting an entire forest is perfectly normal. What about you, Scott?"

Scott simply snorted at the question. He used his machete to cut a path, slicing apart vines and bushes. Slowly the party made their way deeper into the jungle, past the point where the Rifters had cleared out all the roaming monsters. It didn't take them long before they found the Rift-event. It was located amidst old ruins that the jungle had reclaimed. Lance could make out enormous stone walls, buildings, and tall towers in the distance. Much of it was in ill repair or even in ruins. Trees had grown through roofs. Moss, vines, and other signs of nature had covered entire buildings and had swallowed up former roads.

"It looks ancient . . . and quite similar to what we used to see on Earth," Iyas pointed out as Lance agreed with him. "It looks like it used to be a large city. Positioned near a river. Perhaps a trade hub at one point?"

"Could be. But who knows what the Rift really is? It isn't the first ruin I've seen," Lance said. They had no way of finding out. Either the Rifts created places and ruins like these for Rifters to fight in, or the Rift connected them to actual ruined worlds somewhere. Both scenarios were equally terrifying for him.

"I can't wait to burn it to the ground," Scott stated as he swapped out his machete for a shovel before he faced the other two Rifters. "Get to work."

I need to remember to thank Daniel for his gift. Lance made a mental note. They had spent the last few hours digging up dirt and cutting away vegetation to make a fire line around the city. It was arduous work, with two Rifters digging and the third on watch, but their increased Strength and Endurance had allowed them to make a lot of progress. That there were only three of them made it less likely that monsters would spot them.

Eventually, Scott had grown impatient and started a few fires near the city before Lance and Iyas joined him. The three of them had watched the flames quickly spread toward the ruined city. The fire lines would prevent most of the fires from spreading toward the Rifter's camp. It would've taken them several days to make a perfectly safe circle around the city to contain the fire properly, but the three of them figured that this would suffice for now. Still, there was plenty of smoke that occasionally reached them. During those moments, Lance was glad that he had Daniel's scarf wrapped around his nose and mouth to filter out the fumes.

The fire was already engulfing the outer walls of the ruined city, blocking any monsters from getting to the Rifters from that side, or risk getting burned. In a few hours, the entire city would become a bonfire and take any monster along with it. Those that survived the fires by cowering inside the buildings would die from smoke inhalation. Those that escaped the city would find most of their forces incinerated.

"That's a pretty sight," Scott said finally, seeing the fire now spread beyond the walls and enter the city. Their heightened hearing could make out the cries of monsters. "I love it when a Rift has an environment we can use to our advantage."

Iyas nodded as he slammed his shovel in the ground. "Well, it beats having to deal with hundreds of monsters all at once. No doubt it will make it easier on the others."

"Bah, sod the others. If they can't handle a Level Three Rift, they shouldn't have come in the first place," Scott barked as he grabbed his shovel and continued digging, slamming into the earth with tremendous force.

For someone who wants to be a leader, he cares little for the wellbeing of others, Lance thought. He remembered how often he had seen types like Scott in his childhood. The bullies that wanted to be seen and heard but didn't know how to behave when they finally got the position of power.

As much as he wanted to berate Scott, Lance knew he himself was also a part of the problem. All three of them had set fire to the forest. All three had done so to "lessen" the enemy numbers and make it easier to clear the Rift. But starting that fire also meant that the Experience it produced from killing the monsters would go to them. He grabbed his canteen and threw some water over his face, temporarily removing a bit of the heat he was feeling. *No doubt that's why Scott was so eager to be the first one to start the fire.*

Still, Lance was fine with it. Every Rifter was going to get paid upon completion, not to mention gain a Level from clearing the Rift. He needed the Experience more than anyone else there, and fast! If he wanted to catch up with the three Rifters who had caused Thomas's death, he would need to cut corners and lower himself to these types of tactics. If burning several forests inside Rifts would help, he would burn them all.

"Time to swap," Lance said, patting Iyas on the shoulder, rotating him out.

Lance was glad that Iyas was there to remind them they were doing this for the sake of the other Rifters. *At least one of us has a conscience*, he thought as he slammed his entrenching tool into the dirt.

Mira watched the black curtain of smoke rising in the distance when Lance, Scott, and Iyas had returned to camp later that night. "Man, that fire is wild!" she exclaimed. Even from base camp, the Rifters could see the devastation it had caused. "Greenpeace is going to love you guys."

Both Lance and Iyas had to laugh at that comment. They knew how people would have reacted to what they'd done if it had been on Earth. They'd be criminals. "At least we'd make the news," Iyas said as he finished his meal. "Tomorrow is the day."

"That it is," Lance said, knowing full well that they would face the remaining monsters and the Guardian. *I wonder if it's just one or multiple Guardians this time?* Lance thought before finishing his own meal and washing it down with fresh water. The GRRO report he had read mentioned that the number of Guardians varied in this Rift.

The three of them had bonded a bit during these last few days, and Lance had learned more about their pasts. Mira had lost her leg and her uncle during her first Rift. Her uncle had been her caretaker and had been the one who had taught her how to hunt with the air rifle. After the Rift, she had struggled to adjust to her new prosthetic leg and take on smaller jobs as a Rifter. She had endured a lot of discrimination from other Rifters, with most of them seeing her leg as a liability.

Iyas had revealed that he was traveling the world, looking for some purpose in life. His initial Rift hadn't been as gruesome as most initial Rifts, but he was struggling to unite both his previous life and that of a Rifter. He explained he wanted to see a lot of countries, meet new people, and try to find some balance and purpose.

Lance had shared some memories from his initial Rift and those after that, admitting that he had experienced good and bad ones. He hadn't mentioned losing Thomas, preferring to keep that part to himself. He was still struggling with what he had been through. Lance knew he didn't have the time to make new friendships, because he was constantly rushing from one Rift to the next one. Still, Mira and Iyas were good people in his book, and he was glad to have met them.

"I can't wait to have actual nighttime again," Lance said. He hoped that would increase the quality of his sleep again. The constant daylight wasn't the thing that was bothering Lance the most. Fragmented memories haunted his dreams, in he was constantly soaring or plummeting through the air. He assumed it was a side effect of the forging process, with him slowly getting more exposed to the previous life of those that he forged into companions.

He had moments when the area around his own white-shard felt painful. He even tasted blood on his tongue now and again. Still, he would choose pain over those dreams of soaring through the sky. There was something unnatural about them, experiencing a freefall only to soar up again mere seconds before slamming into the ground.

Let's just hope that those birds won't be as bad as Thomas's voice in my head, Lance thought as he heard a faint whisper of his former friend somewhere in the depths of his mind, demanding to be heard. Eventually, Lance gave in as he grabbed his phone and found a matching song to fit the mood.

And so, the three Rifters stood there, watching the world in front of them burn while Lance's phone played "Burning Love" by Elvis Presley.

CHAPTER TWENTY-ONE

Skilled Competition

The Next Day
April, 14 AR
Inside Rift Twelve

LANCE

Four Rifters ran up the ruined stone steps, feeling them crumbling underneath their feet as they rushed upwards to stay ahead of the monsters. They could hear the burned Bark-brains behind them, roaring and hissing as they tried to close the distance with their enormous frames. Behind them were hordes of Centaur-toads, equally burned and wounded. "Keep the momentum!" Lance yelled as they rounded another corner just as a few of the monsters slammed into the wall behind them, showering them all in bits of stone and dirt.

They were playing a dangerous game of cat and mouse, with them trying to keep the creatures right on their heels and blinded by rage. The ash and smoke in the air irritated the Rifters' lungs, but none of them complained about it, knowing full well that they had an important job to do.

As they reached the top of the tower, they spotted the hole in the wall, which they knew they had to jump through. *Don't think . . . Just jump!* Lance thought as the three other Rifters made a beeline toward the hole and jumped. The others weren't as physically strong as him, but they were skilled runners and confident enough in their ability to outpace the wounded monsters behind them.

Lance followed right behind them and was airborne for a few seconds before slamming into another ruined tower, barely managing to hold on to the ropes and vines that other Rifters had placed there. The force of the jump caused him to swing wildly for a moment before he could pull himself up and scramble over the edge, aided by several hands. As the four of them caught their breaths, the other Rifters congratulated them, even as they could see and hear the horrible scene that was unfolding before them.

The Bark-brains had underestimated the size of the hole and their speed as they crashed into the wall. With their enormous bodies, they smashed through the stone with ease. Dozens of burned Centaur-toads behind were in a similar predicament as they piled into each other and toppled down the tower in a writhing, hissing mass. The sheer drop had reduced their bodies into red smears on the ground. "Nice job, guys," Lance said as he complimented the others with him.

Across the ruined city the Rifters had created similar scenes like this, taking advantage of traps, ambushes, and brutal tactics. They had crushed monsters with rubble, made them charge into sharpened wooden pikes, pushed burning debris on them, or caused them to plummet to their deaths.

"I could've sworn I felt one of them nibbling on my rear."

"It's a hard target to miss."

"Ah, sod off!"

The runners vented their stress and fatigue, knowing that there was still work to be done. The fire had decimated the monsters' numbers, but the pain from all their wounds and burns had whipped those that had remained into a frenzy. This made things easier for the Rifters if they were smart about it.

Lance peered outwards as he heard shouting. "Lance! We found them!" He could see Mira in the distance, waving her rifle in the air to signal him. She was pointing to the east, toward the ruined keep. He spotted a few Rifters making their way toward it, three shadowy monsters in pursuit.

"Gear up. We have some Rift-guardians to kill."

Twenty minutes had passed since Lance and his squad had joined up with the others. These monsters were floating in the air like weird, ethereal squids. Their bodies, black and shadowy, glowed with a dark mist that distorted the air around them, only to dissipate a moment later. Their many tendril-like limbs were long, thin, and covered in a gray liquid. As far as Lance could see, they had no eyes but were clearly intelligent, judging by how well they could read a Rifter's movements.

These guys are fast, Lance thought, feeling fatigued from the fight as well as pain where their tendrils had hit them. At his Endurance level, he could still shrug it off, but some of the weaker Rifters who had gotten hurt were down for the count with arms or legs that were numb and unable to move properly.

Lance and Scott were each fighting a Rift-guardian, while a smaller force led by Iyas had pinned down the third one. Sounds of combat rang out throughout the ruined keep. Stone fractured and charred wood groaned as the Rifters fought the monsters, with several fighters holding back waves of weaker ones near the main entrance. "Keep it up! Kill them all," Scott screamed as he stabbed a tendril.

Get low! Thomas seemed to cry in Lance's mind.

Lance ducked as quickly as he could, hugging the steel axe close to his body. He narrowly evaded the monster's limb and felt the wind of it against his scalp. *Step in closer.* Thomas' experience continued to guide him, forcing his body to rush forwards.

Thomas's instincts, honed by years of training, surged through Lance's mind. He threw himself aside as another tendril swung for him. He felt it graze his shoulder, but he kept moving, hacking, and slashing at the tendrils with his axe as they sped past him. Lance eventually severed two of the limbs. A torrent of yellow blood spurted from them as they fell to the ground with heavy thumps.

"Not so quick now, are we?" Lance taunted it as he circled the wounded creature. He wanted to finish it quickly to help with the others but froze as he noticed the monster's remaining tendrils trembling. A fireball formed between its limbs, growing larger and larger. *A magic user? This is bad*, Lance thought as he retrieved a javelin from his Inventory. He threw it at the monster.

He watched the crude bone javelin impact with the fireball, causing it to explode violently and burn the monster. Without pausing, Lance rushed forwards and tackled the beast into the stone wall behind it, only to slam through the wall and into the next floor. He hacked and punched at the creature with all his might before it slipped away from him. It was as if the monster sensed the difference in power between the two of them. Before it could escape, Lance threw his axe at it, hitting it straight in the center mass as the momentum forced the monster back onto the ground.

Summoning his entrenching tool, Lance switched it to the pickaxe setting as he slammed it through the monster's torso and into the ground underneath it, pinning it in place. Its strange anatomy made it hard for Lance to judge how much damage he had inflicted and how best to kill it. *Force!* It was as if he could feel Thomas inside of him, fighting for control of his thoughts, breaking apart his concentration.

It felt uncomfortable but proved helpful in the moment, seeing as he was overthinking things again. Instead, he took a page out of Thomas and Dieter's book, as slamming his right hand against the monster's shard, forcing the black-red shard further into its torso before grabbing and pulling on it.

The Rift-guardian bucked like a wild horse. The creature's cold yellow blood poured over Lance's hand as he ripped the shard out, accompanied by a sickening, sucking sound. The stench of the creature's blood was overwhelming, and he fought the urge to vomit. Finally, the shard came free, and Lance stumbled backwards, barely able to keep himself from falling over. And as the monster flailed its limbs one final time, Lance looked down at the bloody guardian-shard in his palm. He was about to store it in his Inventory when he noticed something sticking to the shard—something white. As soon as he grabbed it, a notification popped up.

[Skill-shard found]
[Use] [Store] [Destroy]

Lance blinked a few times. He was hardly able to process the situation, or the rarity of a drop like this. "A Skill-shard?" he said out loud, a smile tentatively forming on his face. It suddenly soured, however, when Scott burst into the room, smashing apart the Rift-guardian he was facing. Like Lance, yellow blood and shadowy gore covered the Rifter from head to toe.

Scott stood up, panting, ready to smash the dead monster one more time. When Scott noticed Lance, his eyes narrowed on the Skill-shard in Lance's hands. "Give it to me."

A few minutes later, two Rifters were holding Scott back, trying to calm him down and talk it out. "Bugger off. That Skill-shard is mine. I killed the bloody thing. It's mine," Scott said, the veins in his forehead pulsing in anger.

The fighting had died down after they had killed all the Rift-guardians. Iyas and the others had finished the third and final one. There were still sounds of occasional Centaur-toads being killed by a Rifter but nothing that constituted a real threat. Most of the Rifters were watching the standoff between Lance and Scott, while others began ripping out black-shards from the slain monsters in what little time they had.

"Says who?" Mira asked. "From where I'm standing, Lance is the one holding onto the Skill-shard and you're making the bold claims. What proof do you have that he took it? Do you have any witnesses?" A few of the other Rifters whispered among themselves, speculating who was in the right.

"I don't have time for all of this. Back off, Scott," Lance said as he felt the earth trembling once more. The Rift was clearly ending. He didn't want a confrontation with Scott. But there was something about the man that he hated—despised even. The man was a bully, a fake leader, and was letting his greed get the better of him. It reminded him of someone. *The more time I'm wasting here, the less time I have to harvest black-shards and store monsters.* The Skill-shard was a precious asset for sure, but Lance was also counting on storing these Rift-guardians and harvesting them back in his lair to make a big profit.

"Back off? Or what?" Scott said, pushing against the two men who were trying to hold him back. The greed in his eyes had changed into anger as he stepped closer toward Lance, as if he wanted to kill him on the spot.

[Use]

The Skill-shard glowed intensely and Lance slammed it against his chest, letting his white-shard absorb the radiation it was giving off. He could feel the surge of energy flow into his body as notifications popped up on his status screen. He ignored them as he took a step toward Scott himself, calm and determined. "Back off . . . now. I'll not warn you again."

The sudden shift in Lance's demeanor and the fact that the Skill-shard was no longer a potential prize halted Scott's advance. His eyes narrowed on Lance's. He was about to open his mouth when a spear slammed between his legs at an incredible speed, ripping apart the stone tiles in a violent display. "Scott, you heard the man. Back off. Or do you want to explain to the GRRO how you broke the single most important rule amongst Rifters? To never fight amongst ourselves?" Iyas asked with a threatening smile, one that almost dared Scott to try.

To hammer the point down further, Mira also stepped forward, brandishing her rifle with both her hands as she did. "This Rift is closing. Either get out with a handful of black-shards or leave on a stretcher."

The fury in Scott's eyes continued to burn for a while longer until he finally backed off, accompanied by even more tremors as the Rift grew more unstable. With Scott no longer there, most of the other Rifters also left the ruined keep, desperate to grab a dozen more black-shards on their way out.

"Are you alright?" Iyas asked, his eyes softening now that Scott was gone.

"Yeah, thanks for the assist. Sorry that you got dragged into this."

Iyas smiled, as if Lance said something amusing. "No worries. A life is worth more than a few black-shards. Besides, you can't put a price on the fear Scott felt when the room suddenly turned against him. It will become a fond memory."

"Yeah, I'd say he was close to bricking it," Mira pitched in as she stepped to the side to dodge a falling ceiling tile. "My daft gentlemen, might I persuade you to get out of this dump before it becomes our tomb?"

At that, the two men nodded and grinned like children, as they grabbed their gear and headed out. Lance timed it so that he was the last one to leave the keep, storing two of the slain Rift-guardians in his Inventory without being noticed. Afterwards, he ran after Iyas and Mira to the Rift-event in the center of the city, only pausing for a moment to note a gray dot in the sky above him. He was still smiling as the world shook under his feet.

As one, the Rifters reappeared in a torrent of black energy. Some Rifters shot back into existence in a stable, grounded manner, effortlessly sliding to a sudden halt on their feet, deftly fighting off any kinetic energy that accompanied Rift travel. Others slammed down on their knees or onto the ground face first. Dazed, they shook their heads and got back up.

The rubble, stone, and dirt that had accompanied the Rifters had showered the Rift site, the protective barriers having caught most of it. Beyond the debris, the Rift had also shot one gray bird outwards, letting momentum carry it upwards before it flew off on its own.

"Fresh air!"

"Finally! Who's up for beers?"

"Pay day!"

The Rifters celebrated among themselves, some going over to the GRRO personnel who were rushing toward them. Beyond a few minor injuries and fractures, the Rift had gone remarkably well. They'd finished the Rift sooner than expected, their brutal hunting tactics and large-scale forest fires decimating most of the monsters.

Lance watched Iyas helping Mira up to her feet while joking with her again that she should weaponize that leg of hers. *If they keep this up, they'll become a couple*, he thought, a soft smile forming while he followed the others toward the cubicles and central office. He slid his hand inside of his scarf to touch Bravo before storing the bird inside his Inventory. With Alpha in the air and Bravo now stored, he had proven that his companions could leave a Rift just like any other Rifter.

The office itself was nothing more than three cargo containers locked together but, compared to what they had experienced with the Rift, it might as well have been a five-star hotel.

"Coffee?" an employee asked as he approached the Rifters with a large tray that held several cups. Beyond that, there were muffins, bagels, apples, and other snacks for them to enjoy.

"Perfect," Lance said as he grabbed a cup and an apple before giving his statement to the site overseer. He identified himself to show that he was still alive and give her a brief report. Beyond explaining that they had burned down the forest and that one Rift-guardian had used a fire Skill, there was little to report. He didn't bother reporting Scott's behavior, seeing as he didn't want to deal with the hassle that would no doubt accompany such an act.

Once he confirmed his payment, he found a chair to sit down in and enjoy his apple. Right there and then he made the mental note to either buy a proper chair or find one during another Rift. *Perhaps even a table while I'm at it.*

He opened his status screen and checked the notifications he had gotten. They ranged from the Experience he had gained, the status of his equipment, his Level Ups, and his new Skill. *Let's check the Skill first.*

[Ricochet: Lvl 1]
[Cost per usage: –25 Stamina per bounce]
[Allows the user to bounce throwing attacks with greater speed
and accuracy]
[Lvl 1 allows one 1 bounce, increasing projectile speed by 5%]

He read the description a few times as he went over every tiny detail. At first, it might've seemed like a somewhat useless Skill to allow something to bounce, but the increased speed and accuracy was something to pay attention to. The description hinted at him being able to bounce even more at a higher Skill level. *Perhaps the speed will increase with Leveling Up as well?* He wanted to test it out immediately, but he knew it would look weird if he suddenly got up and started throwing weapons at trees or bushes.

He then looked at his status screen and noticed the two Levels he had gained. One for killing a Rift-guardian and the other for having cleared and survived the Rift. The number of Levels he achieved from this Rift had been a lot more than his previous Rifts. *Having more companions sure helps,* he thought as he placed three points into Endurance and three into Agility.

[Endurance:] [57] (+3)
[Agility:] [57] (+3)

He then finished his coffee as he made his way over to his private cubicle. He was determined to scrub away every bit of blood and dirt that his body and clothes had collected over the last few days.

Status Compendium

Name:	Lance Turner
Level:	30
Class:	Death Smith

Attributes

Endurance:	60	**Agility:**	60	**Wisdom:**	46
Strength:	60	**Perception:**	49	**Luck:**	49
Health:	1600	**Mana:**	325		
Stamina:	500	**Inventory:**	63		

Traits

Taint of death:	Able to use Rift corpses as items	Prolonged use results . . . ~ERROR UNREADABLE!~
Shard instability:	Prolonged use results . . . ~ERROR UNREADABLE!~	Prolonged use results . . . ~ERROR UNREADABLE!~

Skills

Mend Wounds	Lvl 2	Restores minor wounds	+20 Health +8 Stamina	−15 Mana
Death Forge	Lvl 2	Allows (re)forging of death related items	+2 Items	−Raw materials −Black-shards −50% Stamina regeneration −50% Mana regeneration
Repair Item	Lvl 1	Restores durability on items	+1 durability per 1 item per 1 minute	−Raw materials −Black-shards −25% Stamina regeneration −25% Mana regeneration
Ricochet	Lvl 1	Bounces throwing attacks with greater speed and accuracy	+1 Bounce +5% Speed +5% Accuracy	−25 Stamina per bounce

Retainers

Ash	1x	Human
Icarus	1x	Falcon (hybrid*)
Alpha	1x	Crow
Bravo	1x	Crow

CHAPTER TWENTY-TWO

A Bounce in One's Step

Ten Minutes Later
April, 14 AR
Outside Rift 12
Galway, Ireland

LANCE

Lance felt the warm water wash away days' worth of blood and dirt. The water was hot enough to turn his skin red and make the cuts on his body sting. He had both hands pressed against the steel wall of his private cubicle, supporting his tired frame. His muscles ached in a way that only a Rifter could understand. The water was a blessed relief. It felt like it was washing away everything bad that had happened inside the Rift and gently reintroducing him to civilization.

The water underneath him was a murky brown, tinged with yellow from monster blood. It swirled around his feet like an eddying vortex of filth before going down the drain. *Fewer bruises and cuts compared to normal*, he mused as he studied his injuries. There were only a handful of them this time. Lance was getting stronger, faster, and more durable. Making a fist, he could feel the strength in his grip, dwarfing what he could do in the past. *I'm slowly getting there, Thomas.*

As he stepped out of the shower, he inspected his naked body in the mirror. He ran a hand over the scars and bruises that adorned his frame. He traced his fingers across an old bite wound on his stomach, then followed the many smaller cuts on his chest and arms. The scars were like a roadmap, each one telling a story of a battle fought and won. Some cuts were still healing, the flesh around them pink and tender. *I sure have changed since the hospital days*, Lance thought as he opened the locker and retrieved his shaving cream and his razor.

A few minutes later, he had finished his shave, toweled himself off, and gotten dressed in his civilian clothes. The jeans and shirt felt strange after days of wearing nothing but his combat gear. He finished packing his bags and stored most of his gear in a spare bag. It was easier to store it inside his Inventory, but Lance had filled that up with monster corpses.

He retrieved his smartphone from his Inventory and heard it buzz mere moments later now that it finally had the chance to connect to a cell tower on Earth. He spotted several emails from Oliver with questions about the Rifts, suggestions for cool weapon names and several music samples that were attached as files. The last email he got from Oliver was about something major that was happening in Paris with a link to a speech. *I'll look at that tomorrow*, he thought as he had just gotten out of a Rift and was too tired to watch a long speech.

Beyond the emails, he had also received several text messages from both Dieter and Daniel. They were interested to hear how the Rift in Ireland had gone and were asking him to contact them when he got back. *It's like having two additional mothers. I swear, Dieter is becoming more like Daniel.* He smiled as he read their messages, feeling both uncomfortable at their meddling nature and glad that they took the time to do so.

Several other messages were from the GRRO about recent updates to the app on his phone, a transfer of funds, and several open requests for parties that were being formed to take on a Rift. "Not today," he whispered as he ignored their requests. He scrolled down his contact list and spotted the last message he had received from Kate. It was a picture of her orchestra during practice, with Kate looking smug as usual.

Lance felt conflicted about his feelings for Kate. On the one hand, he thought it would be disrespectful to Thomas's memory if he got close to his sister. But, on the other, he also couldn't forget the way she kissed him and the evening they spent together. A part of him longed for her. He had fond childhood memories of when she would flirt with him and how blissfully confused it would usually make him. He finally stored his phone again as he reminded himself that his focus should be on the oath he had sworn to Thomas. So, Lance grabbed his bags and left the cubicle.

After closing the door behind him and letting a GRRO employee know he was leaving, Lance made his way over toward his van in the parking lot, which was only a short walk from the Rift itself. The dull gray material of the vehicle was comforting, although it looked anything but flashy compared to some of the other cars surrounding it. A bright red sports car stood out the most and it was absolutely screaming "Scott."

It's almost like status and money turns most people into bloody peacocks, Lance thought as he imagined the smug face Scott would have while driving the car. He then picked up several small pebbles from the ground and spotted two nearby trees that he could use as a target. He made sure there wasn't anyone around him before he aimed the first pebble at the tree on his right and activated his Skill.

Ricochet
[You have used Ricochet Lvl 1 at the cost of 25 Stamina]
[Current Stamina 117/500]

As soon as he activated the Skill, he noticed a faint black line connecting with the right tree. It then jumped and continued toward the other tree, precisely where he had wanted it to hit. Lance was sure that only he could see the line. Just in case, he grabbed his smartphone, peered through the camera, and snapped a photo of the trees. Like he had guessed, there wasn't a line in the picture.

He tried to aim along the black line as he threw the first pebble and missed completely, much to his own amusement. *It's like with the bloody bow all over again*, Lance thought as he remembered the dozens of arrows he had missed in the beginning before he had even hit a single target.

Ricochet

The second pebble had hit the tree, but on the wrong side, forcing it to bounce off to the right and into the dirt. It was hard to judge the Skill's effectiveness. Lance thought it had gotten faster after he had hit it, or at the very least it hadn't lost momentum. He threw the pebble two more times, with his Stamina nearly running out. The second one had finally hit the first tree in the right spot, following the vague black line, only to speed up before it hit the second tree. This time, the effectiveness of the Skill was clear, as Lance heard the pebble violently hitting the wood.

He realized that it wasn't an automatic aiming Skill, nor something overpowered. It simply showed Lance the best spot to hit something and make it bounce perfectly while increasing its velocity. *If I Level this up further and use knives, this is going to be quite handy.* He activated the Skill again and tried shifting his target from the trees to a car, or the side of the pavement. Each time, Lance could vaguely see the black line shift and change, forming a new line.

Sometimes he noticed the line going downwards, only to bounce upwards and hit the underside of a car. Other times, the line pointed at a signpost in the back in order to bounce and aim at Lance's van. It was silly, but when he imagined these objects being monsters, it suddenly made sense. All of this meant that he could now target monsters on their exposed flanks, or even ignore a shield as he bounced a knife or javelin from the side. *Now I just need to get good at throwing. No pressure.*

A throwing knife was less effective compared to a bow or a javelin, despite how Hollywood and games portrayed it as this amazing "one-hit kill" weapon. But, with his increased stats as a Rifter, the Ricochet Skill, and a large Inventory, Lance was certain he could make it deadly. He remembered just how brutally effective Daniel was with his daggers when the man imbued them with a lightning Skill that electrocuted monsters upon contact.

He dropped the pebble as he grabbed his car keys to unlock his van. He was about to signal to his remaining companion in the sky to dive into the car quickly without being spotted when he heard someone behind him.

"That's an amazing ride," Iyas said, his words dripping with sarcasm as he approached Lance and inspected the van, emitting a mocking whistle. "I get the whole low-profile thing, but this might be going a bit overboard." He chuckled as if to let Lance know that the comment was intended as playful.

"It beats the overcompensating red monstrosity there," Lance countered as he pointed at the car that no doubt belonged to Scott. Lance was suddenly aware of just how well-dressed Iyas was. The man was wearing a tailored suit that emphasized his tall frame and tanned skin. Lance suddenly felt extremely underdressed. For a moment, Lance wondered if the red car belonged to Iyas.

Iyas grinned as he nodded. "That it does. Overcompensating might not even fully cover this. By the way, I'm sure you were just going to store your gear and not leave already, right?"

"I . . ."

"Come on, a goodbye isn't that bad, right? Might I remind you that the lovely Mira is a skilled sharpshooter and can use explosive projectiles?"

"Fair point," Lance replied. He had gotten used to being on his own, both to protect himself and others. He knew he didn't have time to make new friends, not while he was on the path of seeking justice for Thomas. Still, Iyas was right about saying goodbye. It would be rude not to, seeing as the three of them had fought side by side for several days and they had backed him up.

"Smart choice." Iyas leaned against the metal frame of Lance's van as he closed his eyes and relaxed in the morning sun. "So, what are your plans next? To celebrate on your own, or to find a new Rift to jump in?"

Lance smiled at the last bit, knowing full well that he had been constantly throwing himself into Rifts. "Probably sell what I collected and upgrade my gear a bit. Afterwards, I'll enjoy a proper night's rest without a second sun dangling above me."

The two men continued to chat for a while. Lance enjoyed it, hearing Iyas go on about a Rift he had been in Morocco that had dumped him into a world in constant darkness, where the wind played tricks on your senses. It had been a Level One Rift with incredibly weak monsters, but the world itself and the sound of the wind had terrified Iyas to the point that, afterwards, he had taken several months off from being a Rifter before he had built up the courage again.

Lance found it easy to talk to Iyas, or at the very least, listen to him. Iyas had seen a lot of the world but had a well-grounded mindset about the type of Rifter he wanted to become. Iyas asked Lance about the Workshop back in London and was comparing it to other places like it all over the world, including the one in Dublin called the Foundry. It was Lance's next stop.

Lance had a backpack full of Items to sell, and, safely stashed inside his rented "lair," he had even more Items already processed and tucked away. "Tell me," Lance pressed, his voice teeming with curiosity, "what tales can you share about the Little Market?" He looked to Iyas, eager for a firsthand account and a potential lead to its whereabouts.

Iyas froze at that, and Lance immediately felt bad, wondering if he had soured the mood permanently. "I'm just curious. I overheard other Rifters talking about it, but I don't have the faintest idea of what it is exactly and how to get there," Lance said quickly, hoping to mend things.

"I see," Iyas said. It seemed like he was thinking about something before he spoke up again. "I suppose it's a healthy curiosity. But you'd be better off at GRRO-sanctioned locations."

Lance smiled, hoping to calm the tension. "Like I said, it's just a curiosity. I've been trying to expand on my traps and figured the Little Market might have more 'effective designs' that a typical GRRO-sanctioned market might not be willing to sell."

"I'll think about it," Iyas said before he nudged Lance in the ribs and pointed at the direction Mira was coming from. "Let's shift the conversation toward something else for now."

A while later, Lance was driving back to Dublin. He had a little over two hours left on his journey to the Foundry. The wind was whipping through the van, pulling at his clothes and hair. Both windows were open, and Ash sat next to him, wearing a hoodie to hide most of his pale features. Alpha and Bravo were in the back, watching a long documentary about birds hunting in groups. Icarus was flying above the van, occasionally diving low or landing on Ash's arm.

Lance was still tired, but the occasional "Mend Wounds" Skill helped stave off any fatigue he was feeling. The idea was to sell some of the monster parts he had harvested and quickly make his way home to eat and take a quick nap. He had wanted to sleep for several hours, but Mira and Iyas had tag-teamed him into agreeing to meet up later that evening for some drinks.

A part of him wanted to refuse, seeing as he wasn't there to make friends. But both Mira and Iyas stood by his side when Scott had confronted him. In the end,

Lance had agreed to their demands, knowing it was the least he could do to thank them.

"Alright, Ash, call him back," Lance said as he watched the man stick his hand out of the window and slap it against the metal door. Seconds later, Icarus landed on Ash's arm and hopped into the back of the van to join his brethren.

Lance was proud of his companions. Their first Rift together had been a tremendous success and field-testing them entering and leaving a Rift had opened several new opportunities. Already, Lance was eager to try his hands on a Level One Rift on his own, just to see how quickly he could solo it with his companions. *The Experience gained might not be great, but all the black-shards would be mine.*

"So, any preference for the type of armor I'm going to get you?" Lance asked as he nudged his companion in the side. Ash barely reacted. Instead the pale man simply observed how Lance was driving. Lance had instructed Ash to do so previously, telling him to pay close attention.

"No . . ."

"Again, try to sound less like the devil himself. But I was thinking of thick steel plates and sturdy leather. Sort of like a mobile tank," Lance explained as he tried to imagine just how much more effective Ash would be when armored. The protection would help, but he still wanted Ash mobile and stealthy. Most of Ash's kills had been because of traps and ambushes. "You've been practicing your boxing and fighting styles, right?"

"Yes . . ."

"Good work. I'll teach you some chokeholds and takedown techniques when I have time. That should be useful for you when fighting against a stronger opponent. You did great in the Rift near the water. Truly." He patted his pale companion's knee playfully before he pointed at the steering wheel. "Want to try driving for a while?" he asked with an innocent smile.

At that point, Lance was still blissfully unaware of just how scared he, as a veteran of twelve Rifts, could truly be in a matter of minutes.

CHAPTER TWENTY-THREE

An Eye for Change

Several Hours Later
April, 14 AR
Inside the Foundry
Dublin, Ireland

LANCE

It hadn't taken Lance long to arrive at the GRRO-sanctioned location near Dublin. He had stopped once to fill up his van's tank and another time when he had allowed Ash to steer the car. The result had been the van nearly crashing into the side of the road and Lance having to take several minutes to calm himself down.

The GRRO place he had stopped at had an official name, but most Rifters referred to it as "The Foundry." Although there were others in Ireland, this was the largest; it was where most Rifters went to buy and sell supplies and equipment, or form parties.

The Foundry was a bustling marketplace full of people and activity. Rifters of all shapes and sizes milled about, haggling, and bargaining over prices. The air was thick with weird unidentifiable odors, along with those of metals and oil. Lanterns hung from the ceiling, casting a warm glow over the scene. Loud laughter and shouting filled the air as parties met up or formed on the spot.

The Workshop in London was far larger and more expansive, but Lance had taken a liking to the Foundry. Some savant of structured architecture had designed the place in precise lines. Every shop was of a similar size and stood next to one another with a clear purpose. It lacked the Workshop's intrinsic warmth, but Lance had only walked around the place for a few minutes before he understood the complete layout and knew where to find everything. Thomas would've hated it, but to Lance's introverted nature, all of this made sense.

He had first sold the stuff he harvested from the monsters in his last Rift. Most of it were things like hides to make into leather, along with claws and teeth. He had stuffed his rucksack full of those sorts of things until it had threatened to rip apart at the seams. More fragile or squishy materials such as their eyes and meat Lance had stored in his Inventory, preferring not to carry around constantly due to the smell. As horrible as it seemed, a collector or Rifter with an Alchemist Skill would pay quite a penny for it.

He hadn't brought his bulk goods back with him during his last Rift. He had wanted to stay light on his feet and had gone in that Rift purely to train and observe other Rifters. Even with just his Inventory and rucksack, he had made a decent amount. He had sold most of his black-shards and the single guardian-shard to get a little spending power. He had promised Ash that he would get him some decent gear, finally. He was surprised by just how much more a guardian-shard was worth compared to a regular black-shard. A thousand times as valuable. It made sense, since they were rare, and the Rift-guardians were tougher foes to kill. Beyond that, their shards could be used to breach unstable Rifts at the cost of one shard per Rifter. The latter was something Rifters rarely did since the price of a guardian-shard was usually too high to justify it.

The gear he had bought for Ash in the Foundry was basic steel and leather equipment that offered a lot of protection without hindering Ash's mobility too much. Ash's equipment had very different requirements to his own. For his own gear, he wanted as much protection near vital organs, but for Ash, it was mostly to prevent the loss of limbs and mobility. An arrow to Ash's heart or lung was less damaging than his losing a hand. Overheating, chafing, or discomfort were also things that didn't affect his companion.

Although it tugged at his guilt and grief, he made sure he equipped Ash with equipment that was worthy of Thomas. The armor contained thick steel plates riveted with leather straps and additional leather padding. Lance had also bought boots, gauntlets, and leg armor for Ash, all made from thick steel plating and sturdy dark leather. Ash would now also have a proper helmet to cover the top and sides of his head. An adjustable sturdy leather neck and face-guard would allow Ash to cover most of his face, leaving just his eyes exposed.

The metal had a dark coating on it, preventing it from reflecting light as much as possible, while also making the armor look more intimidating. Wearing it, Ash would look like a walking tank, worthy of Thomas's approval. It had taken a bit of guesswork to get all the right sizes, but the seller he had bought it from was used to people buying armor for other Rifters. In the eyes of the merchant, Lance was no doubt just another underling sent out on a task.

At other shops, he had replenished his food and water supplies, along with several steel throwing knives, a sturdy backpack for Ash, and a few longer cloaks. He had bought knives and cloaks bulk, hoping to destroy them and gain their template. Lance figured he could replace bone knives far more easily when he learned to use his new Skill. And with his "Death Smith" Class, he could pump out bone knives if he had the black-shards and the bones to do so. The cloaks, he had purchased for a special project.

Lance had thought about either joining a party that would tackle a Level Four Rift or instead attempting a Level One Rift on his own. The Level Four would offer far more Experience and allow him to see how Rifters dealt with a more dangerous Rift. A Level One Rift would mean that every black-shard retrieved would be his. For now, he shifted his focus on harvesting the monster corpses he still had inside his Inventory. That and getting some rest before he was to meet up with Iyas and Mira later that evening. *Experience or wealth?* Lance considered as he made his way out of the Foundry and into the parking lot. *I'll tackle that problem tomorrow.*

Ash and the birds were still in Lance's Inventory, as he didn't want to chance someone looking inside and spotting them. He placed the crates that contained the daggers, cloaks, and Ash's new armor in the back of the van and was about to load up the food and water he had bought when his phone buzzed. He noticed two messages from Iyas. One contained an address and instructions, while the other was a simple message:

Not a word to Mira. And don't let curiosity get the better of you. -Iyas.

"Yes!" Lance said, slamming his fist against the side of his van because of his excitement. He still had to verify it all, but if the address was legit, it meant that he now was one step closer to finding the black market. If it all worked out, it meant that he could unload even more monster parts without the GRRO or anyone else getting suspicious about how a single Rifter could carry so many individual hides, bones, claws, and other parts from a single Rift each time.

He quickly texted Iyas back to let him know he was grateful for the help and that the first drinks were on him. Then he loaded up his van and eagerly made the trip back to his base of operations.

Several hours had passed since Lance had returned from the Foundry. And although he had showered since he emerging from the Rift that morning, a fresh coat of blood and filth already covered his body. To his side stood Ash, equally filthy, as the two of them carefully removed the dark, shadowy skin of a Rift-guardian. The skin was tough and leathery, and it took a lot of effort to peel away from the underlying flesh. The smell of blood and death was overpowering, and

Lance had to take breaks to gag and catch his breath. Not even the filtering properties of the kaffiyeh wrapped around his face seemed to help. Luckily, Ash didn't seem to mind and had done most of the work.

They had just finished with the second Rift-guardian's skin, letting it drape over several chairs. Even now, peeled off of their former bodies, the skin continued to distort the very air, as if a dark smoke was continuously forming and dissipating. "It's like looking at the world through a funhouse mirror. Everything looks twisted." He let his hand run over the skin. He could feel its warmth and how it made his hand seem warped. *I was lucky to have gotten my hands on two of these Guardians.*

"Ash, cut up the rest of the Guardian and put those freeloaders to work," Lance said as he handed his companion a sharp knife. As ordered, Ash pointed at bits of meat and removed organs, marking the separate piles whilst grunting verbal commands. It still sounded horrible and demonic, but the birds understood Ash just fine. It was a bloody task, but Lance's companions didn't flinch or hesitate when faced with the savagery of this world or that within a Rift.

Lance rubbed his eyes with his thumb and forefinger, feeling the grit of sleep and the sting of exhaustion. Although it was still midday, it felt like he had already been awake for much longer. Long days of brutal combat, rough living, and constantly harvesting monsters had taken a toll on him. His sleeping bag had tempted him several times from across the room. Still, the desire to finish his special project was far more alluring.

Lance picked up another cloak he had purchased in the Foundry and grabbed a knife as he carefully made alterations to it. He cut the edges and bottom to give it a tattered look, while making arm slits at the side to allow him to wear it like either a cloak or an improvised coat of sorts. "I'm just throwing away money here," Lance said as he inspected the finished project one last time. He had done the same with four other cloaks already, destroying each of them while hoping to get their template. "Lady Luck, don't fail me now."

**[Unknown template. Base 13% chance of discovery
when destroying this Item]
[Do you wish to destroy this Item?]
[Yes] [No]**

He paused as he noticed the increased chance of discovery. It had started out as a mere five percent, but it had increased during the last few attempts. *At least my familiarity with the Item has increased. But I'm running out of cloaks.* He chose "Yes" as he continued to hold on to the cloak, seeing a countdown appear near the item. He spent the time he had to wait by observing Ash and the birds.

The pale man had made substantial progress already on the second Rift-guardian, and Alpha and Bravo were working in unison to drag a large piece of meat toward the storage pile. Icarus was in the back, struggling with a Rift-glider's eyeball that had gotten lodged in the back of its beak. "Icarus, if you break it, you'll have to buy it," Lance said. He enjoyed the bewildered look that the creature was giving him. Even Ash gave him a confused stare at that moment.

[Success]

The Item disintegrated in his hands, but the process had been a success. He could see the status screen mark the addition of another template that he had learned. His eyes immediately lit up as he rushed toward the chairs that contained the shadowy skin, quickly storing them one by one while he activated his Death Forge ability. It took him a few minutes to figure it all out and to double check it once more. Upon accepting the forging process, his status screen notified him of the cost of it all. The process had used up an entire Rift-guardian's skin and a chunk of his black-shards.

"Good?" Ash asked as he made his way over toward him, still covered in yellowish blood.

"Yes, it is. Amazing even."

Ash nodded at that, doing his best to share in Lance's excitement, but lacking the knowledge and ability to join him properly. And so, minutes passed as the two men waited patiently while the timer slowly ran out.

[You have finished forging an Item]

Within a second, Lance had retrieved the Item from his Inventory, and it appeared in his hands. The tattered cloak looked like something out of a horror movie, as the black smoke distorted the air. He wove it around a few times to see the strange effect it had. It was hard for the eyes to follow, but he found he got used to it after a little while. It felt even stranger as he draped the cloak around his shoulders.

[You have named this Item 'Shadow cloak']

Lance gave the cloak its own nickname, showing how impressive he thought it was. "I look like everyone's childhood nightmares combined into one. This is perfect," Lance said as he waved his hands a few times before retrieving three throwing knives. "Everyone, think fast."

Ricochet
Ricochet
Ricochet
[You have used Ricochet Lvl 1 3x at the cost of 75 Stamina]
[Current Stamina 231/500]

The steel throwing knives left his hands and flew toward the nearby wall. Instead of losing speed or sticking into the wall, they increased in velocity as they bounced off it. A single knife hit one of the monster corpses that Lance had piled on the floor. The other two flew wildly toward Icarus. The peregrine falcon flew to the side quickly, dodging the knives, but accidentally swallowing the eye it had previously held within its beak.

"Sorry about that," Lance, holding up his hands in an apologetic stance. He felt bad about doing it but also ecstatic at how cool his new cloak and knives worked with one another. He could already imagine the fear and confusion he'd force upon monsters as he entered the next Rift like the bloody reaper himself. "Let's see if you need repairing, alright?" He made his way over toward the startled Icarus and picked it up. He nearly dropped it when he did so.

[Do you wish to reforge this Item?]
[Yes] [No]

He let his fancy shadow cloak fall from his shoulders as he stared at Icarus and the notification that was hovering above him. None of it made any sense . . . until it finally did. It was as if all his experimentation earlier with the javelins and other upgradable items had prepared him for this moment. "This . . . this was the missing thing," Lance said as he carefully opened Icarus's mouth and confirmed that it had indeed swallowed the Rift-glider's eye. "The Item and the upgrades need to be combined first. They have to eat the flesh of the fallen!"

[Yes]

He noticed more black-shards get removed from his Inventory while Icarus trembled for a moment, as if feeling something happening to it. Although he had seen the notification and had accepted it, it was still baffling to see the timer appear above the bird's head. "This will change everything," Lance said as he heard Ash move toward him. *They all have three upgradable slots. That means that I can upgrade each companion with an appropriate Item. I still don't know if this is even a good thing. But if it is . . .*

His mind went numb at the dozens of potential outcomes, both good and bad. The process could simply not work, it could damage Icarus, or it could do exactly what he wanted it to do. If it proved to be good, it would mean that he'd need more black-shards. Like with the javelins, the first upgrade was ten black-shards, while the next one was a hundred and the third one a thousand. *If this works, I'm going to need a lot more black-shards. I'll never want to sell them again.*

Slowly, the seconds went by as Icarus continued to tremble, as if going through some change. It finally went limp in Lance's hands, as if unconscious. *Please don't break,* Lance pleaded with whatever force or deity that might hear him at that moment. Finally, the timer ran out and Icarus stirred again, slowly stretching its wings as it stared back at Lance not with a dull gray gaze but with bright blue eyes instead.

[Item upgraded]

"Ash, harvest as much as you can. Quickly!" Lance shouted with joy, kissing Icarus on the beak before making a mad dash toward the crates and plastic bags used for storing the harvested monster bits. And in that moment, he felt anything but tired as he began storing and retrieving monster parts in his Inventory before sealing them in plastic bags. He did so to get rid of any bits of gore or tissue that would've otherwise remained attached to the harvested parts.

The only thing on Lance's mind in that moment was the desire to gain more black-shards and the address of the black market that Iyas had texted him.

CHAPTER TWENTY-FOUR

Golden Goose

Later in the Afternoon
April, 14 AR
Inside the Little Market
Dublin, Ireland

BRIAN

The man fiddled with his empty Jägerbomb as if it might hold some answer to his problems. His fingers traced the rim of the glass out of pure boredom. Already he felt irritated that he had gone for the combination of alcohol and caffeine, rather than just doubling down on the alcohol. The last thing he wanted to be at this moment was drunk and alert. His Jägerbomb had seemed like an good idea twenty minutes ago, but now he just felt jittery and on edge. The bar was too loud, and the music was awful.

The man appeared to be in his early thirties, although the deep lines around his steel-blue eyes made him seem much older. He ran a greasy hand through his hair, pushing the matted brown curls away from his face. His stubble was thick and uneven. He clearly hadn't shaved in days, nor did he look inclined to do so. His clothes were dirty and wrinkled, as if he had been sleeping in them the entire week, and the stench of alcohol and his sweat permeated the surrounding air.

He tapped twice with his index finger when the bartender approached him, signaling that he wanted another drink. Although he had only been coming here for a few weeks, the bartender already knew his routine by heart. The man watched as the bartender grabbed a clean glass from under the counter and placed it in front of him before reaching for the bottle of whisky. *What a dump*, he thought, scanning his surroundings.

The bar was right in the middle of the small market. It was square in design, with many smaller shops lining its walls. The scent of spices, fish, fruits, and other perishables hung thick in the air. To him, it felt stifling, hot, and heavy. He took a sip of his drink and grimaced, feeling the cheap, watered-down alcohol burning his throat. The worst part was the fact that he needed a lot more to even numb himself properly. Subconsciously, he scratched his chest, feeling the hard, crystalline object there underneath his clothes.

"Brian, what about them?" a bald man asked as he approached him, his finger pointed at several newcomers to the market.

"Could you be less of a loud idiot about it? Or just scream it next time while waving a sign?" Brian replied with his thick Australian accent. He shook his head as he placed his drink down. "That or try throwing yourself down a—" He paused for a moment as he calmed himself. "Just get back to the shop." If he was being honest, he was venting his frustration a little. *Daft bloke. And who names their child Fergus? Why not a proper name like Bruce or Jack?*

The only reason he had him on his payroll was the fact that Fergus looked half grizzly bear, had a face that screamed "bully," and had survived a Rift. Fergus was barely stronger than an average human, seeing as he was too scared to go back into a Rift. Luckily, Brian didn't need him to be a strong Rifter, only look the part.

Brian measured each of the newcomers in his mind, judging whether they were simply there to buy some spices, fish, and other items, or if they were there for a different reason. Greenrock Market was a tiny place just at the edge of Dublin. Only locals really visited, and it wasn't popular at all. That fact made it the perfect temporary front for an underground black market. Nearly a third of the stalls there were owned by a Rifter or those in the business of procuring and selling Rift items. He himself owned a fish shop that was merely a front.

Like most underground markets Brian knew of, it would constantly change location. Sometimes it was in a matter of weeks, other times it took months. The authorities and the GRRO did their best to find places like this, but it was hard to discover contraband on someone if they could store items within their Inventory.

Brian ignored the buzzing of his phone, knowing full well it was one of the people who he owed money to. Even before he had survived his first Rift, he was in a lot of debt. Afterwards, that had increased exponentially due to his making several poor deals with dangerous individuals. Luckily for Brian, he possessed the ability to never see any flaw in his own actions.

He watched as the newcomers stopped at different shops or took a seat at the bar. He recognized a few of them from the previous week. *The same two Rifters from last time and that weird Swiss bloke who works for a private collector*, Brian mused as he got up and paid for his drinks. He was just about to call today a bust when he noticed a tall young man walking past several stalls before making his way over to the fish stall. That fact alone was curious, seeing as most of the produce on display was giving off such a pungent smell that no one in their right mind would ever want to buy something there.

Brian observed the young man discussing something with Fergus, who was staffing the stall. The hulking man looked confused, standing there behind the counter as this young man continued to ask questions, pointing at the fish behind the display cases. Brian almost felt sorry for Fergus, knowing full well that the man barely knew what a bloody fish finger was.

Brian noticed Fergus staring at him. The man's gaze was one of irritation and confusion. Brian was about to shake his head, giving Fergus the green light to chase the young man away. He stopped when he noticed something weird. In a blink of an eye, the young man suddenly had a smartphone in his hand. He had done it subtly, keeping his hand near his pocket when Fergus had looked away for a moment. Any other person would've assumed he had simply grabbed it from his pocket and not from some ethereal Inventory system. *A Rifter? He doesn't look the part*, Brian thought and then smiled before he finally signaled to Fergus to let the young man inside.

That phone alone would be worth thousands of pounds . . . at the very least.

A few minutes had passed since Fergus and Brian had let the young man inside the back of the shop. Compared to the open design of the stall in front, the back was fully closed off and had several sections, including a freezer and a small office. Besides Fergus, two of Brian's other associates were also there. They weren't Rifters, but they knew their way around the underground market and were local hires.

"So, Señor Rifter, what can I do you for today? I wouldn't recommend the fish, seeing as there are easier ways to kill yourself," Brian said as he stepped behind his desk and took a seat. Mentally, he was already conjuring up plans to liberate the young man's smartphone at a cheap price. *Hopefully, he is as green as he looks.*

"Monster parts for black-shards. Beyond that, information, and window shopping for now," the young man replied as he looked at the other people in the room.

Brian had trouble figuring out the young man's deal. Like so many others before him, he seemed uncomfortable at being there and surrounded by strangers. But he didn't seem scared. It was as if the social part was more troublesome for him. "Monster parts for shards? Do I look like the bloody GRRO? Why not exchange them there?"

"Because they'll ask questions when a large quantity is involved." The young man took a step forward as he grabbed the rucksack from his shoulder and retrieved two full plastic bags. He had filled one with monster claws, while the second contained bones and teeth. "And I have plenty more where that came from," the young man said, holding out his hands and producing several hides and even an eyeball or two before storing them again.

Brian was silent for a moment as he inspected the many bones and teeth. Each Item he touched with his fingers produced a notification, letting him know they were legit. "How many are you looking to sell?"

"Several 200-liter storage crates. Three crates filled with monster meat, one with hides and leather, two with bones, and one partially filled with unsorted organs," the Rifter explained as if he were simply reading a shopping list out loud. "I'll have twice that amount in a week or two."

"Twice that, huh? What crew are you running with?" Brian inquired. Everyone lied at the black market, but there was something off about this young man. He placed the bag of bones and teeth back before opening the second bag.

"If I wanted to answer questions, I'd have gone to the GRRO, remember?"

Brian chuckled at that as he grabbed the first claw and twirled it around his fingers. *Sharp little bugger, I'll give him that.* He checked each talon and claw to make sure they were authentic. He knew he could leverage a deal here to work as a middleman between this young man and the GRRO, taking a healthy cut for himself for little to no work. He'd just force Fergus and the others to sell it now and again. "And you just want black-shards? Cash could be easier."

"Just shards for now. But I'm interested in other things as well. Unstable black-shard powder, a trustworthy Smith who does private work outside of the GRRO, Guild-credentials, and contacts for other unofficial markets in Europe."

"Well, not only am I a great fixer, but I also have the Smith Class. Not sure about the trustworthy part." Brian said before he noticed something strange. "Where did you get this?" He pointed at the claw and locked eyes with the young man. Everything about Brian's demeanor suddenly changed, his tone now sharper and almost feverish.

"Like I said before. If I wanted to answer—"

"Kid, don't test me on this one," Brian said harshly. Picking up on it, his two associates stepped closer while Fergus took up a position near the door, making his colossal frame look even more intimidating.

"From inside a Rift."

"Don't lie to me!" Brian said as he threw the bags back toward the young man. The Rifter easily caught them. Brian then held up the claw he had been pointing at, letting the Rifter see the sliver of skin and muscle still attached to it. "This was pulled from a monster and not stored inside an Inventory. You can't take corpses from a Rift, only harvested items. How the hell did you get your hands on a monster outside of a Rift?" The young Rifter paled at that, as if he suddenly felt the rug being pulled out from underneath his feet. "You got this from a Rift outbreak. Which one of the seven did you get access to?"

"I'm done here," the young man said suddenly as he stuffed the Items into his rucksack. He was about to leave when he felt a hand on his shoulder—one of Brian's associates.

"Sit down or we'll make you," Fergus said as he walked away from the door and made his way over toward the Rifter. It was the sort of slow walk that bullies had perfected over the years. "Don't make me repeat myself."

That should do. Just count the people in the room, kid, Brian thought as he smiled, interested to see how the young man would react. They outnumbered him, and the Rifter didn't know how strong Fergus or the other two were. "How about we start over? You were about—"

The young man suddenly attacked, breaking Fergus' nose with a well-placed elbow. Before anyone could react, a bright, blinding blue light engulfed Fergus. Then chaos ensued as the two men on his flanks charged him, wielding brass knuckles and a knife.

Brian just sat there in confusion as this previously quiet Rifter suddenly changed into something fierce. The young man dodged several jabs and straights while countering twice. Just his punches alone were enough to shatter his opponent's ribcage. A knife then grazed his shoulder, only for the young man to duck underneath a second strike as he grabbed onto his attacker's wrist and shoulder. A moment later, there was a horrible popping sound as the young man dislocated his attacker's shoulder. *It's like the kid is playing with Legos.*

When the blinding light stopped, Fergus was back in the fight. "I'm going to f—" He stopped talking as the young Rifter suddenly threw his rucksack to the side, only for it to bounce off the wall with increased velocity and hit Fergus in the face. The impact distracted Fergus long enough for the young man to make his move. He threw a straight right against Fergus's chest, only to flinch when his fist struck the white-shard in his opponent's chest, hidden by clothes. "You're mine now!" Fergus roared as he rushed at the young man to tackle him to the ground.

But the young man ducked at the last second, using Fergus's own momentum against him. He grabbed hold of Fergus's arm and swiftly twisted, sending the larger man crashing down to the floor with a flip. The large man hit the ground with a loud crunch so hard that it shattered several tiles underneath him.

Not giving him a chance to recover, the young man quickly got up and started raining down blows on Fergus's prone form. The young man aimed for the liver, stomach, throat, and even Fergus's groin. At that point, it wasn't even a fight anymore. The young man was simply making sure that Fergus wouldn't get up soon. Afterwards, he pulled Fergus onto his knees before placing him in a chokehold from behind, cutting off his oxygen.

The large man desperately tried to free himself, but everyone in the room knew what the outcome would be as his face turned purple.

This is an experienced Rifter. He's had training and isn't hesitant about putting it to use,' Brian thought as he accessed his Inventory and materialized a large weapon in his hands. Although you could classify it as a shotgun, he had designed it to be wielded by Rifters, due to its sturdy nature and the large size of the slugs that it fired. He pumped it once as he pointed it at the young man. *Fergus might as well have been a sack of wet rice during the fight. Who is this kid?*

"Enough. You made your point, and you humiliated the brute there long enough. Here," Brian said as he opened his desk drawer and pulled out a small bag that contained several black-shards. He threw it at the Rifter's feet in a way that he hoped was nonthreatening. "This should cover any inconveniences my associates have caused you, and serve as a token of goodwill. You're free to sod off and come back when you've cooled off."

"And what's stopping you from shooting me in the back?" the young man asked as he held Fergus as a shield between the two of them.

"Nothing, but be reasonable, kid. Either I get a lucky hit and spend the rest of the afternoon cleaning up blood, or I miss, and have you go postal on my face like you did with him. And I like my teeth where they currently are," Brian said, wondering how this was going to play out. He lowered the weapon slightly, hoping it would be enough to calm the young man down. He wasn't even sure how effective it would be against the Rifter, seeing as he didn't know just how durable and fast his opponent was.

Fergus then lit up in another flash of blue light as the young man threw him forwards, nearly hitting Brian. During that, the Rifter grabbed the black-shards and his rucksack and rushed out of the room.

It took several minutes for the men to pick themselves up again. Brian shook his head as he looked at his hired muscle, hearing them groaning and moaning after the fight. A part of him was irritated at the young Rifter for having done all of this, but Brian knew they themselves were mostly to blame. *We pushed and expected to find a kitten. How were we supposed to know he'd have the temperament of a bloody honey badger?*

"You two, get yourselves checked out by a doctor," Brian said to his two wounded associates. The dislocated shoulder would no doubt hurt like hell. The ribs would take far longer to heal and prevent movement in the next few weeks. *I can't rely on those two anymore. It's better if I move on.*

"What're we going to do about him?" Fergus asked as he limped over to Brian's desk. Fergus was a mess of bruises and two of his fingers were sticking out at weird angles. His nose, however, already looked partially healed. "I might know a guy who—"

"No need for such a thing. Besides, I'd rather keep the kid as an asset," Brian said as he handed Fergus the claw he had kept on his desk. He made a mental note of Fergus's injuries. *Was the blue light a healing Skill?* he thought as a smile formed on his face. "He might be our golden goose. A violent maniac of a goose, but still one that vomits gold. If I could convince him to join me or learn how he can retrieve monster corpses from a walled-off outbreak, I could pay off my debts within a matter of months."

"How much debt do you even have?"

"Enough to buy a small island at this point, but that isn't the case. Private collectors will pay a fortune for intact monster limbs, let alone an entire corpse. I'll be rich," Brian stated, grinning all the while.

"You mean we'll be rich, right?"

"Naturally," Brian lied before he pointed at the door. "Try to follow the bloke, see where he'll go. We need to learn everything we can about him before we make our next move." He recalled what the young man had asked about, from underground contacts and Guild-credentials to off market powders. *Did he get the monsters from the outbreak in Paris? It's the closest one to Ireland, and it has been in the news a lot lately. Either way, he's an interesting enigma.*

As Brian stored his weapon inside his Inventory, he leaned back in his chair. His smile widened with excitement before it soured as his phone rang again to remind him that he still owed people a lot of money.

CHAPTER TWENTY-FIVE

Alcohol and Brotherly Love

Later in the Afternoon
April, 14 AR
Inside Lance's Hideout
Dublin, Ireland

LANCE

Lance cautiously peeked out the door as he tried to see if anyone had followed him back to the building he was renting. He scanned the street, looking for any sign of movement. It was empty, but that brought him little relief. The anticipation was getting to him, no matter how much he tried to persuade himself that he was in the clear. His heart was beating like a drum in his chest, each thump echoing his fears. He was sure that even Ash and the birds inside the building could hear it.

He had fled the black market after the fixer had pulled a strange gun on him. He had tried to remember where he had parked his van while constantly looking over his shoulder. Lance had walked for blocks, turning this way and that, until he eventually found the right street. He had felt like someone had been following him for a while, even thinking he saw someone dash around a corner at one point. When he finally reached his car, he felt a wave of relief wash over him. His hands were shaking when he fumbled for his keys, and he had half-expected someone to jump out and attack him. But when he got the car started, he breathed a deep sigh and drove away.

That relief had been short-lived, however, seeing as uncertainty was gnawing at him. Although he had taken care of those three goons, he didn't know how many there could be out there. Searching for him. And while he felt confident in his fighting abilities, he also knew just how one-sided a gunfight could be.

He could still feel the ache in his right hand from when he punched the man in the chest and hit the white-shard. The whole fight had been a blur, instinct taking over when Lance had felt pressured. He had brought down three people in a matter of seconds, including a Rifter. He had felt Thomas's anger and rage surging through him, feeling the need to protect a friend. It was based on previous memories of how Thomas had protected him in the past. Lance had been so focused on the fight, on winning, that he hadn't fully realized what he was doing.

He had always felt that he was above hurting people. He thought he wasn't a bad person. Not like the three Rifters he was trying to bring to justice. But it surprised him how little the fight had shaken him. He had broken ribs, dislodged someone's shoulder, and knocked people unconscious, but he hadn't hesitated. *I'm a good person, having to do bad things to fight bad people. But I'm still a good person*, Lance told himself, not knowing if he was reassuring himself at that moment or holding onto a facade. He fought and killed monsters, but that felt different compared to the fight he had just been in.

I messed up. I'm so stupid. Lance locked the door tightly, knowing full well he'd feel the urge to look outside again in a few moments. *Why didn't I double check my work? I had one job: store it inside the Inventory and retrieve it again to get rid of any evidence.* Lance remembered the way the man in the black market had pointed at the single monster claw.

The bit of skin and flesh still attached to the claw had been a dead giveaway that he had butchered the monster outside of a Rift. *That Rifter . . . that fixer took one look at that single claw and nearly figured me out. I'm not sure what he would've done if his mind hadn't gone toward an outbreak.* Lance swore to himself that he wouldn't make the same mistake again. He knew why it had happened, a combination of excitement, lack of sleep, and greed.

Ireland is over for me. Despite what that man said, there is no way I'd be able to trade at that black market now. It's better if I leave the country. Perhaps find a different market elsewhere, he thought before he turned his gaze to his side, seeing his companions all lined up and waiting for him. He had explained to Ash what had happened in the Little Market and the events that had led up to it.

Both Icarus and Ash were staring at Lance strangely, as if they could see something more than just his body. Their eyes were now a bright blue instead of the dull gray they had been before.

Upon returning home, he immediately given Ash two upgrades. One was a Rift-glider eyeball and the other a bit of Centaur-toad muscle. Visually, the Rift-glider's eyes had turned Ash's eyes blue, like what had happened to Icarus. The Centaur-toad's muscle hadn't changed Ash's appearance at all, or not that Lance could see. He figured most of the changes had happened internally. It was hard to see if Ash looked stronger or not when his baseline was that of Thomas's already powerful frame. He opened his status screen and observed his companions' increased stats and speculated on how it might improve their combat capabilities.

Retainers

Ash	1x	Human	<u>Rift-glider eye</u>	<u>Centaur-toad muscle</u>
			+2 Sight	+4 Speed
			+Heat vision	+100 Durability
Icarus	1x	Falcon (hybrid*)	<u>Rift-glider eye</u>	
			+2 Sight	
			+Heat vision	
Alpha	1x	Crow		
Bravo	1x	Crow		

It was hard to judge just how much more useful his two companions had grown, seeing as their stats didn't improve like a Rifter but instead like an Item. The most noticeable was Ash's increased durability. Just looking at Ash's stats, Lance could see that his companion could now sustain a hundred more points of damage to his durability before he'd break and no longer function. That meant that Ash could be out in the field longer without Lance having to worry as much each time Ash took a hit.

The four extra points in speed looked useful, but it was hard to judge that now. If it were anything like that of a Centaur-toad, it would increase Ash's speed and ability to evade. Lance figured he'd need to test it out extensively before he'd feel comfortable trusting his silent companion in the field.

The increased sight and heat vision for both Ash and Icarus were the most exciting. The extra few points in sight would help in ranged combat or in scouting. Still, with two crows and Icarus's already-good eyesight being what it was, Lance wondered if it would even make that much difference in the grand scheme of things. The heat vision was the true gem in all of this.

Although the Rift-gliders were very weak monsters, they had a knack for always being able to spot a Rifter. *I will need to test that when I have the time. If they truly can see heat signatures, it means that Icarus as an airborne hunter and scout will be even deadlier, and Ash will become even better at ambushing.* The thought of Ash going out at night to kill monsters while wearing his new armor and shadowy cloak was enough to calm Lance down temporarily.

The first upgrades for Ash and Icarus had cost ten back-shards each. Ash's second upgrade had been a hundred shards. *I only have a handful of shards left. Enough for minor repairs, nothing more,* Lance thought as he looked at Alpha and Bravo. He felt a pang of guilt for not being able to upgrade them. Still, for all the courage he was feeling in that moment, he also remembered the size of the gun that the fixer had pointed at him. Higher-Leveled Rifters might shrug off small caliber bullets, but Lance was far from that stage. He knew that an angry thug from the black market with a rifle and a lucky shot could easily end his life. *I need help.*

He then grabbed his phone and texted Mira and Iyas, asking them to meet up early that evening.

Three hours had passed since he texted Mira and Iyas. During that time, they met up in a pub for drinks and Lance came clean about what had happened to him in the black market, although he kept the part about the claw, as well as anything that might hint at his class as a Death Smith, to himself. What he said instead was that a greedy merchant had wanted to intimidate him, or worse. Both Mira and Iyas were silent throughout his story the first time through, but by the time Mira demanded Lance explain things for the third time in a row, Iyas was laughing nonstop.

"Admit it, you nearly wet yourself when you ran over here," Iyas said, as he threw another peanut in the air before deftly catching it in his mouth.

"I drove here."

"I hope you placed plastic sheets on the seat beforehand," Iyas said, as his grin widened even further. He was quite pleased with himself, balancing a peanut on his index finger as if to emphasize the point.

"Come on, Iyas, this isn't funny. And might I remind you of the fact that you were the one who gave Lance the address in the first place? Why would you even know such a thing?" Mira asked as she pulled the bowl of peanuts away from him, giving him a stern look.

"I . . . well, I know a guy who knew a guy. Wait . . . why am I on trial suddenly? He's the one who went on a rampage," Iyas said as he feigned innocence. "Besides, this will blow over in a few days. I think the whole idea of a black market is to remain hidden, not attack Rifters in public. And Lance gave them a proper scare, right? If not, imagine what three Rifters will do to them!"

Lance smiled at that as he finished his beer and cradled the empty glass in his hands. He found comfort in discussing the situation with them. Not only was it reassuring having two Rifters at his side, but discussing things with Iyas was particularly helpful. "I'll get us another round," Lance said as he left the table and headed back to the bar.

By the time he got back, Mira had partially covered Iyas in peanuts. Again, Lance noticed the chemistry between them and occasionally felt like the third wheel. He handed them their drinks just as Mira was explaining her desire to try some GRRO-sanctioned work to broaden her experiences. Iyas replied by saying that he was thinking about taking a holiday to Spain with family or at least some time off before jumping in his next Rift.

Lance tried to calm his nerves. He forced himself to trust in Iyas's words that people from the black market wouldn't be gunning for him, or at least not so publicly. He'd still leave the country as soon as he could, but now he'd do so knowing that these underground markets were all over the world and that Iyas might find the location of another one.

The plan for now was to pour a few drinks into Iyas and either learn how the man usually found them or try to get a contact from him who'd know. That would get the ball rolling again. Lance wouldn't mess up the next time. He was about to plan his "Iyas beer strategy" when Mira suddenly jumped up from her seat and pointed at one of the many bottles lined up on the wall behind the bar. "Guys! They have my favorite drink here. We should do shots!"

"The night is still young, how about—" Iyas started, only to be silenced by Mira's determined gaze.

"I yield," Lance said as he held up his hands, not wanting to test Mira's resolve.

"Shots it is! Besides, we still need to celebrate properly that we made it out of the last Rift in one piece," she said, while signaling for the bartender to make his way over to the table. "Besides, what's the harm in a few shots?"

An hour later, Lance stepped out into the alleyway from the bar's rear exit. He had told Mira and Iyas that he was going to empty his bladder. Truthfully, he had simply wanted some fresh air, seeing as he needed to decide when to leave Ireland. *Should I go in the morning or join a party and clear another Rift first?* He took a few steps further into the alleyway. Looking back, he could see a CCTV camera hanging above the bar's entrance. Beyond it there were a few empty bins and a decent amount of graffiti sprayed on nearby walls.

He knew he was safe there because Icarus was flying in the air above. He brought the bird out before he had first entered the bar and had instructed it to attack any threat when he gave the order.

Lance began to ponder the pros and cons of his decision. Leaving in the morning would be the safest option, but if he stayed, he'd be able to upgrade Alpha and Bravo with the possibility of giving Icarus a second upgrade. Giving Ash a third one would probably take Lance several Rifts, seeing as the cost of upgrading him further was up to 1,000 black-shards already.

Upgrading my companions would also boost my protection. But relying on them alone will expose my unique Class to people. Not that I myself even fully understand it. Even now those error notifications don't make any sense. He opened his phone and checked the time. He considered purchasing a plane ticket for tomorrow morning when he heard the bar door open behind him.

Iyas emerged with a handful of peanuts and an amused grin on his face. "Are you done watering the plants? Mira was getting worried about the state of your bladder."

"I think Mira is too busy with other things," Lance parried as he turned to face the Rifter, matching his grin. "Or other people."

"Ah. Well, she is a lovely lass, and who doesn't like a woman who is also a skilled shot?"

Lance nodded in agreement as he wondered if Iyas might have similar feelings for Mira. He then placed his smartphone back in his Inventory before he and Iyas started walking toward the door. "She'd probably punch us if she found out we were gossiping about her."

"She'd probably do worse. Speaking of women, who were you calling or texting?"

Feeling the need to come up with an excuse, Lance used the last email he had gotten from Oliver as cover. He figured it was better than to spoil the mood by telling him that he was thinking of skipping the country. "No girl. Just the little brother of a deceased friend of mine. The lad occasionally sends me music or weird Rift-related headlines. Sort of a personal fan and surrogate younger brother. He's a good lad," Lance said with a smile as he and Iyas neared the door.

"Ah, being a replacement brother is a tough job. Hell, just being a brother is a chore. Trust me, I have a sister," Iyas said as he threw another peanut in the air, catching it in his mouth again. "But you grew up with a brother, so at least you have some experience, right? You'll do fine—"

Lance halted abruptly, a perplexed look etched on his face. "Wait, I never mentioned having a brother, Iyas," Lance said, prompting Iyas to freeze as well. A small cascade of peanuts slipped through Iyas's fingers, and an uneasy silence settled between them. Then, without warning, the tall man vanished, only to reappear beside Lance in a swift motion, plunging a knife into his stomach.

"Well, I'll be damned. My sister wins again," Iyas muttered, his hand twisting the knife before swiftly pulling it from Lance's body. A sense of apprehension settled over him as he observed Lance fall to his knees, as if paralyzed. "She'll no doubt lord this victory over me, just like she always does. Twins and their relentless rivalry, am I right?"

"W . . . wh . . ."

"Don't bother speaking or moving. The poison I coated the blade with works quickly, even on Rifters," Iyas explained, squatting to look Lance in the eyes as he slowly pressed the tip of the knife against the young man's chest. Moments later, Iyas pressed it inwards, not stopping until he fully sheathed it in Lance's flesh. "I heard you had a fire in your eyes, but she omitted the fact that you have sharp ears as well. Still, we had fun with our little play while it lasted, right?" Iyas twisted the knife sadistically before he dragged it out. Then he stabbed Lance's left shoulder, which flared with more pain.

"You know, I was actually worried when you started asking me about the black market. I thought you had caught on," Iyas admitted, his tone surprisingly composed. He chuckled softly, though the amusement didn't quite reach his eyes. "Yet, here I stand, exposed due to a simple slip of the tongue. Ironic actually, seeing as compared to my sister, I'm the professional and level-headed one. The irony isn't lost on me. Trust me. Funny how things—" His voice trailed off as his attention snapped to the sound of the door swinging open behind him.

"Lance, Iyas? What is taking you guys so long?"

Lance's eyes went wide as he heard Mira's voice in the distance and the sound of her prosthetic leg on the pavement. He wanted to cry out, to warn her, but no words left his throat. Iyas's body was blocking his line of sight, but he knew she was getting closer.

No! Lance thought as he tried to fight the effects of the poison. He could feel it hinder him both physically and mentally. He tried accessing his Inventory to get Ash out to defend Mira but found that it was nearly impossible to keep his mind concentrated long enough to access the options. *Mira, run!* Lance screamed internally as he watched the amused expression on Iyas's face before the man vanished and appeared right next to her in a flash of movement and steel.

In the blink of an eye, Lance bore witness to the devastating sight of Mira's collapse beside him, her hands desperately clasping her slit throat, crimson streams slipping through her fingers as her life ebbed away. The mixture of pain and confusion etched onto her face tore at Lance's very core, nearly undoing him. Utter powerlessness gripped him, rendering him impotent to offer any aid, to alleviate her suffering, or even tend to his own. He tried retrieving Ash again but failed. He tried signaling Icarus in the sky but lacked the voice to call out for him. *I'm going to die here!*

"Look what you made me do, Lance," Iyas said as he squatted in front of him, the gleaming blade stained with crimson held aloft. The grin on Iyas's face was the same one he had shown Lance when they had been laughing and drinking together. However, now that smile sent a chill coursing through Lance's veins, unraveling any remnants of affection he had once harbored for the man and replacing it with a vile sickness.

"W . . . why . . ." Lance finally managed to whisper past his throat as he watched Iyas toy with the knife.

"Simple." The tall man paused for obvious dramatic effect as he placed a finger underneath Lance's chin, forcing him to look the assassin in the eyes. "Because Kira asked me to."

CHAPTER TWENTY-SIX

Rage of the Departed

Mere Seconds Later
April, 14 AR
Outside of the Pub
Dublin, Ireland

LANCE

A few seconds later, Iyas leaned closer to Mira to confirm that she was dead. His voice was strangely soft, like a lover's whisper. "Sleeping beauty?" His fingers delicately swept a stray lock of hair aside, revealing her lifeless features.

Mira's eyes were open, staring sightlessly at Lance. Her pale flesh was a stark contrast to the pool of scarlet that surrounded her. Lance could see the mixture of terror and confusion still lingering in her lifeless gaze. It was as if that moment had become frozen in her eyes forever. A deep rage roared inside of Lance, demanding that he act. He tried to struggle and fight off the poison, but it only resulted in him rolling over to his side in agony.

Iyas shook his head. "You know, I never wanted this for her. The poor girl had been through so much already. But sadly, business comes first."

"P . . . ay . . . ," Lance forced the broken words past his lips, ignoring the pain he was in as he locked eyes with Iyas. He knew it was futile, but he refused to die without offering resistance. Iyas only chuckled in response, the sound cold and heartless.

"Yes, yes, very tough and scary," Iyas said as he knelt closer to Lance, a relaxed expression on his face, as if they had been childhood friends. "Now, despite what you might think of me, I'm not the villain here. Our young friend here died quickly, and I would've offered you the same fate had it not been for the contract dangling over your preciously confused head." Iyas then produced a smartphone out of thin air and pointed it at Lance's wounded frame before sinking the knife back into his torso. After that, he took the time to snap a picture. "I'd say 'cheese,' but at the rate we're going with our steel friend, you look similar to Swiss cheese yourself right now."

Lance struggled to access his Inventory system or even his Skills. He had fought monsters before and had gotten hurt plenty of times, but there was something crippling about getting stabbed. The feeling of steel ripping apart flesh as it bit deeper and deeper. And the poison on the blade made things even harder for him. It was as if the pain and mental fatigue prevented complex thoughts or movements. *Is the poison designed to subdue Rifters?* Lance thought as he forced himself to focus on details rather than the torture he was enduring.

"But we're done with the worst part of the contract. Kira wanted proof of the kill, and she likes her victims to have tasted fear. Don't ask me why, but it's her thing. And the last thing me and my sister want is to do something that might make Kira angry. So, while my sister is off completing her contract in France, I'm going to complete this one," Iyas said as he stored the phone in his Inventory again and pulled the knife out of Lance's torso. "I feel sorry for you since you were just in the wrong place at the wrong time. Perhaps you were born under a bad sign. You could've picked any Rift, but you had to choose the Rift Kira was using to broker a deal between a powerful guild and herself."

He paused for a moment, as if contemplating something. "How about I show you something cool before we end this? Think of it as learning a trade secret."

Lance watched a grin spread across Iyas's face, leaving him feeling utterly powerless as the man moved toward Mira's body. His inability to move forced him to watch as Iyas sank the blade into Mira's chest and carefully cut into her. The tall man slowly unearthed the white-shard from her corpse in a horrible display of precision and gore. Lance forced himself to look at Iyas's hands as he desecrated Mira's body. *He's done this before. He knows exactly what he's doing.*

"Now, in my honest opinion, the best part about being an assassin is when you have the chance to take down a Rifter. Or in my current situation, two. You see . . . killing a Rifter is different from killing a monster." Iyas pulled out the white-shard and held it out in front of Lance, letting him see the bits of Mira that were still attached to it. Both men could see a piece of the white-shard fragment into a Skill-shard.

'What the hell is this?' Lance thought as his face paled from both blood loss and shock.

"There is the expression I was hoping for," Iyas said as he placed Mira's white-shard on the ground and placed the Skill-shard on top of it, just out of Lance's reach. It was as if the assassin was building a grotesque tower. "There is a reason Rift-guardians give way more experience and have a higher chance of spawning a Skill-shard compared to normal monsters. The secret is in the amount of energy or radiation that their shards contain," Iyas explained with a warm and almost eager expression.

"A white-shard contains even more energy, especially if the Rifter died with a full Inventory." He smiled as he pointed at the shards. "That means a lot of Experience and an even higher chance of getting a Skill-shard. Efficient, right? Now, with any luck, I will have inherited Mira's lovely 'Item explosion' Skill." The tall assassin then flashed Lance an amused expression. "So smitten with me . . . She would've wanted me to have it, right?"

"P . . . ay . . ." Lance tried to force the word past his lips as he stared at Iyas. *I'm going to make him pay for this!* He felt the rage inside of him explode as more of Thomas's memories flared inside him, as if his dead friend were equally outraged at what he was witnessing. Beyond that, there was also a soaring, unfiltered, animalistic urge to retaliate and fight off this predator.

"I know. You'll make me pay. But I've got to be honest here. You're not really instilling me with fear right now. Amusement, yes. But not fear." The assassin then sighed as he got up and looked around him, checking to see if there were any witnesses. "I usually hate finishing a mark inside a city. Too many potential witnesses and surveillance cameras," he said as he pointed at the camera installed above the door that the two of them had used to get out of the bar.

"Still, it could've been worse. With you jumping in and out of Rifts, you nearly forced me to use bait. But then I'd feel the burden of choice, right? Would I have picked the White Clovers? Your number one fan, Oliver? His older sister with that alluring smile? Their mentally compromised mother or their crippled veteran of a father?" Iyas asked before he leaned forward, watching Lance's face go through a dozen of emotions at the same time. "I wonder which one of them would've made you run toward me the fastest?"

Whatever was left of Thomas's mind and memories that now lingered inside of Lance lit up in a fury akin to something that could only described as a primal rage. It dwarfed anything Lance was feeling. It fused with his own anger, becoming one. That intense hatred suppressed his own pain and mental fatigue as it burned through him. He tasted blood in his mouth as his mind cleared up in a blazing inferno of outrage and a demand for retribution.

Mend Wounds
[You have used Mend Wounds Lvl 2 at the cost of 15 Mana]
[Current Mana 306/325]

Although the Skill blinded him, it also lessened the effect of the poison that was coursing through his body. He flailed all his limbs toward Iyas until he felt one of them connect.

Mend Wounds

Lance rolled away from the blinded and illuminated Iyas as quickly as he could, hearing a steel blade slam into the spot where he had been bleeding out previously. *Now! You only have a few seconds!* Lance internally screamed at himself as he slid backwards, feeling the wounds on his body open again and get worse by the second. As his vision returned to him, he noticed Iyas calmly make his way over to him. The man appeared to be amused by Lance's resistance. He felt his body struggling to even move, but his mind remained focused on just one thing before he passed out.

[You have combined and retrieved Items]

As Lance fell backwards, he noticed Iyas stop in his tracks as a strange figure suddenly appeared between them. The figure wore black steel and dark leather. The black cloak hid most of the man's features in a dance of shadows and mist.

"Who the hell are you?" Iyas asked as he took up a defensive stance. The newcomer stood at the ready, armed with a broken shield and a steel axe. The man's blue eyes took in the sight around him as he tried to make sense of the situation.

Lance felt the pain and mental fatigue returning as the healing effect of his Skill wore off completely. He had just enough energy left to point at the assassin and utter a single word before his world turned to darkness.

"Kira . . ."

Lance could hear fighting going on around him, steel hitting steel or even flesh. He felt himself drifting in and out of consciousness, hearing snippets of words and seeing brief flashes of light. At one point, he thought he saw a figure looming over him, holding a knife, but then it was gone. His wounds woke him up again, stinging his body before fatigue and blood loss nearly forced him to pass out again. Still, the rage that burned inside of him forced him to stay awake this time and get his revenge.

Mend Wounds

As he clutched the wounds on his chest to staunch the bleeding, the pain and fatigue eased slightly. Once the healing light had faded, he could see properly again. Signs of combat surrounded him, from a cracked wall that showed signs that it had met something heavy at a frightening speed, as well as spots on the ground that appeared as if something hot had scorched it. Beyond that, there were places where it looked like metal had scratched apart bits of masonry. There was even a spear embedded in a nearby dumpster.

Lance noticed Ash and Iyas circling each other. Both bore injuries from their duel thus far. They could've been at it for mere minutes or an hour. Lance couldn't tell. The assassin was a mess of minor cuts and bruises, while Ash's armor contained numerous puncture holes, and the left side of his body looked as if fire had engulfed him at one point.

While the assassin was still wielding his blade, Ash was using just his shield in his left hand and striking and grappling with his right. The two of them rushed at each other again. Iyas was skilled with a knife, but Ash had a strong defense and dodged most of Iyas's strikes or blocked them with his shield. The assassin was relentless in his attacks, seeking to find an opening in Ash's defenses, but the pale warrior was just as determined to not let that happen.

Each hit that landed on Ash seemed to irritate the assassin further, as if he were taking great offense at the fact that his poisoned knife wasn't working on the newcomer. This was even worse when Iyas vanished from sight, only to have Ash still track him with his bright blue eyes. *I made the right call in upgrading his speed and giving him heat vision. He wouldn't have lasted as long otherwise.* Lance found himself struggling with his thoughts in his suppressed state.

One moment, Iyas would attack with quick flurries of strikes, switching stances rapidly and making feints with his knife, while the next he would switch the knife to his other hand to strike lefthanded, or suddenly use a fireball Skill. Lance could see how Iyas was slowly overwhelming Ash's defenses with quick attacks. Eventually, the assassin cut apart the tendons in his right leg in an orchestra of violence and precise cuts, severely limiting Ash's speed and fighting potential. Most people would've screamed at the painful and crippling injury. Ash simply registered it while he kept his guard up.

This is bad, Lance thought as he noticed that the balance of power had shifted. Ash's protective gear seemed to counter Iyas's speed, and Ash could take a surprising amount of punishment, but he was still outclassed. Iyas held the advantage with his Level as a Rifter and his combat experience. Even Lance wasn't sure if he'd be able to win against the assassin in a fair fight. *He's weaker than Dieter and Daniel, but stronger than me. I need to do something, fast.*

Lance searched around desperately, trying to find some way to turn the tide. Icarus was still in the air and could no doubt help, but a Rifter of Iyas's Level would shred Icarus apart in a second. *I need a distraction.* Just then, Lance spotted Mira's shard and the Skill-shard on top of it. *There.*

[You have retrieved an Item]

Alpha suddenly materialized near Lance's bloody hands, only for it to fly immediately upwards, as Lance had taught it. "Protect Ash," he groaned as he felt the sting of his wound lead him back to the point of passing out. He activated his healing Skill again as he burned through his Mana, forcing himself to crawl toward Mira's body. He could hear combat all around him, and occasionally feel the sting of heat and debris as one of Iyas's Skills nearly swept him up. When Lance's healing Skill had worn off, he spotted Ash countering Iyas's attack with a perfectly executed counter to his throat. It clearly disoriented the assassin, but the man remained focused enough to send Ash flying backwards with a powerful kick.

Iyas rushed toward Ash to finish him but was stunned when an avian adversary suddenly attacked him by scratching his face. The distraction lasted a second before Iyas cut the bird apart in a single attack. "Enough with these games. Both of you will die and I'll enjoy ripping the shards from your chests!" Iyas said venomously. Ash ignored the man's words as he got back up again, holding the damaged steel shield at the ready. Ash was obviously in a bad state, but the determination in his eyes said otherwise.

"Those . . . are big words . . . coming from someone . . . who is barely . . . holding on," Lance said as he forced more healing light and energy to envelop his body. He got back up, gritting his teeth as he felt the wound open again, but it was a price he had to pay. "Iyas, has no one ever told you the tale of Icarus?" He noticed Ash changing his stance when he spoke those words. Lance knew his companion grasped that something was about to happen.

Then, with a bloody smile, Lance held his right hand near his chest and opened it up slowly. He showed Iyas the Skill-shard that was now held between his fingertips before he slammed it against his chest. It connected loudly with his whiteshard. The Skill-shard glowed intensely, disintegrating as Lance's white-shard absorbed it all, storing all the energy. Lance didn't have time to check the effects of the new Skill, nor did he have the time to see just how much it would cost him. He had to act.

[You have retrieved an Item]
Detonate
Ricochet

Lance watched as Bravo materialized in his hands. The bird's gray-shard started glowing and giving off light. He threw the bird as fast as he could while Bravo did its best to increase the speed further. Bravo hit the ground just in front of Iyas. The Ricochet Skill activated when the bird slammed into the pavement. The Skill forced the bird to bounce upwards even faster as it bypassed Iyas's guard. Bravo then slammed into Iyas's chest while it detonated.

The power of the explosion threw Iyas backwards as if a small grenade had gone off right in front of him. The sheer violence of the detonation tore most of the man's clothes to shreds and damaged the skin and muscles around his arms and chest.

"Ash!" Lance screamed as he watched his companion rush forwards, unbothered by the strain he was putting on his mangled leg. Ash rammed the sharp edge of the shield into Iyas's right leg with every ounce of power he had. The impact forced the dazed, wounded Iyas to his knees before Ash grabbed Iyas's hair and left arm, struggling to hold the assassin in place.

"Icarus!"

Lance roared as he pointed at Iyas, giving the command for the Peregrine falcon to attack. In unison, Ash pulled with all his might, forcing the dazed and secured Iyas to bend backwards and look upwards. "Now!"

The last thing Iyas saw was the gray falcon dive-bombing him at a speed that only the fastest bird in the world could achieve. It hit Iyas head-on with its small beak, delivering every bit of kinetic energy it could produce. The end-result was Thomas's rage made manifest as Icarus and Iyas became undone. The peregrine falcon's indestructible gray-shard carved a deep, deadly path through the body of the assassin due to sheer momentum.

Lance collapsed shortly afterwards, seeing Ash grab the broken shield and sheath it into Iyas's body repeatedly, still determined to end the fight even though there was none left to have. And as Lance lost consciousness, he and the city of Dublin could hear Ash's demonic victory roaring through the night.

CHAPTER TWENTY-SEVEN

Holding a Grudge

Mere Seconds Later
April, 14 AR
Outside of the Pub
Dublin, Ireland

LANCE

Lance . . . wake up . . ."

Lance could hear someone call out for him, easing him out of his slumber despite his protesting body. He opened his eyes and noticed a familiar face looking back at him. "Thomas?" He could hardly believe it but his best friend staring back at him. His familiar bright blue eyes meeting his own. He smiled for a moment, before he became conscious enough to shatter his happiness. The man above him was too pale, his eyes too strange a blue, and his face absent the teasing smile that was Thomas's trademark. "What happened?"

"Bleeding . . ." Ash said, his voice unnaturally deep and as demonic as ever. He brought his gauntleted hand toward Lance's body, pointing at the makeshift bandages and tourniquets that were in place. From what Lance could see, Ash had made them from pieces of torn clothing. Blood seeped through the fabric, staining everything crimson.

Mend Wounds

"You did good," Lance said as the healing light did its work for a moment, stemming the flow of blood as he went over his injuries again. His medical training kicked in as he adjusted the bandages to the best of his ability. *I would've bled out already if it weren't for him*, Lance thought as he waited for his vision to return.

He remembered flashes of him going in and out of consciousness, giving Ash instructions as best as he could. *Grab their shards . . . grab Iyas's body . . . and take me to the Little Market. He did all of that?*

When his vision returned, he realized he was in the passenger seat of his van. Ash had his hands on the steering wheel. The windscreen bore cracks in it, and the front of the van showed damage. Smoke was coming out from under the hood. The cheap GPS device inside the van indicated that they had arrived at their destination. *Ash must've used the coordinates that I used last time.*

Looking past the cracked windscreen, Lance could see the entrance of the Little Market from where he was sitting. "Help me out of the car," he asked. In response, Ash forced open the driver door before making his way around to his side.

Lance then looked behind him and spotted Iyas's partially destroyed corpse, which Ash had dumped in the back. The assassin was barely recognizable in his current state. Lance shifted in his seat for a moment as he reached backwards to touch a part of Iyas's skin.

[You have stored an Item in your Inventory]

A moment later, Iyas's body was gone. His discarded clothes were the only bloody hint that the man had been there. Lance hated the fact that he had gotten a new Item notification. *Just deal with it. I'll live longer if no one ever finds his body*, Lance thought as he carefully emerged from the van, with Ash's help. The bit of movement was enough to open his wounds further, forcing him to activate his Skill once more and blind him temporarily.

"The shards?" Lance asked as he held out his hand. He felt a wave of disgust as the weight of a hard object suddenly appeared in his hand. It was only a few grams, but to Lance, it felt indescribably heavy. *I'm sorry that this happened to you, Mira. I'm sorry that everyone that gravitates toward me ends up dead.* Moments later, he felt the shards of Alpha, Bravo, and Icarus join Mira's. It reminded him once more of the price that they had paid for him to live.

[You have stored several Items in your Inventory]

He steeled himself as he ignored the notification. Instead, Lance shifted his gaze toward his status update, showing that he had gained several Levels. He was now Level Thirty-Two and had several unspent Attribute points on his hands. *So much experience from killing a single Rifter?* Lance thought as he forced all the excess points into his Wisdom stat, knowing that increasing the rate of his Mana regeneration could be the difference between life and death. Spending it on Endurance tempted him for a moment, but he knew that the increase would be useless for already sustained injuries.

[Wisdom:] [48] (+6)
Mend Wounds

Again, Lance lit up in blue light as he pointed at the entrance of the Little Market. "Ash, put on your helmet and help me inside of the fish store." Lance was hesitant to go further, remembering clearly how it had gone the last time. But he had little choice. He was bleeding out but couldn't risk going to a hospital or the GRRO. If he did, then Kira could find out and send more assassins after him, or after those close to him.

Lance groaned as he made his way past the dirty fish stall and into the store behind it. He watched Ash slam apart the lock with the steel shield that had belonged to Thomas. He felt more blood pour down his side but ignored it for now. Upon opening the door, he spotted the two startled Rifters he had encountered before. *That fixer . . . That drunk is in charge. The other is just the muscle,* Lance thought as he forced himself to stand up straighter and move toward them, ignoring the fact that his bloody footprints were singing tales of the unknown.

"Listen, kid, I told you we should cool off, right? And from the looks of things, you look anything but cooled off," the fixer said hastily. No doubt the man intuitively knew that something was wrong here. From the many filled crates in the room, it was clear to see that he was busy packing up, no doubt intent on setting up shop elsewhere. "Look, how about we talk—" He halted as he noticed the newcomer stepping in behind Lance.

If Lance's roughed-up and bloody visage was enough to unnerve the fixer, then Ash's appearance was enough to terrify him to his core. Wrapped in shadow and covered in fresh blood, Ash stepped forwards like death itself, wielding a dripping, red axe and a shield. There was too much blood on Ash. Too much for someone not to realize that Ash had just killed someone up close. "Kid . . . please. I've got children . . . I mean . . . I don't know for sure . . . but I might have them . . . I—" He stopped as Ash slowly slid the desk to the side, removing the last obstacle between them.

"Get out of the chair," Lance said as he flared up in a blue light. It temporarily blinded him as his wounds tried their best to close on their own. When it faded, he noticed that the fixer had jumped out of the chair and had rushed to the bulky Rifter he had hired to be his muscle. Lance let Ash help him in the chair as he sank down, suddenly feeling just how tired and injured he was.

"Kid, if you wanted to settle a score . . . you've succeeded. I'm freaking out here and I doubt I can ever get these stains out of my pants again. Please . . . don't kill me. If you want blood, take Fergus's over here. He's the true mastermind behind all of it. I'm just—" He stopped talking when Ash slammed the axe against his shield, silencing the room in an instant.

"A deal . . . I'm here to offer you a deal," Lance said as he forced the words past his lips. The blood loss, the pain and the lingering poison in his system were draining what little energy he had left. He again lit up in a blue light as a bit of color returned to his cheeks. "I need . . . multiple forged IDs and Guild-credentials . . . off-market gear . . . transportation . . . black-shards . . . and immediate . . . medical help and Mana crystals."

The fixer, to his credit, calmed down, once his shrewd mind had begun to understand that the options of diplomacy and manipulation were back on the table. "Call me Brian," he said as he took a step away from his scared companion, as if to distance himself from those emotions. "I can get you all of that, no problem. But a deal has two parties, so what am I getting out of this, kid?" Brian asked with a smile, as if he could smell an opportunity. That smile vanished when Ash took a single step forward in an orchestra of intimidation, blood, and ethereal shadows. "I mean, besides your demonic friend there not ripping me apart?"

"I don't . . . have access to . . . outbreak sites," Lance said as he clutched his side again, feeling the blood pour out. He focused his thoughts and activated his healing Skill again, halting the life-threatening injuries for the moment as the blue light wrapped around him. His wounded state and the constant flash of light reminded him of that fateful day when Thomas had bled out in his arms. It was almost poetic that a knife had caused his injuries as well.

"I've something got better . . ." He forced himself to stand up to his full height. Both mentally and physically he towered over the others in the room at that moment as he held out his right hand to his side. "I have this." Suddenly, three intact monster corpses materialized underneath his hand, stacking on top of one another. Both Fergus and Brian nearly fell over backwards, their faces twisted in a mixture of awe, fear, confusion, and greed.

"Deal," Brian said suddenly before he kicked his companion in the shin. "Fergus, on your feet! Fetch the doc."

"You mean the veterinarian?" Fergus asked as if confused, while Brian pushed him toward the door.

"Stop talking. Just get her. Drag her out of her house if you need to. You have five minutes," Brian hissed as he slammed the door shut behind Fergus and composed himself again.

"Trust me, she is brilliant. She has done a lot of work for me in the past," Brian explained as he rushed over toward several crates and withdrew several Items. Most of them contained a mana crystal with some charge. He carefully began handing a few of them to Lance. "Just drain all the Mana out of them. The doc will be here soon. She's a brilliant doctor, really. Works wonders with dogs and horses. I mean, how different can they be from humans, right?"

Lance ignored the man as he depleted the Mana from the first Item and basked in another wave of blue light that struggled to stem the bleeding. "Ash, kill him if he tries anything," Lance said, closing his eyes as he drained the Mana from another Item. He ignored Brian's obvious pleading, knowing the weasel would try anything to stay alive. Still, he needed a sly animal like that now.

Ash took up a protective stance near Lance, placing the broken shield next to his chair. Ash inspected each Mana-filled item that Brian dug up from his many storage containers before he handed them to Lance, taking his role seriously.

Lance tried to ignore the pain he was feeling as he opened his eyes and accessed his Inventory. He felt the embers of Thomas's fury at seeing Iyas' mutilated corpse stored within. He hated having it there but knew it would be better than the authorities finding Iyas's body and linking it to him. Or worse, Kira finding out about the body and figuring out that her target was still alive.

Next to the icon of Iyas's body was a single white-shard. Having it there disgusted Lance. He wanted to mourn Mira properly. To weep at the knowledge that this monster of a man had cut her life so short and that he had left her body behind in that alley. *At least her family will have a body to bury,* Lance thought, hating himself for not being able to shed a single tear. *It's more than what Thomas's family had.*

Knowing his own personality and the weight these topics had on his conscience, he forced himself to close the Inventory. Then he stared at the television to distract himself for a while. "Ash," he asked his companion as he pointed at the remote control on the table. *Is that the thing Oliver mailed me about?* Lance thought as he watched a press summary about what was going on in Paris.

Ash increased the volume, so he could better hear the French president and a general going on about retaking Paris. They spoke of the hundreds of brave Rifters who had already pledged themselves to fight alongside the army, and a great experimental weapon that was going to destroy the Rift itself. *What the hell is going on in the world? Closing an outbreak? Is that even possible?*

"The doc should be here any minute. She'll patch you up nicely. Might even stitch a smiley face if you want her to," Brian said nervously as he handed Ash another item, eyeing the bloody, armored man like one would a feral wolf. "Any preference for pain medication? I have the good stuff . . . morphine, pills, brandy, whiskey, you name it. Even some weird stuff from Egypt that I can't pronounce."

"Nothing . . . just get me the doctor," Lance said as he checked on his wrapped-up chest and stomach. Then he lit up like a blue beacon again. By the time his vision returned to him he could see a list of names being presented on the screen, showing the world the many guilds and Rifters that had pledged themselves to the liberation of Paris.

"Not even a sip of Bundaberg Rum? I cracked open a crate an hour ago. I also have a few local beers lying around, but honestly, I'd prefer your scary friend elbow me in the family jewels a few times rather than drink that swill," Brian said as he pointed at a large crate containing a surprising amount of alcohol. "I might even have—"

"Stop talking," Lance said suddenly as he leaned forward, ignoring his protesting body. Watching the screen, his eyes went wide. The list of names was still going on, revealing the Rifters' nationalities, guild affiliations and, for some, even their world ranking, if they were particularly strong and skilled. Most people would look at that list with awe, but Lance only had eyes for one person on that list. "Louis Vidal."

"What? What's wrong?" Brian asked, taking a step backwards as he saw the sharpness in Lance's eyes and the way his armored friend reacted to the name.

Lance felt his anger reigniting as he remembered the way Louis, Connor, and Kira had left him and Thomas to die in a Rift. Ever since that day, his life had gone off the rails. Now people close to him were getting targeted just for being near him. *Iyas mentioned his sister was going to clean up loose ends in France. Could Louis be her target?* Lance flared up in a blue light to halt the flow of blood again as he grabbed Thomas's broken shield. Iyas's blood still covered it, but Lance paid no attention to it.

"I'm going to need one more thing from you." Lance threw the broken shield at Brian, who was obviously freaking out because of everything that was going on.

"What do you want me to do?" Brian asked nervously. "I mean, I'm built like a Greek god, but I'm no fighter."

"I want you to take that shield and turn it into a weapon that can take down monsters," Lance said. He had endured much since Thomas had died. His body was a testament to that. He had suffered broken bones, claw and bite wounds, and now he had even been stabbed. All that to get justice for his friend. To see Thomas's killers confess what they had done. But right now, having just barely survived an assassination attempt and seeing Louis's name displayed as a noble hero broke something inside of him. Relying on justice and good intentions wouldn't work, not with people who were more than willing to lie, hide, or kill to escape it.

His problems had only gotten more numerous and problematic since he had started on this path. There had been three of them at first, before Kira had invited Iyas and his sister. *This needs to happen. Overwhelming force is the only thing that will subdue these people . . . these monsters. Before anyone else gets killed because of them,* he thought as he shifted his gaze back toward Brian. "I want it strong enough to take down monsters . . . four of them."

"Sure, kid, whatever you need," Brian said as he held onto the bloody, broken shield. The man didn't yet fully grasp the sheer weight that he was carrying in his hands beyond the metal. He took a few uncertain steps away from Lance and the armored warrior. Moments later, Brian opened the door to let Fergus and a confused woman into the shop.

I promise that I'll keep your family safe, Thomas. Even from me, Lance thought as he leaned back in his chair and closed his eyes, letting the blue light stem the bleeding again. Mentally, he closed himself off from the world around him, from the people in the room, the hands on his body and the pain of his injuries. He found solace in that place, away from the material world, where he could just be by himself, with the faint whispers of Thomas's memories occasionally seeping in.

Paris. Lance uttered the word in his mind, as he could feel the importance of the word and that place. He knew his path would lead him there, as if drawn to it. "Paris," he said aloud as he breathed life and meaning to it in the material world. Unbeknownst to Lance, there were other souls in various locations who felt the same pull to that city.

The broken twin . . . the guilt-ridden soldier . . . the cloaked, golden-eyed stranger. Everyone felt the threads of fate leading them there.

[Two items can be forged. Templates available: 1]
[Required black-shards: 100 x2. Do you wish to proceed?]
[Yes] [No]

Catherina's Smithing Handbook

Smithing handbook #3.
Written by Catherina Melero.

And welcome back to part three!

In part one, we discussed the Smith Class itself, and the Skills usually associated with it. In part two, we took an in-depth look into the licencing side of things and GRRO contracts. Boring, I know. But we had to get it out of the way. In part three, four, and five, we are going to go over the tips, pointers, and outright sneaky tactics to exploit the crafting system as much as we can. And remember, it isn't cheating if it will save someone's life.

Tip #1—Producing in bulk.
Depending on the Skill level of a Rifter, they can produce items one at a time or a bunch of them at once. The latter is obviously more useful, but it is still ineffective when having to deal with an order to produce hundreds of arrows. No matter if someone can produce one or five at a time, a big order still takes a boatload of time.

The trick here is to make them in bulk by abusing the system. For this to work, we can create a template where multiple arrows are all connected to each other with a thin strip of metal. A strip that a Crafter can snap in half afterwards and grind down the edges to create the finished product. It's easier to grind down a hundred arrows than to spend all that time waiting for five arrows to get produced through normal Skill use.

Tip #2—Double time.
It surprised me to learn just how few Rifters with a Crafting skill know about this one. When someone levels up their Smithing or Crafting skill and can create two

or more items at the same time, they should try to use the Skill on something they are currently crafting. They'll find out that they will speed up the process quite a bit. It is still less effective compared to creating two items at once, but it can work wonders in a pinch. Sometimes speed wins over quantity.

Tip #3—Upgrades people!

We've got to choose our upgrades carefully, and at the same time we don't. No? Not clear enough? Alright. So, after a few Skill levels in Smithing or Crafting, a Rifter can fill a few slots on a piece of equipment. There are ludicrous numbers of rare metals, gems, and other materials to use in these slots. It makes little sense to spend these rare materials on a dagger or gauntlet that isn't something that we'll use ten levels from now. Save them for high-tier equipment to boost it even further.

But at the same time, don't shy away from upgrading weaker or normal weaponry and equipment with basic materials. Giving an iron breastplate three additional upgrades of iron will not bankrupt a person. But it can prove the difference between life and death for Rifters that are just starting out. We can always swap these upgrades out later for better materials. Just remember, replacing an upgrade with another will destroy the old one. So be careful about upgrading rare/expensive stuff!

Tip #4—Saving on Templates.

When first starting out, most Rifters that have gained a Smithing or Crafting Class will start out with just one template. A Rifter that just picked up a Smithing or Crafting skill will start out with zero templates. Ouch!

And they'll soon find out that creating templates by destroying items is an awfully expensive path. I've seen so many of them take out loans in the beginning just to get a few templates on their hands. And the downside is, they will limit their templates based on the items they can afford to destroy.

Suggestion? Wood, clay, cardboard, plastic, Styrofoam, paper, etc. If a Rifter is careful and lucky enough, they can find a Rift where there is still an abundance of materials like these lying around. Most Rifters don't loot this type of garbage, but for us it can be gold.

Bring it home, mould it, carve it, melt it, hammer it, cut it, pray to it. Just get it into the shape of an item that looks right and then destroy it by using the Skill. Do it often enough and a Rifter might get a template that looks exactly like it. And then, forge it with actual metals and fabrics this time. This obviously works better for armour and equipment, seeing as most weapons would need a sharp edge. Still, a Rifter could always get it close to sharp and afterwards just sharpen it by hand.

Tip #5—Recycle the rubbish.

Let's be honest. Most of the items that a Rifter loots from a sentient monster are god-awful. It just is. A rusty dagger? Trash! A half-dented breastplate that wouldn't even fit a child or bent arrows that were made from bones. Yuck!

A Rifter could sell these things, although I still can't understand for the life of me why someone would want to buy it. Don't get me started on the personality of most collectors! The better option is to destroy these things. Sure, no sane Rifter would want the template for a tiny, dented breastplate. But destroying these items boosts one's familiarity with its type. Destroy a dozen of these crappy breastplates and a Rifter will slowly see their familiarity with other 'decent' breastplates also improve, allowing for a much higher chance at gaining their templates.

I don't know about all of you, but I'd rather destroy rubbish and save cash for the good stuff.

<Link_previous_page> <Link_index> <Link_next_page>

Endurance Attribute

GRRO Manual part 9b.
Written by Herman Gros.
Chief physician Berlin branch.

Greetings <insert_firstname>,
In the previous part, we went over the six different Attributes that define a Rifter: Endurance, Strength, Agility, Perception, Wisdom, and Luck. In this section, we will examine the Endurance trait further, discuss the benefits, and explore certain hypotheses regarding this Attribute.

Endurance, like other Attributes, will improve over the course of a Rifter's life. Either through smaller gains by leveling up, or through active input from the Rifter. Because of the latter, there is an unpredictable variant in play since a level 25 Rifter that specializes in Endurance could technically be just as durable as a level 100 Rifter who does not.

Beyond this, there are also the elements of basic human biology, genetics, lifestyle, and environment at play. Studies have shown that a Rifter's Attributes can drastically improve their capabilities by building off the Rifter's natural physical and mental state.

Example: An already healthy individual with a strong immune system shows far more beneficial gains from the same amount of Endurance points when compared to an unhealthy individual.

Combat related benefits:
In terms of combat-oriented benefits, extensive research has shown that most Rifters with a high Endurance Attribute see a drastic improvement in Health regeneration and damage resistance. See the link for more Health-related information. **<Link_document_#4-b>.**

Lesser documented cases have shown that some Rifters have even reached the stage where small-arms fire proved ineffective at fully piercing their skin and muscle, or that the Rifters could even shrug it off. Beyond that, there have been extensive studies that show that the effectiveness of toxins drastically decreases the higher someone's Endurance Attribute is. Because of ethical concerns, researchers have tested this field of study on Rift-animals, so results might differ for human Rifters.

Rift related benefits:
Beyond the benefits during combat, Endurance is a great Attribute for surviving a harsh Rift. The increased Endurance allows a Rifter to adapt to extreme temperatures and climates, endure Rifts with higher gravity, and allow a Rifter to operate in low oxygen environments.

The increased effectiveness of a Rifter's immune system also lessens the risk of poisons, contaminants, and even decreases the negative effects of digesting rotten food. It is still unclear how exactly this is achieved, but many experts believe it has something to do with the radiation emanating from a Rifter's white-shard. It is not recommended for Rifters to ignore the risks of these conditions, but survival rates drastically increase for those with a higher Endurance Attribute.

Recent study has also begun regarding a Rifter's longevity. Although Rifts have been appearing on Earth for several years already, far too little time has passed to monitor the long-term effects that a high Endurance Attribute might have on the human body. From what we have learned from Rift-animals such as mice, they have a far greater lifespan compared to those not exposed to a Rift. The hypothesis is that a high Endurance Attribute might also drastically lengthen the human lifespan by dozens of years, possibly more.

<Link_previous_page> <Link_index> <Link_next_page>

About the Author

Osirium Writes is the pen name of author Joost Lassche, whose urban fantasy LitRPG series, Death Smith, was originally released on Royal Road.

DISCOVER
STORIES UNBOUND

PodiumAudio.com

Printed in the USA
CPSIA information can be obtained
at www.ICGtesting.com
JSHW022335140824
68134JS00019B/1492